Sweet Transgression

Renee Wilde

Literary Wanderlust | Denver, Colorado

Published in the United States by Literary Wanderlust LLC, Denver, Colorado.

https//www.LiteraryWanderlust.com

ISBN Print: 978-1-942856-94-8
ISBN Digital: 978-1-942856-97-9

Cover design: Kylee Howells

Printed in the United States of America

Dedication

To Rory, Edie, and Marjorie,
my own
Happily Ever After

Chapter One

London, June 1815

"But you cannot," Anne Heatherington screamed, running down the crowded hall of the wounded veterans' home turned temporary military hospital, leaping over the legs of men who were sitting propped against the walls.

"Do you hear me?" She stopped short as the physician turned the corner, yards and yards ahead of her. She couldn't be sure whether he was ignoring her or truly hadn't heard, but it was too late now. That soldier he'd been wheeling would soon be without an arm, and there was nothing she could do about it. It wasn't as if the doctor would have listened to her anyway. He'd just yelled at her this morning about wasting his time trying to save limbs that were beyond hope. She supposed he was right. With all the men who'd arrived from Waterloo in the last few days, there was no longer room to administer proper care to the men who weren't yet gangrenous, and since the likelihood was that they would be infected before long, the doctors were saving time and bed space by amputating.

She understood the rationale, but still, she could not get over the twinge her conscience gave every time the doctor wheeled another poor young man around the corner. She turned away and wiped her forehead with her sleeve.

"It's bloody hot in here, isn't it?" A voice rose from the floor next to her, and she glanced down to see a handsome face looking up at her from behind the dirt and grime and blood of the battlefield. She felt no surprise at the curse. Being a military nurse made one immune rather quickly to some things. She was, however, curious about the cultured tone of the man's voice as she took in his large frame. His strength and size were obvious, though he sat with his legs folded cross-legged on the floor. His hair appeared to be a light brown or dark blond, though she could not tell which through the dirt and grime that had accumulated in it. She could see, however, with complete clarity, the curiosity in his dark gray eyes as they stared back up at her.

"It is indeed, sir," she said, one eye brow raising.

"Why are you so puzzled?" The man asked lightly. "Surely, I'm not the first soldier to remark upon the weather?"

Anne couldn't help smiling. "Of course not, but perhaps the first who sounds like he should be over at White's placing a ridiculous bet than sitting on the floor at Chelsea Hospital."

"What makes you so sure my bets are ridiculous?" The man said, laughing softly for a moment before pausing, meeting her eyes, and asking, "Chelsea Hospital, really?"

"Yes, sir," Anne answered. "We're handling the overflow from Waterloo. I assume you came from there?"

She could see the muscles in the man's jaw working as he looked past her shoulder, his smile dropping and his gaze unfocused as if he were no longer seeing what was in front of him. "Yes."

Anne had seen this look before, of course, but she was still puzzled as to why a man who was clearly of a noble class was here at Chelsea. All the officers were taken elsewhere, usually to their homes, for private care.

"What is your name?" She tried to keep her voice businesslike; this was usually the best way to handle a man who seemed about to relive a battle in his mind. Her ploy had the desired effect.

He looked back up at her face, his eyes clear as they met hers and he said slowly, "I'm not sure." Anne couldn't help her sharp intake of breath, though she regretted it. She crouched down to look into the soldier's face. He averted his gaze once again, and her heart ached. "Let me help you find a room and get your wounds looked at." She took him by his upper arm to help him, but he wriggled out of her grasp and slowly made his way to his feet.

She touched his shoulder gently and said, "This is no time to be proud, soldier."

His eyes met hers for a moment before he looked away. "As good a time as any, I'd wager."

"Now *that* is a ridiculous bet," Anne said lightly. "I knew it."

The soldier laughed as well, and she took his arm and led him down the corridor toward one of the smaller, cleaner wardrooms.

"A bit dark, isn't it?" he said.

Anne looked around and shrugged her shoulders. The lighting was poor indeed, and even this room was over capacity with wounded soldiers lying about on palettes, their moans coming from the darkened corners. "It's one of the best rooms we've got," she said unapologetically.

"Yes, I suppose it would be." She wasn't quite sure what he meant by that, but she did not comment as she led him over to a spot by the small, high window.

"You can lie here," she said, gesturing to the clean space on the floor. "I will fetch some linens and inform the doctor you're here." She had bent and begun sweeping the floor with the back of her sleeve to be sure it was clean when his hand gripped her wrist. She was surprised by the pressure from his fingertips on her skin.

"What are you doing?" he asked.

Something in his tone made her look up, though it was not harsh. It was almost defeated. "I'm just tidying up for you, sir."

"Do you tidy up for all these men?" he asked, his eyes narrowed.

"Of course not."

"Then I'll ask again—what are you doing?"

She sighed. She wasn't sure she knew where he was going with this, but she felt patronized. "Then I'll tell you again—I'm tidying up."

He let go of her wrist and rested back against the wall. "It's not as if they have given less than I," he said, his eyes dark as he gestured to include the whole room full of men. "In fact," he said, holding both hands out and turning them palm up, "I still have all my limbs. It could be said many of them have given a great deal more."

Anne had to admit she agreed with him, but it just simply wouldn't do for her to treat a nobleman like a common soldier. It was clear he was an officer and obvious social dictates demanded she treat him with more respect, deference, and gentility. She knew he must know this, but something about his demeanor made her keep quiet on the subject.

"You just stay here, sir, and I'll be back to check you over," she said, putting a hand on his shoulder as she rose. She turned to go, but the man grasped her hand before she could walk away.

"You are beautiful, do you know that?" Anne felt herself blushing. It was not the first time a soldier had said so or called her an angel of mercy or a bright shining joy from the white cliffs of Dover, but coming from this man it was somehow embarrassing.

"I'll be right back," she said, backing away. "Try to get some rest." She turned and fled.

"Where have you been?" The angry physician—she couldn't for the life of her remember his name—narrowed his eyes at her as she ran down the hall toward him, and she could see beads of sweat on his forehead.

"I've been nursing," she bit off, unable to help herself. The doctor did not look pleased.

"We've been running around searching for you for half an hour at least."

She frowned and replied, "I'm here now, aren't I?"

"Indeed," the doctor said as he turned away and motioned with his head for her to follow him. His behavior was infuriating, but she had grown quite used to it over the last few days. She did have some understanding of the difficulty the physicians were having in keeping up with the demand for their services. Many of them had neither slept nor eaten much since the first ship bearing casualties had arrived. She did, however, she thought with a smirk, think they could treat her with a little less spite, considering she had been through the same ordeal they had. She was becoming breathless chasing the man down the hall and was infinitely grateful when they arrived at the large ward. The doctor said nothing and motioned for her to follow him to the bedside of a man whose sheets were soaked with blood.

Anne closed her eyes and turned her head to avoid gagging. It wasn't as if blood really bothered her that much, but since most of the men arriving had been field dressed, it was not often that she saw such a great quantity of it.

"You can see," the physician said with a touch of sarcasm, "there's no saving *this* limb, Miss Heatherington."

She only nodded and began busying herself with her work. She went to the corner to grab a pile of fresh linens and returned to strip away the soaked ones. She could see the gash in the man's leg had been dressed on the field or in Brussels, but that he had somehow torn it open again to create a fresh wound. In the days since he'd done so, it had become infected and turned a ghastly shade of gray-green. The smell was overwhelming, but this, as opposed to the great quantities of blood, was something she had grown somewhat used to, though it seemed impossible that one could ever become immune to the scent. Even the doctor winced when she pulled away the old dressings.

She took the pitcher of water and began bathing the area so they could see exactly where the wound was. It was well below the knee, and Anne was relieved they wouldn't be amputating at the hip. Perhaps with a wooden attachment, this man could walk again. She doubted he'd understand the good news if she told him. He was writhing and muttering from fever. The doctor did not need to tell her to fetch the laudanum. She administered a hefty dose, gathered the tools, and then stood by to assist the doctor in his surgery. Her mind wandered as she pondered again who her mysterious lord was while she went about the rote task of answering requests with actions. She supposed she would find out soon enough. A noble family whose son was not on the rolls of the dead and who had also not returned home would make inquiries. She supposed it was only a matter of time.

"Miss Heatherington?"

"Mm?" She looked up from the bandages in her hands and realized the doctor had finished and needed her to dress the wound. "Yes, Doctor," she said and began to go about her work. It didn't take long for her to complete the familiar task, but when she had finished, she sat next to the man's bedside to hold the long vigil until he awakened.

When his eyes finally fluttered open, she quickly dipped a towel in the cold water and held it to his forehead. She asked him if he'd like a drink, and when he nodded, she slipped a hand behind his head, her fingers pulling him up so she could hold the cup to his parched lips.

"You'll be fine, soldier," she whispered. "Drink and then we'll get you some more laudanum. The best thing is to sleep now."

He opened his mouth to speak, but she hushed him. "No need to talk now. Be restful."

But he shook his head. "Miss, please . . ." his voice was the barest croak of a whisper, and she had to bend down to hear him. "My lord . . ."

She turned her head quickly to the side to meet his eyes. "Your lord?" she asked hesitantly. Could he be speaking of her mystery man?

"Who is your lord?" she asked quickly, "Where could I find him? When did you last see him?"

But the young man's eyes closed again, and his head fell to the side as he slid back into sleep. Anne took a deep breath and continued swabbing his forehead, but it was apparent his fever had broken and he would sleep now. She cleaned up what she had been doing and checked on a few of the other patients in the ward before she went to the stores, took a large pile of fresh bread and cheese, and made her way back to where she'd left His Lordship.

Jonathan—he knew that was his Christian name, though he knew precious little else—sat up and leaned back against the wall, thinking about the young nurse who'd raced out the door of the wretched little room he'd found himself in. He wasn't sure why he'd told her she was beautiful; he just knew it was true, with her slim figure and the hint of a curve in her hips, her chestnut hair escaping haphazardly from her chignon, and her dark brown expressive eyes. It had felt like the thing to say. He admitted to himself that he hadn't wanted her to leave him here. She was the first person he'd actually spoken to since he'd been dropped off in that corridor hours before.

He closed his eyes and took a deep breath. If he could only remember his surname, or his estate name, or his dog's name, or anything besides the rank smell of the ditch outside Hougoumont where he'd lain for three days before being found by the medics. He'd have thought he was dead if it wasn't for that smell. He'd been near-naked, stripped of his jacket and boots by the looters who could always be found combing battlefields for valuables, and he'd been numb, unable to feel or to remember who he was or what had happened to him.

He opened his eyes, trying to escape the cacophony of sounds and images that assaulted him when he tried to remember. He saw little bits of battle, heard the endless booms of cannon, and the smells . . . He could smell gunpowder and flesh and mud and—

"Stop," he whispered to himself. He felt a shuddering sob in his chest. "*Stop.*" He was breathing heavy and fast, and he forced himself to take big, slow, deep breaths while he focused on a spot on the floor in front of him.

"Stop what?" came a gentle voice from the doorway. The nurse was standing there, arms loaded with linens and what looked to be bread and cheese. His stomach released a very ungentlemanly roar, and he could tell she heard it, for she smiled a wide, genuine smile. He had not been exaggerating earlier when he'd said she was beautiful. There was a simplicity about her, a frankness that added to her beauty. She was quite unlike any woman he'd met. And he'd known many, especially during his days at the balls.

"I had one," he said, smiling up at her.

Her eyebrows arched in question. "One?" she asked.

"A memory," he said, pondering it. It was not just one memory really, but a whole host of images that played in his mind. "Balls, parties. I've been to balls, and I've waltzed."

The nurse came toward him and crouched quite nearby. She laid down her armful of goods and placed her hand on his forearm. "That's good," she said, her eyes widening with encouragement.

He looked into her eyes and smiled. "It is, isn't it?" His gaze could not resist traveling to the food and he motioned to it with his head. "That for me?" he asked.

"And me," she said with a matter-of-fact grin. "I haven't eaten since midnight."

"And what time is it now?"

"Near on teatime," she said, looking up at the window and down at the bread. "Quite fortuitous, really. Now if only we had a nice hot pot with a cozy and—"

"Stop, you'll drive me mad," he said, reaching for one of the loaves.

She laughed and then stopped, opening her mouth a little and then closing it. It was a lush, wide mouth, the sort of mouth a man wanted to ravish.

"Do you mind if I sit?"

He let out a snort, and then realized she might take it as derision. "Of course not, Miss . . ."

"Terribly sorry," she said, making her way rather gracefully, he thought, considering the circumstances, to the floor, where she managed to fold her feet just so beneath her voluminous skirts and then deftly picked at the fabric to arrange them around her. When she was fully seated, she reached out her hand, "Anne Heatherington."

He took it and made a great show of bowing over it as he placed a gentle kiss on her knuckle. "Jonathan," he said, wincing a bit at the absence of a last name.

"You remember your name," she said.

"Yes, and I've been to balls," he said, smirking a bit. "We've almost reproduced my autobiography."

"Don't be so pessimistic," she said before she took a bite from her roll. She munched in silence for a moment, swallowed, and said, "It seems to me if you are beginning to remember things, the rest will come in time."

"I certainly hope so," he replied, but inside he really wasn't sure he was telling the truth. Did he hope to remember even more of Waterloo than he did? What really had happened to him there? Had he made mistakes that cost lives? Or, worse, had he run from the battle? What if his family here in England were detestable? What if he had done detestable things? How many men longed for a second chance, a new beginning? He shook his head.

"What is it?" Anne asked.

"Nothing," he said, his voice clipped. "I'm being ridiculous, that's all."

"It must be terrible not knowing who you are," she said. "Unless, of course, there are things you'd rather not remember."

His eyes shot up to meet hers. "What did you say?"

"Just that everyone has things they'd rather not remember, I suppose," she said, her dark brown eyes even larger than they'd appeared before. "But look at me, that's a terrible thing to say."

He couldn't help but let out a wry laugh. "No, Miss Heatherington, not terrible at all. In fact, I thank you."

"For what?"

"For making me feel less monstrous."

"Well, you're quite welcome," she said, and she swept her hand in a mock-operatic bow. "Though I've only known you a short while, my lord, I'd say you are far from monstrous."

"Thank you again," he said, nodding, "and just call me Jonathan."

"Surely you know you are a nobleman," her voice was gentle, and she shook her head. "How did you end up here at Chelsea, I wonder?"

"I pretended not to be noble."

"You what?"

"I pretended. I faked an accent. I must be terribly good."

She looked shocked, and he wondered how he could explain it to her. "What would they have done with me, Miss Heatherington?"

"Anne, please," she said, her voice going soft again. "I imagine they'd have at least taken you somewhere else. The college of physicians perhaps? Somewhere where they could put out a bulletin for your family?"

"How many men around you were under my command?" he asked. "How many men still lying on the field? What did I do to protect them?"

She did not answer right away, but she did not drop his gaze. He continued, "How many of them are here without arms, legs, without lives, because of what I might have done or not done?

Why should I be treated before them?"

"You're right, of course." Her answer shocked him. Not because he didn't want her to agree with him, but because she'd been so kind. He hadn't expected that type of frankness from her.

"I see it all the time." She looked down, and he could see tears glisten through the lashes resting on her cheeks. "Most of them are just boys, some conscripted, leaving families behind. It's truly a tragedy."

He was silent. The weight of his guilt felt as if it were pressing in on him from all sides. It became difficult to take a deep breath. He kept looking at her, the wisps of hair that had come loose from her chignon, the flush of her cheeks, the rising and falling of her bosom as she sat and contemplated war. She looked up and he was startled again by the way she managed to hold his gaze without flinching.

"But you, sir, only did your duty, the same as them," she said, gesturing around her. "You took orders and defended England, the same as them. And you'll never be the same, just like them. What good does it do to wonder what your role in the battle was? Everyone here had a role, and here you sit."

He remained silent, though her words were comforting. She leaned forward, her hand almost searing him this time when she rested it on his arm, and her voice became so soft he had to lean forward to hear her, "some wounds are easier to see than others, Jonathan."

He felt his eyes moisten, and he looked away. "Maybe you're right," he said in a strained voice. "But all the same, I'd prefer to wait here and serve my turn. There are others who need your help more than I."

She finished her bread and wiped her hands on her skirts in a businesslike manner. "There I cannot disagree with you, but nonetheless I would like to check you for wounds or infection. A quick swab now could save your life in a few days."

He nodded. "I'll allow it, I suppose," he said, hoping his

levity would break the heaviness of the atmosphere. It seemed to work because she bestowed one of her dazzling wide smiles on him and bent forward to roll up his sleeve.

"Any pain at all?"

"None that I've noticed," he said. "I feel filthy more than anything."

She smiled and looked back up at him. "Welcome to Chelsea."

She went about touching him gently, moving his arms to test his elbows and shoulders and moving her fingers through his hair. He had to admit her closeness was causing an uncomfortable, but unavoidable reaction in him. He tried to defuse his thoughts with conversation. "How did you become a nurse, Anne?"

She continued her examination as she spoke. "To tell the truth, I wish to become a physician." She paused as if she'd expected him to laugh or make a comment, but he remained silent. "I know it is really quite impossible, but I like to feel I'm helping people. When the war broke out, it seemed natural for me to come and volunteer my services."

"Naturally," he said wryly, wondering how many of the women at those balls he remembered would feel so "natural" about coming to this dirty, awful, reeking place.

"I know what you're thinking," she said, smiling. "Do you?" His eyebrow arched in challenge.

"You're thinking," she sat back on her heels and looked up with that direct intense gaze again, mocking a male voice, "this one is not of the ranks of noble ladies I have known."

He laughed outright at that. "How did you know?"

"It's written all over your face." She began moving his feet in circles to check his ankles. "And I've heard it before."

"So, who are you then, Miss educated, ambitious, cultured Anne Heatherington?"

"Ambitious I can see, but where do you get educated and cultured?"

"The same way you knew I was a nobleman," he laughed.

"Instinct."

"I, ah . . ." she dropped her eyes now, and he noticed slight recoil in her shoulders, though she continued her ministrations. "I had a governess."

"And where do you live? Who are your parents?"

She smiled but he knew she had said all she wished to. "I had a governess."

He had to admit he was curious, but he left it at that, after all, it wasn't terribly unusual to run into women who lived in limbo between the upper and lower classes. Perhaps her father was a merchant or attorney. In any case, she didn't seem willing to discuss it, so he stayed quiet.

She seemed uncomfortable, and she changed the subject to small talk. "How long did it take you to get here after they found you?"

He had to think about that for a moment. "I'm not entirely sure," he said. "I tried to sleep through most of it, and took any laudanum they offered."

Her eyebrows came together as she stood and crossed her arms. "You don't have any wounds," she said. "You shouldn't have taken any laudanum."

"Some wounds are less obvious than others," he said, looking her straight in the eye. "You said it yourself."

"I'm sorry, sir," she said, "but I must return to my duties. Please accept these linens, and know that I'll return with water as soon as I'm able. If you need me, ask anyone walking by for Anne. They'll know who you mean."

"Thank you, Anne," he said. "Truly, I thank you."

"Just doing my duty, my lord."

"I thought we had agreed upon Jonathan."

"Very well, Jonathan," she said, and her tone had chilled. "Be well, and I will see you again soon."

With that, she turned, and when he could no longer see her shadow in the hall, he felt as if a light had been extinguished in the room. He sighed and leaned back again. He wasn't sure what he'd done to upset her, but he hoped he would not repeat it next time. He very much hoped to see more of Miss Anne Heatherington.

Chapter Two

It was a horrifying jumble of images, yet he felt he was there, despite the fact that he could make no sense of the scene at all. He neither knew where his feet were nor which direction was up. The sky was black and the ground was dark with mud—or was it blood—as he tried to make his way through the wasteland of debris. There were large chunks of wood crossing his path, and he felt as if something was beating him around the head and shoulders as he tried to clamber around them. Then he was lying in the mud. He could smell it, thick with excrement and death. He writhed and tried to stand, but the mud was sucking him in. He tried to scream but no sound was coming out. He was kicking and trying to escape, but every move he made seemed to stick him more firmly into the muck. At last, he stopped struggling and turned his head to the side, only to be face to face with—

"Wake up," the voice was gentle and female.

"Wake up," it came again, more insistent this time. "You are having a dream. Wake up." His shoulders were being shaken, and he opened his eyes with a gasp.

"*Good God,*" He shouted, but he regretted his outburst when Anne stumbled backward. Her eyes were wide, and she'd brought one hand to cover her mouth. He watched her lower it as consciousness made its way through his mind, and he tried to smile at her to set her at ease.

"Thank goodness you're awake," she said, moving her hand to her chest with a sigh. She turned away and began busying herself with a large pile of what looked like fresh cheese.

"I'm so sorry, Miss Heatherington."

"Please," she said, her deep brown eyes meeting his gaze, "do not apologize. You gave me a start, is all. It's not as if I haven't seen men in the throes of a nightmare."

He took a deep breath. Yes, he supposed it had been a nightmare. It had felt so real, yet also unreal. He could still smell the gunpowder and the blood, both tangy with iron, even though he knew he was fully awake now—grounded in the room at Chelsea, hunger pangs rumbling in his belly, and the form of this beautiful nurse bending over food.

"You look more rested, at least," Anne said as she laid out three hearty slices of bread with a plateful of cheese before him.

Jonathan didn't know what to say, so he nodded and took a bite of his bread and cheese. "This is delicious," he said, his mouth half full before he took a swig of the water she'd brought. He hadn't realized how hungry he'd been. He almost felt ashamed of himself as he gulped down another bite, but when he looked up, he saw Anne eating with relish as well. She smiled as she poked a piece of bread that had missed the bite back in between her lips. Instead of appearing unladylike, as he was sure she would be concerned about in another situation, she appeared to him to be hearty and earthy and *real*. It was the strangest feeling, but he almost thought he'd known her all his life. With his memory loss, he supposed, anything was possible. But she seemed so concerned with helping him discover his identity that he was certain she would have told him had she recognized him in any way. Besides, the feeling he had was more than one of recognition.

"You know," Anne said bringing her eyebrows together, and holding a piece of bread between bites, "I feel quite comfortable with you. Isn't that odd?"

The more they spoke, the less odd it seemed. "I was just thinking the same thing. You seem so . . ."

"Familiar," she said, nodding as if she'd hit upon the perfect word.

They both laughed. "What a pair we make, don't you agree, Miss Heatherington?"

He watched her as she looked around the room, where he now noticed far fewer soldiers than had been lying there earlier. "I suppose we do, Lord Jonathan," she said, her eyes twinkling. "There's nothing quite like a war to bring people together, is there?"

Jonathan smiled, but he didn't feel any joy as he grabbed another hunk of bread and cheese from in front of him. "No, I suppose there's not."

"It seems the ranks are finally dwindling," she said, looking back at him. "The corridors have been cleared, and many of the men who were waiting here have been treated already. You've slept long."

He flushed. He didn't want her to know he'd found more laudanum. It had seemed to upset her so when she'd left earlier. Was she angry with him for wasting it on himself, or was she worried he'd become attached to it, as he'd seen other men become? He thought of her worrying about him, and the flush made itself felt again, right around his collar and slowly spreading to his cheeks. He pulled at the neck of the loose shirt he wore and looked away, hoping to cool the warmth a bit before she noticed.

"I dare say," she said, looking up at him through lowered lashes, "I'd give *more* than a penny for your thoughts."

If it had been possible, he'd be flushing an even deeper

shade than before. "I'm afraid," he said, trying to match her light tone, "they are worth far more than that." He took a deep breath and looked back at her, but he found he couldn't stop himself from imagining the sleeves of her bodice pulled down past her shoulders, baring her neck.

As if sensing the direction of his thoughts, she looked away, then stood quickly and began tidying up. He felt like an ass, but there was no helping it. She was beautiful, she was kind, she'd given of her services and time to help him, and he felt so damned comfortable in her presence. When she returned with a small basin of water and some fresh linens, he took her wrist before she could leave his side again.

"Do you think you could help me?"

Her sharp intake of breath provoked a reaction somewhere deep inside of him. He realized that, though he was drawn to her physically, it was more than that. He just didn't want her to leave.

"Please," he said. "I don't want to be alone."

Her eyes widened with sympathy, and she nodded, her lips pressed together as if to acknowledge that he needn't say anymore. She knelt down next to him again, and he closed his eyes when she ran her hand through his hair.

"You aren't," she said quietly. "Not tonight."

Anne wasn't sure what fever had taken hold of her brain to allow her to think it appropriate or proper for her to spend the night in an empty, darkened wardroom with a healthy, handsome young soldier, but she pushed the niggling voice of reason out of her head as soon as it appeared. She sensed she had been more accurate than she'd thought when she'd said that his wounds were still deep, though they were not visible. She was a nurse, after all, and she felt a deep compulsion to keep by his side through the night, to help him through the nightmares. She wanted to affirm, as much to herself as to him, that there was some goodness and light in the world.

Still, she had to admit to some extreme discomfort with the feelings that he had awakened within her. She found herself, more than once as she helped him rinse his hair and scrub the back of his neck, wishing to touch him elsewhere—even kiss him. She'd never kissed a man in her life, nor had she desired to on any other occasion. In fact, she'd sworn never to feel those feelings for any man. She felt her heart ache as an image of her mother swam through her mind, but she pushed it aside.

"I'll just be over in the corner," she said, standing and picking up a load of soiled linens. "You may call when you are finished."

"Thank you for your modesty, Anne," she heard him say as she walked away, though she didn't dare turn back, despite the hint of wry sarcasm she thought she heard in his voice.

She bent over the pile of linens in the opposite corner of the room, trying to put them in a pile and separate the ones that had been used only for cleaning from the ones that had been bloodied or soiled in other ways. She heard Jonathan shuffling over by the window and couldn't resist peeking every now and again, though she flushed and cursed herself each time she did so. Mostly she could only see the rough shape of him outlined in the darkness, but once she looked up and had to stop herself from gasping when she saw the broad plain of his naked back. It was muscled, sinewy, and tanned. She supposed he'd had to lie on the battlefield in the sun before anyone had retrieved him. She watched him, fascinated, through narrowed eyes as she tried to clear her vision. The muscles across his shoulders rolled beneath his skin as he bent to wash his legs, and then he sat up straight and lifted his arms in front of him, causing all the skin of his back to go taut. Out of nowhere, Anne found herself wishing to run her hands across those muscles, to feel them move beneath her palms. She looked down quickly as his head turned toward her. She prayed the darkness in the corner obscured the blatant fact that she had been spying on him in his nudity. What kind of a wanton had she become?

If he had noticed her looking, he gave no indication, but she kept her eyes averted after that to avoid any more potentially embarrassing situations. She felt a strange, warm tingling sensation spreading through her body at the thought of him so close. She could hear his breath as she went about her work, could hear the washcloth rubbing against his skin. Her own breathing became faster, and she felt as if she might faint if he didn't finish soon.

"Very well, then," his spoken voice startled her so much that she dropped the pile of cleaner linens she'd been carrying and a terribly unladylike swear escaped her before she could help it.

"No need for such vehemence, Miss Heatherington," he said, laughing. "I can take longer if you need more time."

She looked up at him and frowned, motioning to the haphazard heap of linen piled around her feet. "Thank you, but I think I'm finished here."

"Excellent," he said, "then you can come over here and keep me company."

Anne took a deep breath to steel herself before she walked over to where he was sitting. She couldn't help a tiny gasp when she saw that, though he'd replaced his shirt, he'd left it unbuttoned, and she could see tantalizing glimpses of the hair on his tanned chest. It looked so soft. She averted her eyes and sat down next to him where she wouldn't have to meet his perceptive gaze. Just when she thought she'd made it safely into place, he annoyed her by chuckling.

"Surely," he said, "you must have seen a man without his shirt buttoned before this."

"Of course," she bit off. "But, pardon me for saying, they are usually unconscious at the time."

"I will button it for you if you wish," he said, and the corners of his eyes crinkled in merriment, "but you will pardon *me* for saying that it is still bloody hot in here."

She had to give him that. She hadn't stopped sweating all day. Still, a peevish streak made her retort, "and you're not even wearing two petticoats, chemise, and stays."

"You don't need to, either." He was still laughing, but something in his tone made her uncomfortable.

"Are you trying to seduce me, Mr. Jonathan?"

His gray eyes narrowed as he leveled his gaze at her. "Truthfully?"

"I think we've moved past niceties," she said, trying to remind herself to breathe.

"Indeed," he answered, looking at the ceiling and sighing, "you are right."

"So?"

"I am not trying to seduce you."

She felt relieved and deflated at the same time. Then she scolded herself for the latter. She frowned, and he must have seen it, for he asked,

"Truthfully, Anne?"

"Yes?" She gulped, trying to keep her eyes on the floor in front of her.

"I am completely happy sitting here with you, happier than I thought I would ever be again just a few days ago. You are so fresh and honest," he said as he put a finger under her chin so he could bring her gaze back up to meet his own, "I find I very much enjoy being with you."

"So," she began, narrowing her eyes, "You would like me to remove my undergarments, and yet you are *not* attempting to seduce me."

"Quite right," he said, clapping his hands together and then bringing them behind his head. He leaned back against the wall, looking up toward the ceiling. "I simply want us both to be comfortable."

She brought her lips together in the primmest look she could conjure and said, "Thank you, my lord, but I assure you I am most comfortable with all of my clothing *on*."

He shrugged. "Suit yourself."

"Thank you, I usually do."

"Do you always have to have the last word?"

"Yes."

"Really?"

Even though she knew he was baiting her, she couldn't help herself. "*Yes.*"

He just laughed. "Come," he said, "we're at odds and evens. Let's tell stories, or devise a game—something."

She moved a few inches away from him for good measure and said, "Very well."

"Why don't you tell me all about your life?"

She cringed. Why did he have to ask her something like that? "There's really nothing to tell," she said with a frown.

"Oh, come now," he said, "there must be some fascinating sibling who left cheese in your shoes."

"No, there wasn't." She could see him narrow his eyes, but she sighed in relief when he didn't press the topic further.

"Very well, you won't tell me about yourself, and I *can't* tell you about *my*self, so I suppose we're at something of an impasse."

"I'm sorry," she said, and she meant it. She took a pause and then continued, "It's just that my life has not been all sweetness and light."

"Very well," he said with a smile. "Since we can't talk about the past, let's talk about the future. What do you dream of being?"

"I've told you," she said. "A doctor."

"Of course. City or country?" Nothing he could have said would have surprised her more. She was grateful to him for indulging her and not making fun.

"City, I believe," she said, though she realized she had never thought about it before. "Though I wouldn't mind mixing my time between the two."

"You'd do well to marry a nobleman, then."

She couldn't help her snort of derision. "Not likely."

"Believe me, Anne," he said in such a quiet tone that she

looked up into his eyes again, "you are the most fetching woman I've ever met."

She smiled, but couldn't resist teasing. "You don't remember any of the other women you've ever met."

"Trust me," he said, "if they were anything like you, I'd remember."

She felt herself blushing, and that strange tingly feeling settled in her stomach once more. He put his finger under her chin again, and she felt the pressure of his touch like a fire burning on her skin. It was nothing compared to the burning she felt when her eyes met his. Now that he was clean and washed, she could see the chiseled planes of his face, and his dark gray eyes seemed even more piercing than they had before. There was something in them, something she couldn't quite understand.

"Anne Heatherington," he asked, his tone soft and gentle, "may I kiss you?"

She swallowed and paused. "I'm not sure."

He chuckled but didn't take his finger from her chin. "Shall I endeavor to find out?"

She shook her head, then nodded, then shook her head again. Finally, she looked back into his gray eyes. "I thought you weren't trying to seduce me."

"I'm not."

She looked around her at the empty room, and up at the window where the bright moon told her it was late into the night. She looked back into Jonathan's eyes and wondered if he would ever discover who he was, and something changed within her. She didn't pity him, no, it was deeper than that. She wanted to comfort him, but more than that, she wanted to comfort herself. She wasn't sure why she assumed kissing this man would be comforting, but she knew it felt right. Surely her virtue would not be in question if she only kissed him. Who would ever know?

"Yes."

"Yes, what?"

She frowned, "Yes, you may kiss me."

"Ah," he said, smiling. "Just what I was hoping to hear."

Anne closed her eyes as Jonathan leaned forward, but she was a little unsure of what to do. She licked her lips, almost from instinct, and he kissed her with just the lightest brush of his lips against her own. Her eyes flew open to see him pull back and smile. He stroked the side of her head with his palm, smoothing her hair, moving his thumb over her cheekbone, and then the corner of her lips. She looked down again, blushing, wanting more, but not sure how to ask for it. When she looked back up into his eyes, he smiled again.

When her hand reached tentatively up to touch his cheek, he turned his face to lay a gentle kiss on her palm. She realized the best way to ask was just to be honest.

"Now may I kiss you?"

She saw his jaw tighten, and she worried for a moment that he might not want her to kiss him, but his slow nod told her otherwise. His body was taut and tense as she kissed him. She began moving her lips along his own, placing small kisses on the corners of his mouth, and then on his upper and lower lips. His breathing quickened, and he cradled the sides of her face with both his hands and drew her even closer, his tongue tracing around her mouth. Her lips parted to allow him entry and she was surprised by how good he tasted. She could feel herself melting open, wanting him to hold her tighter, and she could feel warmth spreading deep down in her belly.

"Anne," he whispered against her lips. "Oh, God, Anne."

She could only whimper in response, and the sound of it seemed to spur something in him. He moved one hand behind her neck and began to pull out her hairpins. His fingers moved up into her long hair as it began to spill over his arm, and his other hand moved down to her shoulder and then to her waist before it traced the path up her torso toward her breast. She gasped as he cupped her in his palm, and she could feel the heat of his touch through the layers of chemise, stays, and dress she wore. He ran his thumb across a taut nipple, hardening even more beneath his touch. Her hips bucked, and her tongue darted into his mouth as he kissed her even more fiercely. Her hands were stroking his back, and he turned himself toward her so he could pull her down to the palette beneath him. When he did so, caressing her hip and laying on his side next to her, she pulled away and looked at him. She was panting and unsure of what she was feeling, but she was absolutely positive she wanted more.

"Anne . . ."

She touched her index finger to his lips. "Hush, Jonathan," her voice was husky as she whispered, "tonight we're here. I want you to kiss me again."

He bent his head toward hers, and she gave herself to the sweetness of his kiss again as he stroked the side of her face, her hair, her neck, her shoulder. "I want you to be sure," he said in a low tone as he laid his cheek next to hers.

"I don't know if I've ever been more sure," she replied as she put both her hands on the sides of his face and brought him down to kiss her again.

Anne couldn't quite explain to herself what she was feeling, but she was quite sure she had never experienced anything like it. Jonathan was touching her in ways that were so good, so delicious, though she knew in her head they must be terribly wicked. Something about the night kept prodding her to throw caution to the wind and to take what he was offering her. The war was finally over, hopefully for good this time, but a struggle was just beginning for him, she knew, and she herself would be adrift without the daily need for her presence here at the hospital. It was the end of something old and the beginning of something new, and she knew she would never see this man again. Once he found out who he was, they would move in very different circles, and somehow that made this moment all the sweeter. It was a night stolen from time when her life didn't matter and he was unknown. The moonlight cast a strange glow to the wardroom, and it seemed to Anne as if she were living in a dream, a dream that she could cherish for the rest of her life.

These thoughts raced through her mind, interrupted and crowded in by Jonathan's tender kisses and caresses. When his hands brushed across her breasts, she could feel the calloused fingers through her thin chemise and dress, could feel them move across her nipples, and every time he did so, they seemed to become even more sensitive to his touch. She couldn't keep herself from moaning when he caressed her neck and pulled the shoulder of her dress down the side of her arm, baring one breast in its path. The fabric slid against her skin, and the delight of his fingers over the cloth was nothing compared to the feeling of Jonathan's lips as he bent over her and nipped at her skin everywhere he'd bared it. He pulled his head up and looked right into her eyes as he gently blew on the now hardened little bud, and Anne writhed beneath him. Her wriggling stopped when he brought his mouth down upon her and began to suckle. Her whole body bucked upward in response, wanting to push more of herself into him.

Jonathan tormented her for long moments before he came up to kiss her once more and hold her tight against him. He kissed her cheek, her ears, her neck, and his breath was hot against her skin as he shushed her and told her to be patient, then yanked down the other side of her bodice, pulling her chemise with it. He pulled back, and she could feel the air, now cool in the evening, against her nakedness, and it was delightful. She looked up at Jonathan and saw that he leaned on his elbow, gazing at her with a strange look on his face.

"You're so beautiful, Anne," he said almost reverently as he ran one finger down the side of her face, then her neck and shoulder, passing under the curve of her breast before tracing over the fabric of her dress and down the side of her hip.

"Please, Jonathan," she pleaded. "Please."

"What?" he said, leaning down once more to kiss her. "What can I give you?"

"I-I-I don't know," she stammered, flushed, hot, and expectant.

He smiled against her lips before pulling the lower one in his teeth and suckling it. "Be patient, Anne. It is worth the wait." All she could do was kiss him in response, feeling almost as if a fever had overcome her, producing within him what sounded like a deep growl as she placed her hand on his naked chest and ran her fingers through the soft hair that grew there. His fingers tightened where they gripped the fabric of her skirts, and he began to bunch them up in his fist, pulling them in great handfuls until they were pooled around her waist. The air on her legs was another shock, but she felt her hesitation melting away when Jonathan touched her again. He was running his hand down the length of her hip and thigh, stopping to unfasten her stockings before he methodically pulled each one off. Never had the soft silk of her stockings felt so wonderful against her skin as when it was followed by Jonathan's even softer touch. When each of her stockings had finally slid from her toes, Jonathan's hand moved its way upward again, taking time to caress the back of her knee, moving slow circles up the inside of her thigh, before finally resting on the mound above her most private place. Her hips seemed to rise toward him of their own volition, pressing herself against the palm of Jonathan's hand. He did not move his arm, but he leaned his mouth to her once more.

"Don't rush," he said.

She could only moan in response, though she tried to nod her head. Before she knew what she was about, Jonathan was kissing her again and moving his palm up and down. She writhed with an agony sweeter than she'd ever imagined. When Jonathan moved his finger against her opening, she cried out, begging for something, though she was unsure what she was asking for. She just knew there was more. She gasped as Jonathan slid his finger into her. He stroked her as one would take care to stoke a fire, slowly, deliberately, igniting a passion within both of them that could not be contained.

When she cried out for release, he slid his thumb across the tiny nub at the top of her womanhood, bringing the sensations nearly to a crest before stopping to kiss her and suckle her nipples, one by one. She returned his kisses and caresses with fervor, her innocence, and confusion forgotten in her blatant need. She tried to wriggle herself against his hand, to elicit more from him, but he expertly controlled her movements and responded only enough to tease her until she could stand no more. He stroked her with a deliberate rhythm then, using his finger and thumb and kissing her lips until she shuddered around his finger and clawed at his back, pulling his mouth closer to hers as she moaned in release.

His voice was husky and pained as he pulled back to look into her eyes. "You are amazing."

She smiled, her eyes half-lidded in her languor, and she whispered, "No, it is you who are amazing."

He only groaned in reply and kissed her on her forehead, her cheeks, and again on her mouth. "I'll be right back, sweeting," he whispered against her lips as he rubbed his nose against hers. "Don't go anywhere."

When he rose, she stretched out in a yawn like a comfortable cat. She pulled her dress back into place to cover herself. "I don't believe I will," she said before closing her eyes.

He took long moments in the corner, and Anne felt cold until he returned, stretching out his long frame behind her, pulling her close against his chest. She smiled and snuggled herself up against him before they both fell into a dreamless slumber.

Chapter Three

Six months later

Anne stretched awake, squinted at the bright sun coming in through her windows, and she knew she had overslept. She turned over and, sure enough, saw Mildred's white cap bob hello.

"Millie?" She asked, yawning. "How long have you been standing there?"

"Only a moment, Miss Anne," the maid replied as she sat the tray on a side table and made her way to the bed to assist her lady.

Anne stood up and pointed to her wardrobe. "I think it'll be the yellow morning dress today, Millie."

"Yes, Miss Anne." The maid bobbed her head again and went off to fetch the gown. Anne made her way to her washstand and felt a good deal better once she had splashed cool water over her face and neck. When she turned around, she saw Millie had returned with the gown and was busying herself with Anne's toilette. Anne waved her maid away. "No to-do today, Millie.

I'm staying in and going over the accounts."

"Yes, Miss Anne." Millie retrieved Anne's stockings, chemise, and stays, and together they got her dressed and ready for the only excitement her life had now. Each day was much like the last, and she actually welcomed a task, no matter how boring or menial.

How much her life had changed, Anne thought with a sigh. She'd barely had time to mourn her mother's death while working in the hospital, and then had kept busy with the management of the household. Though on the fringes of society, her mother had left her a sizeable fortune, and Anne had realized, had taken care to allow her daughter to lead a charmed life in which she could do as she pleased. Now that Annelise Heatherington was gone, it was up to Anne to take over the considerable duties that woman had managed during her life. There were a dizzying number of tasks to attend to, from the hiring and management of the servants to the decisions about what to do with the remainder of the estate. Annelise had been a fiercely independent and opinionated woman, the fact of which had plagued Anne for most of her life. Anne had loved her mother, and she mourned her loss, but she had to admit to a feeling akin to relief to finally be out of the scandalous wake the older woman had left everywhere she went.

Scandal, Anne thought with a frown, was precisely what she wished to avoid, though whenever she thought of it, she remembered that strange and wondrous night in Chelsea Hospital and wondered if it was just in her blood, this wickedness, this propensity to wanton acts. No, she thought, she had control over her life now. That one night was almost a dream and would become more so as it faded from her memory. But she thought as she watched the snow falling softly outside the window, time had passed from late spring to early winter, and the memories had done little to fade. They seemed in fact, to be more lustrous than ever. Every day the memory seemed to become more bitter than sweet as she went from hoping to never see him again, to wishing she might, to realizing she almost certainly would not.

She stood and allowed Millie to pull her morning dress over her head, shaking her previous thoughts out of her mind. She was mistress of her house now, and she would do well to remember that she had more to think of than a single act of transgression, memorable though it was.

When she reached her morning room, she went directly to her escritoire, waving her hand absently at Millie, who followed close behind with a tray of coffee and coddled eggs. She didn't feel hungry this morning and didn't much see the point in partaking in breakfast merely for the ritual, as there was no one else for her to share it with. She sighed and pushed back from her desk. It couldn't hurt to at least have some coffee. She smiled at Millie, rubbed the bridge of her nose, and nodded her head so the maid would curtsey and leave.

She had not been sitting back at her escritoire for five minutes, steaming coffee in her hand, her brows furrowed as she peered down at the books in front of her, when Hillyard, her butler, announced a visitor. "A gentleman here to see you, Miss Heatherington."

Anne looked up, pursing her wide mouth in a frown before asking, "Whoever could it be?" No gentleman that could properly be called such had visited Heathermere since the initial flurry after her mother's death. She'd had secretaries and barristers, servants and workmen, to be sure, but no gentleman callers.

Hillyard cleared his throat. "An earl, Miss, and he says it's rather urgent." Hillyard paused and frowned. "Shall I show him in?"

Anne was mildly annoyed at her butler's obvious show of his own opinion on the matter, but she had to agree it would not do to turn the earl away. "Yes, thank you, Hillyard."

Anne stood and tried to remain composed as her mind raced. Who on earth could he be? She didn't have long to wait, however, before Hillyard appeared again in the doorway and announced, "The Right Honorable Earl of Norwich."

Anne came forward, curtsied, and extended her hand. "Lord Norwich," she said before looking back up to his face. He looked familiar in a way Anne could not quite place. His dark brown eyes were deep-set and were full of emotion. A handsome man in his late fifties or early sixties, he appeared to be healthy and hale, though there was telltale gray throughout his dark hair. When he bent over her hand and muttered, "Miss Heatherington, I presume," Anne could not help but hear a slight catch in his voice. She gestured toward the sofa when he straightened. "Please, Lord Norwich, join me. Would you care for any coffee or breakfast?"

"No, I . . . er," he stammered. "Ah, yes, in fact, that would be lovely."

Anne nodded at Hillyard, who disappeared and half-closed the door behind him.

She studied the man next to her and felt a creeping sense of dread as he looked about the room. His face was flushed, and Anne wished more than anything to just ask him what he was doing here, but she had been raised to be polite at the very least and held her tongue at great cost to her nerves.

After a minute or so, Lord Norwich looked back into her eyes and said, "I can't believe it's really you." His eyes scanned her, and she saw with some surprise that he was blinking back tears. Even so, the corners of his lips raised in the hint of a smile. "But of course, it is. *Look* at you."

Her patience was nearing its end. "You'll excuse me, my lord," Anne began, trying to keep her voice low out of deference to the obvious emotions he was feeling, "if I do not follow your conversation."

His eyes snapped back to her own, and he shook his head as if trying to rid himself of his thoughts. "Of course, Miss Heatherington, I apologize." He leaned back against the sofa and sighed, looking up toward the ceiling. "Where do I begin?"

Anne did not reply, but rather kept her eyes trained on his face.

"The devil take it," he said, standing up in a burst of energy. "I'm your father. Can't you see it?"

Anne, despite all her well-rehearsed propriety, could not muffle the gasp that escaped her mouth, though her hand flew up to silence herself should any other untoward sound come out. Lord Norwich strode to the window and rested his hand on the sill. Anne stood and began to pace the floor.

"But you cannot be," she said at last, "my father was an Italian tenor."

A snort from the gentleman caused the frown to deepen on Anne's face. "Mother always said—"

"Deuce it all, girl," the man interrupted, "your mother lied."

This maligning of her mother was more than Anne could bear. She soon found herself standing before Lord Norwich, anger filling her voice with venom. "I'm sorry, my lord, but I must not allow you to say such things in my presence."

When those deep brown eyes looked back down at hers, Anne regretted her tone.

"Please accept my apology," Lord Norwich said as he took her small hands in his larger ones. "I do not mean to speak ill of your dear mother." His eyes were glistening with tears.

When the door opened, it startled both of them, but it was just Millie with a full breakfast tray to complement the cold one she'd already received.

"There," Anne said, clearing her throat, "join me for some breakfast and we'll try to work this out." She motioned to the small table by the large gallery windows, and His Lordship seated himself with a deep breath.

When Anne had served their coffee and sat down herself, she said, "Why don't we start at the beginning?"

Lord Norwich nodded. "I loved your mother very much, Miss Heatherington."

"As did I," she said, looking down at her egg.

"I wanted so very much to know you," he continued, causing Anne's cheeks to begin burning, "but she would not allow it."

Anne was startled by that. "Why ever not?"

"Perhaps it's best if I give you her letters and let her explain it to you." Lord Norwich reached inside his coat and brought out a bundle of papers, tied neatly with a simple brown cord. He sat them upon the table between them and pushed them toward her with his fingertips, but she made no move to pick them up.

"I'm not sure I would feel comfortable reading these," she said.

"I understand. Nonetheless, you should have them now."

Anne looked at the letters and felt a mixture of revulsion and fascination. She took them and deposited them into the drawer of the table they were eating upon.

"Very well," he said, "I hope you'll read them one day. I'm not sure I can explain your mother's reasons adequately as I have never understood them myself."

Anne nodded. "Why don't you try to sum up?" she asked.

"She said she wanted an independent life for you. She didn't want you to be—how did she put it—tied down to connections with the *ton*."

Anne could only smile. Didn't that sound exactly like Annelise Heatherington?

"Your mother was a free spirit, Miss Heatherington," the earl said, not without admiration.

"Indeed," was all Anne could reply. Long moments passed as Anne thought of her mother before she looked back up at Lord Norwich and tried to sort through what he'd just told her. Anne had known her mother was a mistress to many noblemen. A soprano in the opera and sometime actress on the London stage, she seemed like a caricature of the most banal and common of mistresses. But she had made a good living and had raised her daughter in the artistic haven of Bloomsbury, surrounded by comfort, if not luxury, and loved by all in her mother's circle of friends. Her mother had always told her that her father was a great Italian tenor and that he had died tragically and young. Anne had never had any reason to doubt her, given how common such stories were. But now, as she looked into Lord Norwich's eyes, almost a mirror of her own, she knew without a doubt that what he was saying was true.

As if he could read her thoughts, Lord Norwich said, moving toward her, "You can see I have nothing to gain from contacting you," his eyes misted over, and he grabbed her hand again. "Except a daughter."

The emotion of the occasion, the thoughts of her mother, and the pure shock she was experiencing caused tears to fall down each of her cheeks when she blinked. She brushed them away with the back of her hand and laughed. "Wherever do we begin?"

The earl stood and took both her hands in his own. His words tumbled out in a rush. "I'd like to settle a living and a dowry on you, bring you to Mayfair, and introduce you as my ward. Some people will see through the ruse, no doubt, but it's not terribly uncommon, and if you can stomach some gossip, it will be of little import. I'd like to see you settled, Anne."

Anne looked out the window once more, trying to gather her thoughts. Settled. He said it with such finality as if it was all as simple as that. Settled. Hadn't she often dreamed of such a thing? But one small thought kept pushing itself into the back of her mind.

"What of my mother's wishes?" she asked, her voice low.

"Are they your own?"

Anne smiled. He could probably see the difference between mother and daughter. "Not particularly."

"I would never force you into a loveless or convenient marriage," the earl said, his eyes earnest and deep. "You could always return to your independence here in Bloomsbury if that is what you wished." He paused and squeezed her hand. "All I ask is for the chance to know you, and to help you in any way I can."

"Won't your wife disapprove?" Anne asked, shuddering at the thought of a resentful stepfamily.

"She and my firstborn son died in childbirth," he said. "I live alone, so of course we'll want to secure a female companion to chaperon and introduce you to society. I believe my widowed sister Harriet would accept the task with alacrity." He chuckled, and Anne wondered if her Aunt Harriet would be more intimidating than any wicked stepmother.

Though the thought of this was a little amusing, she tried to keep the wry smile out of her voice as she replied, "Very well, Lord Norwich, I accept your offer."

Chapter Four

June 1816, Sutcliffe House, London

Jonathan Marksbury sat in his library, trying to read a novel while his mind raced. Spring was blooming into summer, which meant it had been a full year since that horrific battle at Waterloo, and though the rest of his countrymen seemed to think they had won a great victory and it was a time for heady celebration, the Duke of Sutcliffe remembered the day as anything but victorious. What he could remember of the day, that is. It had been a year since his brother had found him at Chelsea Hospital and he had returned to Sutcliffe Manor, his ancestral home in the rich countryside of Dorset. One year since his life had been miraculously given back to him after lying in that ditch in Hougoumont, and that meant it had been just as long since, in spite of his attempts to forget, he had spent that wondrous night with the elusive Anne Heatherington.

He laid the book face down across his lap and leaned his head back against the high cushions of his easy chair. His eyes closed, and he shook his head as his mind went over all his attempts to find her. His brother knew of no one in their social circles named Heatherington in London, and even his dowager Aunt Margaret had never known a family by the name of Heatherington in all her formidable years. Jonathan supposed she could be from a merchant family, as he had suspected, but he had few inroads in those circles and felt that, once he had recovered his identity and most of his memories, it would probably be more painful to uncover her if he knew they could not wed. For that was what he desired. It was incredible, after all, since he had hardly given thought to taking a wife at all before he'd met her. He'd always known he'd have to produce an heir eventually, but he was still young enough at eight-and-twenty to bide his time on that front, despite his Aunt Margaret's wheedling. After waking up in Chelsea Hospital in that empty wardroom to find no trace of Anne, only a month or two had gone by before he'd realized that, try as he might, he could not forget her. He could not name what force kept her in his thoughts, though he could not deny that lust had much to do with it. No matter the impetus, he had made a valiant effort to find her and wed her. Now, he supposed, after his failure at that and his prolonged recovery upon returning home, he would do well to move on.

In that vein, he had come to London, opened up Sutcliffe House, set up his Aunt Margaret and his younger sister Sarah, and decided to embark upon a lively season in town. Since he'd arrived a week ago, however, his spirits had not perked up as he'd hoped. He'd been listlessly going about the motions, allowing his valet to bring in a tailor, using his innate good taste to choose simple yet elegant cuts and colors for his new breeches and waistcoats, and kindly smiling upon his sister and aunt as they chattered away about the milliner, the dressmaker, and the latest fashion in bonnets. Even the nights at White's with David, his incorrigible younger brother, had done little to enliven him. He was trying to put on a valiant front with his family. He loved them so much, and they were so happy to have found him after the battle, he wanted nothing to dim their spirits. But his nightmares kept him awake at night, and thoughts of his lost Anne Heatherington haunted him during the day.

He had sat back up, picked up his book, and attempted reading once again, deciding firmly to make a real go of it this time, when voices from the hall drifted in.

"Johnnie! Dear Jonathan!" Sarah's voice was breathless and high-pitched as she sailed into the room. "Guess who we met in the park today, traveling with Lady Norwich."

"You're a vision as always," the doting brother said, and it was a heartfelt sentiment, for his gentle sister was as light and fresh as he was dark and sulky. She wore a pale-yellow walking gown, and her chestnut hair was tied back in a very fetching manner beneath a fashionable bonnet. "Now, how could I possibly guess whom you met today?"

"No, of course, you couldn't," she said, draping herself into a chair. "So, I'll simply have to tell you." She leaned forward and dropped her voice to a conspiratorial whisper. "I'm quite sure she'll be the new Incomparable this season."

"Now don't get carried away," Jonathan laughed, "I am sure that title is reserved for you alone."

Sarah laughed but blushed as she rose and came to sit nearer to him. Indeed, her brother thought, she really was quite beautiful. "You are a silly man," she said, dropping a kiss on his head, "but I love you for it."

"So, are you going to tell me who she is, what are her connections, what sort of dowry she possesses, and exactly when I must first engage her for a waltz?" Jonathan teased.

"Well, that's just the juiciness of it," Sarah said. "Nobody's quite sure what her connections are precisely. As to your other inquiries," she said, numbering them each off on her fingers. "The dowry is rumored to be large, her guardian is Earl Norwich, and you may engage her at Lady Weatherby's ball on Saturday."

"All the information I'll need to catch my future wife in my web of cunning and charm. All, except, of course, her name," Jonathan teased.

"How could I have forgotten?" Sarah laughed and stood to leave the room, "A Miss Anne, Miss Anne Batten, though I am quite sure she has only lately been called that."

It was not long after his sister departed that the name of Miss Anne Batten left his mind. He had only just resolved to resume his reading when his Aunt Margaret came in. Dressed in a formidable purple walking habit, bewigged and befeathered in a manner that would be quite ridiculous in a woman any less regal than his tall and imperious aunt, she sat in the chair opposite him and rang for tea. Jonathan thought she would start in on the new Incomparable, so he tried to ignore her for as long as he could. This good-natured ribbing was common between them, and he allowed a small snicker when he heard her tapping her fingernails on the wooden arm of the chair.

"Very well," he said, putting down the book, "what news do you have for me today, Aunt?"

Margaret narrowed her eyes and brought up her spectacles. "What are you reading, there, boy?"

"Shakespeare's sonnets."

The old lady chuckled. "Romantic fare, indeed."

Jonathan folded the Roman history book between his leg and the cushion of the chair, keeping his face poker-straight.

"Indeed," he nodded.

Margaret removed her glasses and leaned back in her chair. "That little chit led me a race this afternoon," she said, sighing. "But I will settle for nothing less than the best. She will make a fine debut."

"I'm sure she will."

"There are other young ladies looking for husbands," his aunt said, her eyes widening in mock innocence as she reached for the teapot the butler brought in.

"Are there?" Jonathan said, feigning surprise. "Well, that shall make Sarah's goal of a proposal from every young man in London quite less achievable."

"Stop being a goat," his aunt handed him his tea, and he

took it with a frown.

"I'm not being a goat," he said, "just rather piggish."

The old lady laughed out loud at that. "Well, to be sure, we had a very nice time in the park today. Sarah is making a good impression, and, as you know, she carries herself with lovely good humor."

"Yes, I know," Jonathan said, leaning back on the cushion. "Just ask David about all the young swains we've had to fend off at White's every evening after you've been in the park."

"You'd better get used to it, my boy," his aunt said. "After Lady Weatherby's ball, the season officially opens, and you know there'll be no end to it all until she's gone on her honeymoon."

Jonathan sipped his tea and watched his aunt as she held her cup and looked up.

"We did meet some competition today, though."

"Ah, yes, the enigmatic Miss Batten."

"So, Sarah's gotten to you already?"

"Indeed. She could hardly have tripped through the house without proclaiming it to the world."

"Well, you know the thing to do would be to offer for this new chit and take her out of the running." Jonathan allowed a real frown at that, but his aunt continued, "Of course I'm only joking, my boy. Though I won't say you won't find an interest in this one. A quick mind and beautiful to boot. As a matter of fact, I think she and Sarah may make fast friends."

"That's the first good I've heard about this Miss Batten all day," Jonathan said, setting down his empty teacup.

Lady Margaret nodded. "Sarah could stand to go gadding about with someone other than her two silly brothers and one forbidding old woman."

Jonathan smiled and stood to kiss his aunt on the cheek. "Forbidding I'll give you, but old I will not allow."

"Quite the charmer," Margaret said, patting his hand affectionately before looking up and adding, "too bad it's wasted on dowagers and sisters."

"You're incorrigible, Aunt," Jonathan said, "I shall have to see what I can do about curbing you. Until then, I'll take my leave and bid you farewell until dinner." He bowed and made to leave the room. His aunt stood and snatched at the book he'd tried to hide.

"I knew it," she said, and there was a little too much triumph in her voice for his liking. "I'd almost swear there wasn't a romantic bone in your body, Jonathan Marksbury."

"Certainly not," he replied and bowed again, turning on his heel and striding from the room.

Anne stood before the pier glass in her dressing room and moved her full skirts back and forth as she and Millie admired the effect.

"Miss Anne, I've *never* seen a lovelier gown," Millie exclaimed, pulling her little white cap askew before she clapped her approval. Anne blushed in spite of herself and looked down at the confection she was wearing.

"I feel rather foolish, actually, Millie," she said. "It's all a lot of fuss over a silly dance party."

Millie gasped. "Best not let," Millie said, mouthing *the dragon,* "hear such a thing."

Anne rolled her eyes. She and Millie had come up with their nickname for Aunt Harriet upon their first meeting with the cantankerous old lady, and though they had developed what could only be called a grudging respect and affection for her, the name had stuck. Both girls would be mortified should Aunt Harriet hear such a thing. Anne nodded at Millie's words. Aunt Harriet had gone to such trouble to help her become accustomed to society, to introduce her to a few select genteel families, and to assemble this dazzling wardrobe, it was ungrateful indeed for her to talk about it being foolish or silly.

"You're right. But don't worry, Millie," she said, bringing her head close to her maid's, "I'm sure she's too busy fussing over her wig and velvets to bother with us just yet."

Millie giggled and came closer to tug and smooth at the deep pink silk that draped Anne's body. Anne indulged her until she yanked at the high waistline in the front. Anne batted the little maid's hand away and blushed. "Now, Millie, that is quite enough. I think we're displaying more than plenty of my . . . er . . . charms already."

"Now, Miss," Millie replied, "I've heard said that a lady can never have enough charm."

"Why, Millie, you insolent chit," Anne said, holding a hand to her chest, "I *do* believe you've forgotten your place." Both Mildred and Anne dissolved into giggles. They had been together since both were young teenagers and had an easy way about their interactions that was much more like friends than employer and employee.

They sobered soon enough, and Millie led Anne back to the pier glass in her tasteful and well-appointed room in Norwich House. Anne still had days when she looked around, disbelieving the changed course her life had taken in the past six months. Now was one of those moments, for not only was she shocked again by her position, but she had to admit a little awe for the figure who stared back at her from the mirror. Millie had done wonders with her dark, unruly hair, piling it in a sweeping mass behind her head, leaving one long curl falling over her left shoulder, which was bare except for the tiniest cap sleeves that clung to the tops of her arms. Her bosom was displayed in fine fashion, her light stays being just enough to create what Millie assured her was a still-modest amount of cleavage. The pink silk was dark and shimmered a little in the light as Anne turned this way and that. It was an unornamented gown, beautiful in its simplicity, and Anne had to admit she must be a vain and horrible girl indeed, for she was quite pleased with the effect.

Both women were startled out of their reverie by a knock at the door. As was customary, Millie went to answer, while Anne stood off to the side, though she knew it was probably the butler come to tell them the carriage was waiting. Millie closed the door when the visitor left and came to Anne. "It's time, Miss Anne," she said, nodding her head. "But your father, the earl, would like to see you in the parlor first." Anne nodded and took Millie's hands in hers.

"Well, here we go." Millie again forgot her place and hugged her mistress before dashing a tear from her eye. "You're a vision, Miss. Take care the gentlemen see you and not your fortune."

Anne chuckled. "You're wise for an insolent little chit, Millie."

Millie nodded, then kissed her hand in a continental *adieu* as Anne made her way downstairs.

Robert, Earl Norwich, stood in his front parlor and paced the floor in front of the fireplace so many times that he could swear he could feel it getting warm under his feet. He felt a great many conflicting emotions, but he had to admit the chief among them was nervousness. He wanted so much to know Anne, to make up to her what he felt he owed to her and—he had to admit—to her mother as well. He wanted her to make a good match so he could see her settled before he left this world. And he wanted a blood heir to dote upon with his fortune, if not his name. He'd given up on ever remarrying when his wife had passed. She was a kind and simple woman, but he'd never loved her, try as he might. Not like he'd loved Anne's mother. It was just like him, he thought, to fall in love with a courtesan. He seemed to always get things wrong. When Anne came into the parlor, he had to catch his breath at her beauty. This, he thought, this is one thing he must not get wrong.

He was not a man of many words, so he came forward and smiled at her, the tears welling in his eyes. She took his hands and thanked him for the gown.

"I would buy a hundred such should they all suit you as well as this, my dear."

"A hundred is probably too many, my lord," she said, laughing, "but believe me when I say you have bought nearly a score already."

He laughed. "I have no need of knowing, my love, for my sister Harriet is quite capable with the handling of finances. I need only to enjoy the effect," he said, stepping back with her hands in his to admire her further. He nodded. "Very passable."

She laughed again and blushed as he let her hands drop. The pink in her cheeks only heightened her beauty. Dash it, he thought, he might have more trouble fighting the young swains off than finding a suitable one for a husband. Her eyes met his own again, and she motioned to the door, "Shall we?"

"Yes, but first," he said, stepping to the side table. He'd been so bewitched by her, he'd almost forgotten his purpose in having her come to the parlor. He picked up the box that lay there and handed it to her. "A little token to celebrate your debut."

She looked up, large brown eyes wide. "Believe me, my lord, the gown was quite enough."

"Posh," he said, closing her hands around the box. "Take it. I only wish there was even more I could be doing for you."

He watched her carefully as she opened the small box. He felt absurdly pleased with her gasp of surprise. Her eyes shot up to his, and he could see tears there. He looked away, for it was his estimation that a gentleman should refrain from crying twice in one evening. His valiant attempt was foiled when two slender arms encircled his neck and a kiss was planted upon his old cheek.

"Oh, father," she said, delighted. "It's beautiful. Will you help with the clasp?"

"Of course," he said as she turned away from him so he could fix the clasp of the necklace at her nape. It was, as he had discerned, Anne's taste, simple but elegant. There were no crusts of gems or curlicues of precious metal. Just one simple chain with a brilliant ruby in the center, falling with simple grace upon her white chest. It had been chosen not only to match this particular gown but also to set off Anne's pale skin and dark coloring. When she turned around, he thought he could almost see flashes of the ruby reflected in the darkness of her eyes. But he shook off such fancy and held his arm for Anne.

"Come, my girl, time to set the *ton*'s collective tongue to wagging."

She smiled and nodded, taking his arm and squeezing it as they made their way out the door.

"La! This crush is even worse than last year, I declare," said Miss Jessica Weatherby, looking up at the Duke of Sutcliffe through batting eyelashes, and placing, in a manner so forward as to be nearly scandalous, a small gloved hand on his forearm. Jonathan smiled out of courtesy but stepped back so her hand fell away from his arm.

"Indeed, Miss Weatherby," he said, scanning the room above his companion's feathered head, "As you hate a crush so much, I wonder that your mother agreed to put on this ball again this year."

Little Miss Weatherby frowned and opened her fan, which she began to wave furiously back and forth. "I declare, Your Grace, you are incorrigible," she said in practiced tones before she spotted her escape. "La! I never thought to see you back in town so soon, Lord . . ."

Jonathan didn't hear the rest or dare to look in the direction of the unfortunate nobleman who'd been next ensnared by Miss Weatherby. He sighed and felt a little ashamed of himself. Jessica Weatherby was no threat to him; he didn't know why he felt the need to behave quite so peevishly toward her. It only seemed to him that the trivial intrigues and gossip of the *ton* were even more trifling than they had been before he'd left. For the life of himself, he could not stop thinking that he'd lain in a ditch outside Waterloo, lost some of his memory, not to mention the lives of countless men, to defend a feathered lady's right to complain about how much disdain and contempt she held her own world in. Of course, Miss Jessica Weatherby had not one whit of an idea what he'd been through, and it was rather unfair to lay all his burdens upon one unfortunate flirt, pig-nosed and shameless though she was.

The duke retreated to the long windows opening upon the terraced garden behind the great house and stood in the comparative coolness and anonymity of the shadow from the long curtains that framed the night air. He put a finger between his neck and cravat and craned his neck around to try and get some relief there, throwing his head back and closing his eyes before downing his glass of lemonade in one gulp. When he had brought himself back to rights, however, it seemed the entire room had gone silent, if only for a moment. The orchestra played on, of course, but a small hush had come over the room as they had looked toward the door and then crushed back upon each other to discuss how crushed against one another they felt. Jonathan's eyebrows came together as he looked toward the door a second later than the rest of the crowd, just in time to see an ample old woman, a grayish but distinguished gentleman he recognized as Earl Norwich, and the flash of a pink skirt as the young lady he knew must be the mysterious Anne Batten disappeared among the crowd.

Jonathan sighed. He supposed he owed it to his sister and his aunt to at least gain introduction to the young lady in question. They all desired so much for him to be settled and happy. In his mind, the two did not necessarily go hand in hand, but he had long since given up trying to convince the ladies in his family of such logic. Scanning the dance floor for his sister Sarah, he found her dancing closely, but still at a proper distance, with the dashing Marquis of Bareham. He felt one eyebrow shoot up as the young Marquis, whom Jonathan considered something of a dandy, spread his hand against Sarah's lower back, but he smiled when he saw his sister retreat and nod her head, smiling all the while. It was a great comfort to him to know the family did not have to worry about the licentiousness of at least one of the Sutcliffe children.

When he saw Earl Norwich and his sister the Lady Norwich approach his Aunt Margaret in the dowagers' circle, he knew this was the time to get over with the inevitable introduction to the young Miss Incomparable. He stopped for one more glass of lemonade and tried to keep it above the crowd as he pushed through the mass of people hovering around the perimeter of the dancing area. The room was lit with what could only be thousands of candles, and the heady scent of fresh flowers was almost overwhelming when combined with the perfumes of all the ladies in their finery. When he, at last, arrived at the side of his Aunt Margaret, he was feeling quite dizzy and in need of a seat.

"Jonathan, so nice of you to come check on me," his Aunt said. "And bring me lemonade." She took the glass he had not at all proffered, and he kept a studied smile on his face as he pinched her shoulder through her gown.

"Lord Norwich," he said, bowing, "and Lady Norwich. How delightful to see you." He took the old woman's hand and laid a light kiss upon the knuckles, which seemed to delight her.

"Sutcliffe," she said, looking down her pince-nez at him, "looking a little gaunt, lad."

Instead of feeling insulted by her comment, he found himself absurdly pleased with her bluntness. It was the first honest small-talk he'd heard all evening.

"Indeed, Lady Norwich, I find the close air here doesn't suit me well at all."

"It does not suit me either, my boy," the old woman said, pursing her lips together. "And I'm not afraid to say it. These things," she waved her arm to indicate the crowded room, "are for the young."

"Speaking of the young," the earl interrupted, "I'd like for you to meet my new ward, Miss Anne Batten."

Jonathan shifted his gaze to where the earl was gesturing,

but saw only the dark brown upswept curls of the young woman in question, as she was engaged in a lively conversation with his own sister and the Marquis of Bareham. Jonathan frowned as he eyed the figure of the young lady in her deep pink gown, the flowing fabric of which clung to her curves as it fell from the high waist. There was something familiar about her, but he couldn't quite put his finger on it.

Both Aunt Margaret and the Lady Norwich seemed to be in a race to get the young ladies' attention and draw them into their circle. Each laid hands upon their young charges' shoulders and whispered to them. Sarah turned around first, smirking as she waved her goodbyes to the young Marquis and grabbed Miss Batten's arm. "Come, Anne," he heard his sister say as the enigmatic young Miss Batten turned her head and smiled at him.

Chapter Five

Anne had no idea that one's mouth could go dry like that, that a shock could be so complete as to render one senseless, until the moment she saw her Lord Jonathan standing before her in the crowded, heady air of Lady Weatherby's ball.

"Lord Jonathan Marksbury, Duke of Sutcliffe," her new friend Sarah was saying with a grandiose flourish, but Anne barely heard it as she stared into his gray eyes. He seemed unchanged from when she'd last seen him, aside from his wearing clothes, of course, she thought with a deep blush. She took a breath and looked down. She must recover. Had any woman ever been put in such a situation before?

"Your Grace," she said, curtsying as she had been taught. She dared not look back up at him. His face had been impassive, and it had been impossible for her to tell what he was feeling or if he remembered her at all, so lost in her own shock was she.

There was a tremor in his voice as he took her hand and laid a light kiss upon her gloved knuckle. "Miss Batten. I hope you won't mind my requesting a dance."

"Of course, Your Grace."

"The third waltz, then," he said. "Until later." There was a question in his eyes as she raised her gaze back up to meet his own.

She forced herself to smile. "Indeed, Your Grace, I thank you." The next thing she knew, she was watching the back of his tailored coat as he away from her.

"I'm sorry, Sarah," she said, turning to her new friend. "I must get some air. Will you join me in the retiring room?"

"Of course, Anne," Sarah said, rubbing Anne's elbow as she maneuvered her out of the ballroom. When they reached the doorway, Sarah tugged at Anne's arm. "Whatever is the matter?" she asked in a whisper.

Anne closed her eyes and said—before she could think it out—"Your brother, I . . ."

"My brother?" Sarah laughed. "Of course, he's quite handsome, but I did think the idea of ladies swooning before him was simply a grandiose hyperbole."

Anne realized she had been remiss in speaking with such frankness, and she quickly lied. "No, it's not that," she said, trying to laugh. "It's just that I'm quite nervous to waltz with him, and I thought you could refresh me before I took my first turn about the floor with him."

Sarah narrowed her eyes, and Anne felt guilty for telling a lie that Sarah could so easily see through. Of course, Sarah and her Aunt Margaret had found it rather odd that Anne had only recently learned to dance, but neither of them had had the indecency to comment upon it. And, Anne learned to her relief, apparently, Sarah was not going to comment further on Anne's strange behavior now. She only stood next to Anne in the hallway and replicated the box step of the waltz with her, peeping up at her through her lashes.

When they had both visited the retiring room and taken stock of their hairpins and flounces, they smiled at each other and returned to the ballroom. Anne scanned the room for the duke, and her heart sank when she did not spy his tall figure among the crowd. She sat with her Aunt Harriet, who was engaged in conversation with the Lady Margaret Marksbury and pondered her situation. It had not been unthinkable, of course, that she would see him since they both knew he was a nobleman even when they knew nothing else. In fact, she had tried to steel herself for the idea, knowing its inevitability. But here she was, having met the event head-on, with no earthly idea of how to comport herself.

When asked by several other young swains to dance, she did so in a daze. She'd met dozens of men tonight, men possessing all sorts of title and property: earls, viscounts, barons, and now even a duke. *A duke,* she thought, *of course, he'd have to be a duke.*

She wondered why he'd asked for a dance. Her mind raced through all possible contingencies as she whirled about on the floor for two country set dances and another waltz, this time with the Marquis of Bareham. He talked quite a bit, but to her racing mind's relief, he seemed content to ramble on only about himself. She frowned as she heard him enter into a discourse on the graces of his tailor, who, he said, was a master in bringing out his own natural good figure. *What a dandy,* she thought to herself, and made a note to talk to Sarah about becoming too involved with such a man. *Sarah.* Anne groaned inwardly. Her closest, no, *only,* friend in London was Jonathan's sister. It was all too much to bear. How would she explain her change of name to him? How would she explain any of this to Sarah? She forced herself to stop thinking about it. She took a deep breath and looked back up into the blue eyes of the Marquis, who was just exclaiming his pleasure at how the bright color of his waistcoat complemented those same eyes, and Anne forced herself to smile. She kept up a light banter through the rest of the dance, but she was nonetheless relieved when it was over and the Marquis handed her off to her Aunt Harriet again.

"Well, dear, you look a fright."

"Please, Aunt, don't mince your words," Anne said with a pointed frown.

"Whatever is the matter, girl?" Harriet lifted her head so she could look down her nose at her newly acquired niece. "One would think you'd seen a ghost or were preparing for the long walk up the Tower."

Anne laughed again. Once more her dragon-like aunt had managed to hit right at the truth of a situation. She *did* rather feel like she was preparing for an execution or a battle at the very least.

"Don't worry about me, Auntie," she said, laying a gloved hand on the old lady's shoulder. "Just a bit nervous about waltzing with the duke."

Anne's eyes lifted when Harriet chuckled. "What can be so amusing about that?" she asked the older woman.

"Nothing dear," her aunt said, patting the younger girl's hand and still chuckling. "I'm sure it will all go splendidly."

Anne frowned and looked at Harriet sideways, wondering what the old woman was getting at now. She had no time to ponder it, however, for the next set was a short one and before she knew it, the orchestra was tuning for the third waltz. Though she had not seen him at all since their brief introduction, the Duke of Sutcliffe appeared by her side just as the dance was beginning and offered his arm. When she touched him, she felt a shiver go up her spine. She cursed herself for her weakness and pasted a smile upon her face. She had done many difficult things in her life; this dance would come to an end and pass as the rest had. It's just one dance, she thought, just one dance.

Just one dance, Jonathan thought, unable to keep his eyes from the top of her dark head. Taking a deep breath, he tried to keep his emotions in check. It wouldn't do for him to make some sort of scene here. He'd spent the entire time since asking her for this dance out on the lawn pondering his position. He'd thought never to see her again. And before he'd resigned himself to that, he'd thought he might try and find her to marry her. But now, he realized, he had no idea who she was or who she'd been. What had Sarah said about her? *Though I'm sure she's only recently been known by that name.* He shook his head. Indeed, she had. So, who was she?

"Lord, I mean, Your Grace, I—"

"Don't know what to say?" he bit off. "Why, Miss—ah, but *there* is a problem—what shall I call you?"

"Batten," she said, and he could barely hear her.

"Strange," he said, hating himself for the coldness in his voice, but unable to change it, "I could have sworn you told me Heatherington in Chelsea Hospital."

A blush covered her face until the tips of her ears became red. She looked back up at him and held his eyes with her own deep brown ones. "Surely it is ungentlemanly of you to speak of such things here."

"Surely it is unladylike of you to engage in deceit and trickery," he countered, finding himself annoyed at her anger.

Her eyebrows came together. "I do not understand," she said. "Why are you so angry?"

"I could ask the same of you, Miss *Batten*."

She sighed. "I am sorry, Your Grace," she said, looking right at him. "You must understand how shaken I am at meeting you here."

"In point of fact," he said, never taking his gaze from her brown eyes, "I do not." He twirled her around the floor and navigated them toward an emptier corner where they'd be less likely to be overheard. "I believe you are at an advantage, Miss Batten," he said in a low tone. "As you know my real name and circumstance, whereas I had given up all hope of ever seeing you again, and have no idea who you really are."

He watched her as she looked at their moving feet and chewed on her lower lip. He could tell she was at a loss for what to tell him, which made him even more determined to find out the truth. He gripped her about the waist more tightly than the dance required, and he placed his mouth close to her ear. "Who are you, Anne, and why did you run away from me?"

When he pulled back, he was surprised to find a tear coursing its way down her cheek.

"I'm sorry," she said, "I cannot say." He frowned.

"Does your unfortunate guardian know the truth, at least?"

She looked up at him through the film of tears. "How dare you?"

He took a deep breath. "I am sorry, Anne, I am not sure how you expect me to respond to all of this."

She took a moment to blink away her tears and let him continue leading her through the dance. When she focused on him again, her eyes were clear. "I am not sure how you expect me to respond, either," she said. "I wish I could tell you the truth, but it is really impossible. I can't ask you to trust me."

"Nor, I suppose, can I ask you the same," he said.

"You have done nothing to make me doubt you," she said, looking away.

"But you know nothing of me," he said, wondering to himself even as he heard his own voice why he was going out of his way to make her feel comfortable.

As the music began to wind down, signaling the end of the song, the small hand that rested in his squeezed gently. "Please, Jonathan, please accept my apology." The tears were welling in her deep brown eyes again, and he realized he was helpless at the sight of them. He cleared his own throat and began leading her back to the matrons who waited for them both.

Jonathan stabbed at the coddled egg perched in its delicate porcelain cup in front of him. Try as he might to hide his dark mood, both his aunt and his sister had commented upon it right away.

"Dear heavens, Jonathan," Sarah had said with a start upon

entering the breakfast room, "are you eating that egg, or making sure it's dead?"

He looked down at the mess in front of him and realized that, in trying to crack the shell, he'd broken it into several pieces, and the soft yolk was seeping out. He tore away the rest of the shell and ate before his meddlesome sister could say another word about it.

"I suppose I'm a bit preoccupied," he said around his mouthful.

Sarah frowned, and Jonathan couldn't help but roll his eyes. "Don't you roll your eyes at me," Sarah said haughtily. "It's not my fault it's so hard for you to hide your feelings."

"What feelings might those be?"

"Well, how on earth should I know? It appears," she said, pausing to smooth her skirts as she took her place at the table, "as if both of you are having a great many feelings these days."

His head shot up, and he tried to pierce her with what he hoped was his most intimidating glare. "Both of us?" he bit off.

His sister was a master at getting his goat, and she certainly had the upper hand this morning. She lifted her napkin and spread it on her lap, avoiding his gaze as she welcomed the egg the servant sat down in front of her. "Why, Miss Batten, of course," she said with a charming smile. "You two seem to have made quite the impression on one another."

Jonathan felt the muscles in his jaw begin to quiver, and he pushed his chair back from the table to avoid an ungentlemanly display of temper. He could not resist throwing his napkin down, however, and as he stalked out of the room, he shot one last glare back at his sister, who sat giggling over her breakfast.

It seemed, he thought as he readied his phaeton for a drive, that all the women in his life were determined to have the upper hand. Perhaps it was the soldier in him, but this fact seemed only to spur him to gain said hand. He frowned. Was he really going to let a gaggle of old women and young misses make a fool out of him? No, he thought, his sister, his aunt, and Lady

Norwich were all harmless and had done little to actually raise his hackles. It was the enigmatic Miss Batten who was making him feel out of sorts, with the memories of their shared night together in Chelsea Hospital, her unwavering refusal to reveal her true identity or situation, and now with all his infernal female relatives determined to throw them together at every ball and roué he attended. Miss Batten was definitely the problem. Being the sort of man who preferred not to bring up the rear guard, he realized Miss Batten was the only obstacle he had to face, and the sooner he did so, the better for his own sanity. His lips curved into a smile for the first time that morning. It felt good to have a plan.

Jonathan paced back and forth in front of the fireplace in the morning room at Norwich House, hat in hand. Every few paces he paused and perused an item on the mantel, then resumed his nervous circuit. He was determined to make a show of courting Anne properly, but he had no idea how she might react. When he finally heard footsteps in the hall, he felt his heart leap and his stomach drop at the same time. He turned and saw Anne come in like a breeze, wearing a shabby yellow morning dress that somehow set off her chestnut hair and lithe figure more than the ballgown she'd worn the night before.

"Good morning, Your Grace," she said as she nodded and offered him her hand, her voice full of saccharine charm. "What brings you here so early this morning?"

As he strode forward to bend in formal greeting, he tried to rein in the reaction he had to her closeness.

"Can't you see?" he asked, pasting a smirk on his face to hide his nerves and placing the lightest kiss upon her knuckles, "It is far too fine a day to spend indoors, Miss Batten."

Jonathan stood and met Anne's gaze, direct and questioning under one raised eyebrow.

"Why do you look so suspicious?" he asked, laughing

outright now. "Is it so very odd that an eligible gentleman would call to offer a drive in the park to a freshly out and eligible young lady?"

"Well, *of course,* it isn't." Jonathan saw Anne wince as her aunt Harriet's voice sailed through the door. "Is it, Anne? It isn't odd at all, my dear." Anne's face transformed to a deep frown as her aunt, previously such a dragon, sailed forth, smiling, to extend her hand to Jonathan.

"How charming to see you again, Lady Norwich," Jonathan said, trying his best to be charming. "How lovely you look this morning."

Jonathan was pleased to see old Aunt Harriet blushing under his compliments, but Anne appeared to be brooking none of it. She placed one hand on her hip and tilted her head to the side, catching his eye, waiting like an audience member at a play. Jonathan smiled and winked at her over Aunt Harriet's old powdered wig. At that, Anne threw up her hands and sat down. Jonathan knew, now that Aunt Harriet was here and had heard his invitation, Anne would have no choice but to go for a drive alone with him.

"Shall we, then, Miss Batten?" he said, trying to keep his voice courteous and soft, hiding the triumphant exultation he felt.

"Indeed, Your Grace," she replied, appearing to force a smile. "Just let me gather my things and I will be right down."

He only nodded while Harriet beamed. "Be quick about it, girl! It won't do to keep the duke waiting," she said, shooing Anne away with one hand. Anne frowned once more as she reached the door before sailing out of it.

Just a few minutes later, Lady Norwich was still prattling on about all the social events of the season as Jonathan nodded away, an awful pasted smile upon his face when he heard the hall door open. He tried in vain not to swivel his head toward the parlor entrance, and he winced as Lady Norwich stopped what she was saying and fixed him with a shrewd-eyed gaze.

"She *is* lovely, isn't she, Your Grace?" The question was rather forward, not to mention quite irritating to him at the moment, but it was said with such adoration that Jonathan could not help smiling and nodding his agreement.

At just that moment, Anne entered the room, and she *did* look rather lovely. She hadn't had time to change the shabby gown, but now she wore a smart spencer jacket, and somehow, she was even more dazzling than before. He took a deep breath. Thinking of how beautiful she was would not help him rid himself of all the matchmakers who surrounded them.

"Ready, then?" he said, trying to be jaunty as he approached Miss Batten and offered his arm.

"I am quite, Your Grace," she said, and he felt that she added the title at the end to annoy him. Nevertheless, he secured her gloved hand upon his arm and began to escort her out. He turned in the hall to give a short nod to Lady Norwich, who curtsied in return.

"Have fun, dear," the old lady shouted after them. "Don't forget to button your spencer if there's a chill."

Anne looked up at him through her lashes and shocked him by winking. He laughed before he could stop himself. Once out of doors, he led her to his phaeton, at the ready on the curb, and helped her up. As he walked around behind to take his place at the reins, he realized he was looking forward to the drive. He supposed it wouldn't hurt him to try to have a nice time.

As if Anne could read his thoughts, he was no sooner seated and taking hold of the reins than she said leaned toward him and said, "I suppose it wouldn't hurt us to enjoy ourselves today." He glanced over at her before he clucked to the horses and allowed himself a genuine smile as they drove off.

He kept the horses at a brisk trot, and the early summer breeze was delightful as they drove the short distance to the gates of the park. Neither he nor his companion spoke, and Jonathan allowed himself to glance at Anne several times. She seemed to be enjoying this as if she had never experienced it before.

Her eyes lit up with childlike pleasure at everything from the children on the street to the hired hacks that drove past them, their drivers shouting fine obscenities at one another. He felt himself grinning at her enjoyment, and he realized he couldn't quite account for the pleasure that the very sight of her was giving him.

"It's a beautiful day, isn't it?" he said, wanting her to include him in her thoughts and observations.

"It's wonderful," she said as she turned to face him, and he was warmed by her bright smile. "I had no idea the view from these—carriages?" She chewed her lip.

"Phaetons," he said.

"Thank you," she said, nodding her head before turning away to look at the sights once more, "as I was saying, I had no idea the view from these *Phaetons* was so much different than from the ground."

"Come to think of it," he said, "I don't think I ever noticed that myself."

She laughed, and he felt that warmth spreading again. "That's because you're always driving."

"I beg your pardon, Miss Batten," he said, with mock outrage, "but even the great Duke of Sutcliffe was once just a child who could, he would be sorry to hear me say, decidedly *not* drive a phaeton."

"Very well," she said, laughing again, "I stand corrected. Now, isn't that the park gate, there?"

"It is," Jonathan said with a chagrin that surprised even himself. He realized he was not at all looking forward to slowing his horses to little more than a stately walk, promenading up and down next to the Serpentine and being forced to pander niceties to all the lords and ladies of the peerage. No, he would much rather have continued on, with Anne, feeling the breeze in their faces and listening to her laughter. He had to sigh to himself when he thought of the matrons and young tittering girls who would be riding in the park at this hour. It was not terribly fashionable, and that almost made it all the worse. He and Anne would be the talk of the day, and he rolled his eyes just thinking about it.

"Is something the matter?" Anne asked, her eyebrows lifting. "If going for a ride in the park proves to be so distasteful to you, why on earth did you come over and ask me to join you?" He would have taken offense at her words, but the lilt in her voice told him she was jesting.

"I, ah," he cleared his throat, not quite knowing what to say.

"Come now, Your Grace," Anne said, adjusting the laces on her bonnet. "Surely there can be no secrets between the two of us now."

Jonathan had to laugh at that. He supposed she was right. Wasn't that why he'd come over to ask her for a ride in the first place? To get at the truth? "Well, if you must know," he began, looking down at her, "I would very much rather not be on parade this morning for all to see and discuss later."

He was surprised when Anne laughed outright at that. "You must not have had the season I've been having so far," she said, as her smile turned more wry than humorous.

"I suppose I haven't," he conceded, "though my bout of amnesia was all the rage for a short while. But war stories are nothing compared to the romantic intrigue caused by a lovely young lady appearing from out of nowhere in the home of an earl."

"Precisely," Anne said, frowning. "I would think that the 'Quality' would have more to talk about than my petty flirtations and romances."

Jonathan felt a strange twinge in his stomach at that. Before he could stop himself, he heard the words coming out of his mouth. "May I ask with whom you've had the time to flirt and romance, however pettily?"

He felt like a dolt the moment Anne's eyes flew to his face. "I'm sorry, Your Grace, but no, I do not believe you *may* ask." She huffed and leaned back against the squabs, crossing her arms in front of her.

"I didn't mean to—"

"No, I'm sure you didn't," she bit off. "I realize our meeting was rather unconventional, but I would nevertheless like to remind you that you have no claims upon my person."

"Of course not," he said, frowning, as he turned to face her. "I really must apologize. I didn't mean to imply—oh, damn it all to hell."

He groaned that last bit as he slowed the horses from their already slumberous walk in order to greet his Aunt Margaret. "Why, Aunt, what on earth are you doing here?" he asked between clenched teeth.

"Just taking my morning constitutional, you know," his aunt said, a mischievous grin spreading across her wizened face. "Beautiful day for it."

"Indeed," was Jonathan's terse reply. "You've met Miss Anne Batten, I presume?"

"Of course," his Aunt Margaret said as she nodded in that young lady's direction. "I do hope you two enjoy yourselves. Be sure to take Miss Batten along the river. It is ever so quiet this time of day."

"I shall take your advice, madam," Jonathan said, nodding his head again at his meddlesome aunt as he clucked to the horses.

"I don't want to come to unwarranted conclusions," Anne said, craning her head ever so to look back at the old woman who stood nodding at them from the side of the road, "but if I didn't know any better, I would say your Aunt Margaret is endeavoring to get us alone together."

Jonathan chuckled. "I don't suppose you *would* know any better, my dear Miss Batten. For that is exactly what she is doing."

Anne laughed. "How very scandalous," she said, turning her head back to look once more at Jonathan's austere aunt, whom he imagined was still clucking like a mother hen.

Jonathan tried to balance focusing on the winding road with his compulsion to keep looking toward her. Her mind seemed to be working a mile a minute. "A penny for your thoughts," he said.

"You know," Anne said, as she looked back up at him, "I think I remember trying to make that deal with you once."

Jonathan met her gaze and did not take his eyes from hers. "I remember," he said, his voice soft.

"Do you remember what you said then?"

"That my thoughts were worth more than a penny?"

"Indeed." She still did not take her eyes off him. He broke the spell when he had to cluck to the horses to take one side of a fork in the path. She took a deep breath as he finally looked away from her.

"You know," Jonathan said, looking back at her again. "I have quite a fortune."

Anne raised an eyebrow.

"For your thoughts," Jonathan said.

Anne smiled and nodded. "Very well, then," she said lightly, looking away and pretending to take in the beauty of the day. "You strike a hard bargain, but I'll acquiesce."

"I'm glad to hear of it."

"I was thinking on the whirlwind of the last few days. The ball, the masses of flowers and notes I received this morning, meeting . . ." her voice trailed off and Jonathan felt an unaccountable heat as he realized they were both remembering that night in Chelsea.

"Meeting me again?" Jonathan prompted. At her silence, he prodded a bit further. "I'm paying a duke's fortune for this, right?"

Anne turned to face him. "Yes, I stand corrected, so sorry to have shortchanged you. Yes, meeting you again last night . . . I have to say it was probably the most whirly part of the whirlwind."

Without thinking, Jonathan placed his hand over hers. "The

whirlies are not all on your side only," he said, removing all traces of jest from his voice. She only looked down at his hand upon her own and then looked back out at the birds dashing between the limbs of the trees.

The spell was broken when she spoke again. "It's lovely to see London in the summertime, is it not?" Jonathan pulled his hand away and faced forward, pretending to focus on the horses again.

"I have lived with it so long I no longer even notice its splendor," he replied without looking over at her.

Chapter Six

Jonathan wasn't sure how he had made an ass of himself so soon, but he felt as if he'd done it, and done it in fine fashion. He already felt like a churl for being so peevish at the ball, and now he felt like a simpering dolt for using a word like whirlies. He just didn't know what to think or say, he realized. What he felt when he was around her—the memories of the hospital, the simple beauty of her face when she didn't know anyone was looking, her lilting laughter—they made him so confused and addled that he could barely form a coherent idea in his head at all.

"Confound it all," he said under his breath at exactly the same moment that she muttered something else.

"What was that?" They looked at each other as they spoke in unison.

"I'm sorry," they both said, and this time their chorus was punctuated by laughter.

Jonathan waved his hand and nodded, gesturing for her to go on with what she was going to say.

Anne smiled and looked down at her lap before she lifted her gaze back to his, and he marveled again at how one full look from her could make him melt in his seat.

"I was just saying I was sorry for being so foolish," she said, glancing back down at her hands as a blush crept up her cheek.

"You were?" He asked.

"Why, yes," she said, "What were you going to say?"

"The exact same thing."

"It seems we are destined to always be at loose ends around one another," he said as he slowed the horses to a gentle stop and turned to face her, holding the reins on one knee.

"I don't know why it has to be that way," Anne replied.

"Don't you?"

"Well, when you put it that way . . ."

"I just want to know the truth about you, the truth about the woman I—." He could not finish his sentence, and he finally broke the hold of her gaze to look back ahead to the horses waiting patiently for his command.

"I'm so sorry," Anne's voice was a whisper but clear on the soft breeze, and his soul ached. "I just can't," she said in the same small voice.

"Why?" He said, and he felt shame again at the plaintive, hungry note in his voice. "Do you not trust me?"

When he turned to look at her, he immediately wished he hadn't, for now, he saw the sparkle of tears forming like dew on her thick lashes. She swallowed convulsively and looked away again.

"Can we return now?" she asked.

"Of course," he said as he clucked to the horses. He looked at her again, and his voice was steady and calm even as they lurched into motion. "Do not think this is over, Miss Batten."

She nodded in wordless response, and he was satisfied that she understood him. He would not let her go so easily.

Anne felt the heft of a full vase of flowers in her hand, testing it before she threw it to splatter against the wall over Millie's head. "You'll pardon me for saying, Miss Anne," Millie began with a frown, "but—" her voice turned into a shriek as an even larger bouquet missed her ear by only a hair. "But," she said more forcefully, "I don't see what wrong these flowers ever did to you."

"You don't?" Anne cried, picking up another and testing its weight. "You *don't?*" she asked again, this time punctuating herself with another hearty heave against the wall. "They nauseate me. *He* nauseates me."

"That's what this is about, then?" Millie said, eyeing Anne out the corner of her eye before sprinting across the room to dodge the next bunch of orchids that was aimed directly at her.

"That is what *what* is about?" Anne asked, breathless, her hair falling around her face in tendrils escaped from her tight chignon.

Millie frowned again and shrugged, looking around them at the broken vases, the pollinated stains covering the wall behind her. She then crossed her arms and looked Anne right in the eye. Anne saw the worry in the line between Millie's eyes, and finally sat down on the edge of the bed and buried her face in her skirts.

"There, there, Miss. It can't be that bad."

"Oh, but it is," Anne cried. "You don't even know the half of it. *He* doesn't know the half of it. How can I be courted by anyone after the life my mother lived?"

"Your mother was a good woman," Millie whispered, stroking her hair.

"That's what makes it so horrible, Millie," Anne said, lifting her tear-stained face to look out the window. "She really was. But her lifestyle was not. And now it's a secret I'll always have to keep. Had I thought of it when the earl asked me to live with him, I may have doubted my choice. Don't you see?" she asked, turning toward Millie and taking her hands in her own. "I'll never be able to tell him the truth, or anyone for that matter. Not only do I have to mourn my mother during the time of my life when I need her the most, but I can't even talk about her. It's like her whole memory is dead."

Anne could see the tears forming in Millie's eyes, and the women fell into each other's arms, each sobbing on the other's shoulder. "No, Miss," Millie finally said. "Her memory is not dead while it lives in us. And live in us it will, I promise you that."

"Millie," Anne said, lifting her head to reveal swollen, puffy eyes, "I think the Duke of Sutcliffe suspects I have a secret."

"Well, of course he does, Miss," Millie said, holding Anne's shoulders. "Everyone does."

Anne sighed, running her hand over her hair to try and smooth it. "No, Millie," she said, "I mean I think he won't stop trying until he finds it out."

"It's only natural, Miss Anne. He's a duke. He's a name to protect."

Anne closed her eyes against the pain. "I know. It's why I must not see him anymore."

Millie squeezed Anne's shoulders. "It's not an easy or casual thing to spurn a duke," she said.

"No, it's not. That's why I must do it as soon as possible before any attachment between us is known or gossiped about."

Millie swallowed audibly.

"What?" Anne asked, narrowing her eyes.

"Well, 'tis too late for that, Miss Anne. It's all any of the servants are talking about. Everyone knows the thing to do is to send flowers and regards the morning after an introduction at a society event. To come calling on you and to take you to the park—well, Miss Anne, to be true—"

"Go ahead, spit it out, Millie."

"Well, Miss, he's made his intentions known."

"Yes," Anne said, "Yes, I suppose he has."

"Oh, how I do love a dropped pudding," Anne said in a shrill tone as she spooned out bites of her dessert and continued to try to avoid the subject of Sutcliffe with the earl and Aunt Harriet.

"Posh," the dragon said, slamming her fork down on the table. "What's this all about, gel?"

Anne lifted her face to meet the older woman's eyes. "I don't know what you mean."

Anne felt gratified when she saw her father chuckle behind his napkin. At least it wasn't as serious as all that, she thought. Surely it was not uncommon for gentlemen to take young ladies driving in the park. It didn't mean more than all the flowers she had received from all the other young men. It couldn't matter *that* much that he was a duke if her father could laugh about it. But she was startled out of her comforting litany of thoughts by her Aunt Harriet.

"That boy is handsome as the devil, rich as Croesus, and kind to boot. Why do you act like you'll have nothing to do with him?"

"Because I won't," Anne said.

"Indeed?"

"He is nice enough, and a good companion about town, but I have no intention of setting my sights on him for marriage."

"And why not?"

Her aunt certainly was direct, Anne thought, as she chanced a quick sideways look at her father, who was watching the exchange from the head of the table like a spectator at a tennis tournament.

"Aunt Harriet, really, shouldn't I be more required to come up with a reason *to* marry a man than with reasons why I shouldn't?"

"Well, yes, and in this case, you have presented two columns: one is entitled 'the Duke of Sutcliffe is the catch of the season' and the other 'my niece has no reason not to marry him.'"

Anne had to laugh at that, and her father even let out a real guffaw.

"While I cannot fault your logic, madam, I am sure that logic has very little to do with the dictates of one's own heart," she said, smiling as she reached across the table to lay her hand over the older woman's.

Aunt Harriet harrumphed, though not without the humor that was never far from the old dragon's words.

"Now, then," the Earl of Norwich said, putting down his napkin, "I do believe those are the wisest words I've heard all day. Shall we retire to the parlor and have Anne play us a tune?"

"Of course, father," Anne said, and she realized the word was rolling off her tongue more easily now than it had before. She looked at the earl and saw that he would not push her to marry Jonathan if it was not what she wished. After all, making a "good" match was not his stated purpose in bringing her here for the season. He had said he only wanted her to be happy, and she could see his sincerity now. She should feel like the luckiest woman in the world. Why then, she wondered to herself, did she not?

"The luncheon fare at White's is nowhere near as good as it was last week, is it?" Jonathan asked his brother David as he picked away at the sumptuous meal on his plate.

David lifted his glass of brandy to his mouth and downed it with such speed, Jonathan's eyes narrowed.

"What?" He demanded.

"Me? Nothing. Nothing at all."

"You're smirking at me, aren't you? Smirking at me, your own brother, behind your snifter."

"I may smirk, I may not. In point of fact, this deception is the very reason I always order a snifter when I'm discussing matters of the heart with another man."

"Matters of the heart?" Jonathan asked. "I was talking about my meal."

"Of course you were," David said with a straight face as he hailed the passing waiter for another brandy. He leaned forward with both elbows on the table and whispered, "Believe me, I've seen enough men talking about their 'meals' to know when I see lovelornity."

Jonathan felt a twinge of tightness in his chest at that but tried to push it down. He knew his brother was only trying to show his concern. Since David had already assisted him in trying to find the elusive Miss Heatherington, it had been no use trying to hide Miss Batten's identity as the same woman. Though David had wisely kept quiet enough about it until now, he seemed intent upon having his say.

"All right, then," he sighed, leaning back in his chair, "What's the big advice you have for me?"

David smiled. "That's more like it." He leaned back in his chair and took the new snifter from the salver the waiter held out for him. "I think if you don't have a situation well in hand, you should grab it by the horns."

"That's what I tried to do this morning when I took her out for a drive."

David narrowed his eyes. "And how did that work for you?"

Jonathan folded his arms across his chest and felt the color rising in his cheeks. "Not well."

"So, what is your next step?"

"The usual, I suppose. Ask for a dance at the next ball, send flowers, and call upon her again."

"Sounds delightfully boring." David sipped his brandy again, looking around the room with one lifted eyebrow.

"All right, out with it. What do you propose?"

"I don't think I'm the one who should be doing the proposing," David laughed.

"I'm interested in the chit, for God's sake. I'm not quite ready to marry her." Jonathan exclaimed, once he finally realized what his brother was saying. "I don't even know who she really is."

"Do you need to?" David asked, his smile disappearing for the first time in the conversation.

Jonathan didn't answer. He was not at all sure why, but he didn't know what to say.

As he sat with the whole family later that evening at dinner, Jonathan felt none of the chest tightness or blushing warmth in his cheeks that he had throughout his lunch with David. "What's on the agenda for tonight, then?" He asked his Aunt Margaret and sister Sarah.

"We're going to the Lighton musicale," his aunt replied. "I'm sure Lady Lighton would be pleased to see you there."

Jonathan frowned at the suggestion. It had been a warm day, even for June, and he was not at all sure an evening dressed in waistcoat and jacket, with a starched cravat, in a crowded music room listening to what may or may not be the least talented young ladies of the season as they traipsed their way over Mozart's grandest works sounded like fun to him. Nevertheless, he had a goal.

"Who else will be attending?" He asked, trying to sound casual, and then grimaced as he saw the look exchanged between his sister and aunt.

Sarah took a sip of wine, and he could swear she was using the same smirk-covering methods as their blasted brother when she said, "Well, I hear Miss Weatherby will be there, as well as the Misses Everington. They're quite lovely. David will most likely make a showing. He's had his eye on several of the performers all season."

Jonathan could not quite believe it. His matchmaking sister was making a jest of his desire for Miss Batten's company. "Blast it all," he said, trying to settle his fork on the side of his plate without smashing it. "Do the Earl of Norwich and his family attend?" He asked, frowning.

His Aunt Margaret never looked more like a sly red fox than when she casually raised her napkin to daintily blot her rouged lips and said, "Of course, the earl will be there with his lovely sister-in-law the dowager countess. Sarah, will Miss Batten attend?"

"I'm not sure," she said, batting her lashes. "I cannot recall if Anne was the musical sort or not."

Jonathan sighed and pushed his chair back from the table. "Is it not time for you ladies to retire to the parlor?" he asked. "Don't I need to stay here and smoke and drink brandy or something? Alone?"

"Yes, Your Grace," his aunt said, rising from her seat and taking her cane. "Come, Sarah, don't we have some japanning or embroidery to do before we dress for the musicale?"

"I'm quite certain we do, Aunt," Sarah said, and Jonathan could have sworn she turned at the doorway and winked at him. He sighed, though he did have to admit he felt a certain satisfaction in watching all of his family members clucking over his love life and making much of him. He knew he had been standoffish since the battle and everything that had gone with his return. He had wanted so much to rejoin his family's comfortable life and come back to society, but he just hadn't had it in him. He knew they loved him dearly, and he loved them at least as well, but he could not just paste on a smile and go about his business as cavalierly as the rest of the *ton* seemed able to. Even before the word of Napoleon's escape had arrived, during the heady time when the war had been won the first time, a time when he had not experienced quite as much devastation or lost his memory, he had been annoyed at all the proceedings in town. Life went on, with everyone acting as if no war had ever happened, despite the fact that everywhere one looked there was a family with members who did not return home. Yet they all kept on, throwing balls, purchasing vouchers to Almack's, gambling at any number of hells, shopping on Bond Street. He had found it disgusting. But he had also known that perhaps they were coping with their grief in a different way. He had felt guilty when he had seen his aunt's perceptive eyes watching him. He knew she just wanted him to be happy, but he hadn't been able to give her what she was looking for. He hadn't been able to fake it, and he'd been happy to retire to the country again—had even felt a sense of relief when he was summoned to Brussels upon news of Boney's return.

Now that he was back, he felt a similar sort of disillusionment and *ennui,* but this time with a dose of gratitude for his life, his memory, and his family, that caused him to try harder than he had before to enjoy the season in London. The presence of Anne Batten had added a certain intrigue into the mix. Not only had he been drawn to her in the hospital at Chelsea, but now he found himself rarely thinking of anything other than what she might be doing, or where she might be going, and when he might see her again. He sighed. He couldn't fault his family for funning him about the entire ordeal. He realized he must be transparent in his interest, even to those who did not know him so well. He wondered if Miss Batten was as aware of it, and found himself both embarrassed and pleased at the thought.

Chapter Seven

Anne felt near to bursting with excitement when she heard the strains of the performers tuning their instruments as she walked through the entry hall to Lighton House, stopping here and there to be introduced or to pay her respects to someone she'd previously met. Her head was in a whirl trying to remember everyone's names. She had decided it was an impossible task, but she knew many ladies of the *ton* had managed it, so she gave her best effort. She was, she thought to herself, getting quite good at the polite smile, curtsey, and "My lady, how wonderful to see you again," without ever hinting that she did not know the person standing in front of her from Eve. Tonight, though, it was increasingly difficult to render such niceties with every step. Her heart longed for music. She had not been to a concert, opera, play, or any other artistic amusement since her arrival in town, so busy had they been with her wardrobe, preparations, and each carefully arranged introduction designed to help launch her into society. She would never have known two years ago just how much she would miss her mother's free-spirited, artistic lifestyle, so she had been thrilled at the chance to see a performance of Mozart's works, no matter how small or intimate the gathering.

She smiled to herself at that. Though "small" and "intimate" were words the invitation had used, she could see now that the gathering was anything but. It was almost as much a crush as the Weatherby ball. She longed to make it into the music room and take her seat, but it felt an eternity before she would ever accomplish such a feat of athleticism and grace. She sighed and fought the urge to cross her arms and tap her toes, pasting another smile upon her face when the earl pulled her toward yet another acquaintance. She stopped when she found herself face-to-chest with Jonathan Marksbury.

"Your Grace," she said, in what she hoped was an even tone.

"Miss Batten, how lovely to see you again," he said, and his tone was so soft and sincere that her head snapped up in surprise. She flushed when she saw the heat in his eyes and began to wave her fan in front of her face.

"It's been terribly hot, has it not?" she asked, and she could have cursed herself for the high pitch of her voice as it came out of her mouth.

"Yes, remarkably so, even for London at this time of the year," he said, then chuckled, "I don't know that it isn't rather *too* hot for a *small and intimate* musicale such as this one."

She laughed in spite of herself and leaned forward to whisper, "One would think the music itself was secondary."

"Why, Miss Batten," Jonathan said, placing one hand on his chest in feigned shock, "Would you imagine that it was not?"

"No," she said, sighing once more, "I only *wish* that it were not."

"You like music, then?"

She smiled at that. "Very much, Your Grace," she said, "In fact, it is one of my few passions in life."

"Is it?" He asked, and the intensity of his gaze made her blush anew. Why was it that every encounter with this man could only serve to remind her of that one night in Chelsea Hospital when she had transgressed? She began to feel annoyed with him for always bringing it up, but she realized they had not actually spoken of it at all. She decided to remain silent and nod, hoping to be interrupted by the next well-wishing acquaintance, but her companion did not let her go so easily.

"Miss Batten," he asked, offering his arm, "May I escort you into the music room? It sounds as if the musicians are almost ready."

Anne bit her lip, torn between her desperate desire not to miss any of the concert, and her almost equally desperate wish to be anywhere but in the duke's company. She didn't see much of a way out, however, so she laid her hand upon his sleeve and nodded, murmuring, "I thank you."

As they entered, she was chagrined to find heads turning and people whispering. She should have expected it. She had learned that, while there may be ostensible purposes for every social event of the season, such as watching fireworks at Vauxhall, dancing at a ball, or attending a musical soiree, each event was really for one purpose, and one purpose only—to see and be seen. At first, she had found this exciting in her girlish happiness at being "out" in society. It had felt gratifying for people to see her, talk about her, and, it seemed safe to say, to like her. Now, though, she had seen enough to know the sinister side of *ton* gossip, and she was not eager to remain in the spotlight for much longer. The Duke of Sutcliffe's interest in her would do nothing but leave her squarely in its harsh path. As if he had read her mind once more, Jonathan turned to her with a smirk.

"It seems we're the talk of the evening, my dear."

"Yes, I suppose so," she replied, being careful to look straight ahead of her as they made their way through the rows of arranged chairs.

"Come, now, Miss Batten," he said, "Surely it isn't so bad as all that to be seen with me?"

Startled, she looked back up at him. "No, of course not," she said, "Why would you say such a thing?"

"I'm only teasing you, Anne," he whispered so no one around them would hear him calling her by her given name. "Surely you must find me capable of possessing a sense of humor."

She laughed and let her shoulders drop, feeling some of the tension leave. "I suppose I don't quite know what to make of you," she admitted.

"But you are not opposed to finding out?" He asked in a whisper, his breath moving the tendrils of hair that hung by her ear.

She knew she should say something cutting, or at the very least off-putting. She knew she needed to discourage this man from pursuing her any further, but somehow the words would not quite make it past her lips. Instead, she found she could only look away and pretend not to have heard. She fanned herself with renewed vigor, then turned to him with what she hoped was a bright smile.

"Are these good seats, do you suppose?" She asked, cringing at the squeakiness of her voice.

"They look as good as any," he said, obviously trying to gauge her demeanor. "I will go wherever it pleases the lady."

"Thank you," she said, avoiding his eyes as she nodded and then took her seat in the row. She murmured a prayer of thanks when the duke turned to greet some friends before sitting beside her, and the music began in earnest shortly thereafter.

Jonathan had to admit the ladies were at least passable in their performances this evening, though there did seem to be an overabundance of sonatas for the pianoforte. He could not, however, keep his attention on the music for long. He stole so many sidelong glances at Anne Batten that he fancied he could feel a pain behind his eyes from stretching them so often her way. Her close proximity to him was more unnerving than he could have predicted.

Her hair was, as it had been at the ball, coiffed in a loose chignon on the top of her head, with lovely curls and strands escaping here and there. Ribbons were bound through it, and, aside from a few well-chosen pieces of simple and elegant jewelry, she wore no other adornment. She had to have been the most simply dressed woman in the room, but either for this reason or for some other he could not explain, Jonathan found her to be by far the most striking. Her gown was of a deep green, simply cut, with no lace or edging to speak of. She waved her fan in front of her face, which bore no rouge or kohl, only the natural blush of her flushed cheeks. He had savored her blush earlier, feeling a tightening in his stomach at the knowledge that she remembered that night in Chelsea Hospital at least as well as he did. Now he savored the delight of her flushed cheeks once more.

He had the distinct feeling he could be suddenly lifted and removed to another planet, and that she would not even take notice, so entranced and captivated by the music was she. Her lips were parted, and she leaned forward in her chair, grasping her fan, but no longer remembering to wave it in front of her face as most of the other young ladies in the room were doing. He watched and noticed that she often blinked her beautiful long lashes just before her eyes widened with delight at a particularly well-turned arpeggio. A soft sigh escaped her lips now and then, and he watched her as she cocked her head to the right and listened with her full attention. Just when he felt he could no longer bear the torture of sitting watching her like this, the music stopped and the audience clapped, signaling an end to the first performance. He leaned in toward her.

"And so that was the Sonata in F major?" He asked.

She looked at him in surprise. "No, you're thinking of the number twelve. That was the number thirteen in B flat."

"Yes," he said, "How foolish of me."

"You're not a fan of Mozart's, then?" she asked.

"Only in so much that I like his compositions and enjoy hearing them performed by competent musicians. Beyond that," he said, that telltale flush rising up his neck, "I cannot claim to have much knowledge."

She seemed a bit disconcerted as she looked both ways, then leaned toward him to as, "Is it unseemly for a lady to be interested in music?"

"No, of course not," he exclaimed, laughing. "In fact, most ladies pride themselves on a purely superficial knowledge, gained only for the desire of impressing gentlemen."

Her light laugh in response gratified him. "Well, then," she said, "I shall endeavor to appear much more superficial about it."

"Indeed," he replied, "You should in fact know that the sonata was the number thirteen in B flat, but you should likewise know which modiste constructed the performer's gown, and to whom the young performer may be romantically attached."

"There I am ahead of you," Anne replied, tapping her fan upon his forearm, "for I ran into Miss Everington with her sister on Bond Street at the mantua-maker's just the other day. *And* I happen to know that at least one of them has her eye on Lord David Marksbury."

Jonathan forced a frown. "Indeed?" He asked. "I happened to hear that very same gossip at my own dinner table just this evening."

"Never say so," She replied, opening her fan once more.

Jonathan's eyes narrowed in a mock show of annoyance, but he felt a strange sensation creeping up his spine. Miss Anne Batten was flirting with him. He knew she'd been avoiding the appearance of impropriety, and trying to keep him at a slight distance all evening, but now they had fallen into that same easy banter they'd had the night the first met. He opened his mouth to speak again, but the crowd hushed as the next performer took the stage. He glanced sidelong at Anne once more before reclining back into his chair to ponder the conversation.

Anne suppressed a frown. She wasn't sure quite how it had happened. She hadn't intended it to happen, but there it was: she had been flirting with the Duke of Sutcliffe. *Flirting,* when she was supposed to be *repelling.* She didn't see herself as the flirting type. Indeed, she had spent a good many years practicing a studied aversion to flirtation, teasing, coyness, or any other such false and feminine wile, the likes of which her mother had perfected over the years. Her mother had often teased her for being so missish, but she supposed it was often the way of each generation to rebel against the one that came before. In her case, the rebellion had been against rebellion itself, a crusade against freewheeling, coquettish behavior.

Now after what could only be described as a sinful night of transgression with this particular man, here she was engaging in the very coquetry she had avoided for so long. There was something dangerous about this man, she thought as she glanced sidelong at him. He had managed to break down the very staunchest of her defenses with little more than light conversation. And now here he sat, appearing deep in thought, or pondering the music, she could not tell which. His gray eyes lightened, like the sky just before the sun rose above the horizon. She shook off the fanciful thoughts about a man's eyes. What was becoming of her?

"And which sonata is this?" Jonathan whispered next to her ear.

"It is the number fourteen," she replied, "And, just to make sure our conversation meets the standards of the *ton*'s gossips, I believe Miss Jessica Weatherby has her sights set on the eldest Marksbury lad."

She laughed as he turned toward her, his eyes wide in surprise. "Surely you jest."

"Come, sir," she said, picking up her fan again, "The man is a duke, a war hero, and handsome as the devil. He's the catch of the season."

Her heart fluttered as Jonathan's gaze became serious. "Is he?"

She looked away, ashamed of herself for being unable to meet his gaze. It seemed, though she didn't know how it had happened, that their conversation had turned from fun to dangerous. "It's what I've heard," she said, fanning herself in earnest now. It had become blasted hot in the music room.

As Miss Weatherby wound down the *Allegro* third movement of the piece, many in the crowd began to rise in order to politely applaud before escaping to the terrace or the dining room, where a light repast would be served for the intermission. Anne stood with the rest of them and had begun to turn to exit when she felt a grip like iron on her elbow.

"Come, Miss Batten," Jonathan whispered. "Join me on the terrace."

Aware that he wasn't giving her much of a choice, Anne nodded and followed him through the large French doors that led out to overlook the garden. Many other couples and assorted groups of guests were there, which lent an air of propriety to their quiet *tete-a-tete,* she was relieved to find.

"So, are you not thirsty, then?"

"Hmm?" Jonathan said, appearing for all the world as if he had momentarily forgotten her presence beside him.

"Why the urgency to come out to the terrace, Your Grace?"

"Oh . . . I . . . ahh," he stammered, and his avoidance of her eyes started to annoy her.

"Well, then, if my presence isn't required, I believe I'll join the earl and Lady Harriet in the dining room." She turned as if to go, but she had to stifle a gasp when strong arms enfolded her from behind and pulled her behind a tall potted topiary. Quite beyond her control, what had started as a gasp turned into a sigh as she felt his lips on her shoulder.

"God, Anne," he whispered against her skin, "I just had to be alone with you again."

Her breathing quickened, but she found herself unable to speak. When his lips trailed up toward her chin, she let her head fall to the side to allow him more access. He turned her around, and she sighed again as his lips found hers. Her mind swam with the sensation. It felt so familiar and yet so new. She knew she should stop; she knew she should act offended and disgraced, but heaven help her, she couldn't. She sank into his arms, her hands finding their way to snake around the wide musculature of his shoulders as he deepened the kiss ever so slightly, his tongue brushing across her lips. She felt her knees weaken and her belly tighten; this time it felt both more wicked and more natural, knowing as she did the bliss that could follow from such an embrace. His tongue entered her mouth, and her fingers wound in the hair at the nape of his neck even as her mind screamed for her to stop. Any moment someone could catch them and her glorious London season would disappear in a blink. How disappointed her father would be, she thought. She placed her hand on Jonathan's chest and pushed him away. His breath was ragged and fast as he fell back against the wall, looking up into the sky.

"I'm sorry, Anne," he said, his voice so low it was almost a growl. "I don't know what came over me."

Whatever happened, she didn't want him thinking he'd taken advantage of her. "Please, Your Grace," her voice was little more than a raspy whisper as she straightened her hair and bodice. "Do not blame yourself—for either occasion."

He narrowed his eyes and searched her gaze. "Are you saying you make a habit of this behavior, Miss Batten?"

She felt as if she'd been physically struck. "If that is what you wish to believe, go ahead and believe it," she bit off as she turned on her heel and stalked away from him. How dare he say such a thing? Did *he* make a habit of this behavior? She ground her teeth together, and, though she tried to hide her anger, she was aware she was making a poor showing of it from the stares of so many of the concert attendees as she made her way through the crowd toward the dining room. When she found the earl and dowager countess, they seemed almost relieved to take their leave during the intermission and make a quick escape. Though her father prattled away about the music as they settled into the carriage for the short ride to Norwich House, Anne could feel Aunt Harriet's perceptive gaze scouring her person. Anne flushed under the scrutiny but said nothing. Let them think what they wanted to think, she thought, it appeared that's all anyone was determined to do anyway.

"Come on, we're going home," Jonathan said when he arrived in the group where his sister and aunt had been chatting.

"Speak for yourself," Aunt Margaret said with a frown. "I fully intend to hear the final two sonatas."

"As do I," Sarah said. "I promised Julia I would stay and be a kind face in the crowd when she takes her place on the stage."

"And I," David said as he joined the group, taking a glass of lemonade from a footman who strode by, "have not yet heard both the Misses Everington play. It is my goal to determine with which to flirt more seriously based on their musical acuity."

David flinched as Sarah's fan came down hard on his knuckles in a stinging blow.

"You are a cad. Do you know that?"

"Of course," he said with a laugh, "How else would I maintain my rakish reputation?"

Jonathan made an unsuccessful attempt at stifling an impatient groan. He could no longer bear the light teasing of his family members just now. Though they usually managed to charm at least a rueful smile out of him, tonight he was in no mood.

"Well, then, if you don't mind," he said, sketching a bow, "I believe I will make my way to the nearest gaming hell and proceed to get good and drunk."

His aunt's lips pursed at his impolite conversation, but Sarah looked at him with narrowed eyes. "Where is Miss Batten?" she asked.

"I am sure I do not know," he replied. "I am not her keeper."

"And a fortunate thing *that* is," his aunt said.

Even as Jonathan turned to take his leave, his brother was at his side, leaning in at his shoulder. "I believe," David said, "the evening may just be more interesting where you are."

Jonathan's voice dripped with sarcasm. "More interesting than both the Misses Everington put together?"

David waved his hand. "Don't worry, they're quite literally everywhere I go these days."

"So, I'm not to be rid of you so easily, is that it?"

David clapped him on the back. "Spot on, good fellow, spot on. Now, lead the way to this notorious hell you've been talking about."

Jonathan rolled his eyes. "You know good and well the only wagers I've ever made were in perfectly acceptable games of vingt-et-un at White's."

"Never say you were lying back there." His brother brought one hand to his chest in mock outrage.

"I hadn't yet decided upon a destination," Jonathan said as they strode through the door, which a footman was holding open for them. He took a deep breath of the cool, fresh evening air and sighed. "I just needed to get out of there."

"And away from a certain young Incomparable of the season?" David asked with a shrewd look in his eye.

"If you will not stop asking until I say so, then yes, that is why I needed to leave."

"What happened?"

"She rejected my advances."

"To put it mildly," his brother finished, in more of a statement than a question.

"Yes," Jonathan replied, "to put it mildly. She reacts to me in the same way I react to her, but when she reaches a certain point, she pulls away, almost like I can see her retreating behind some sort of wall in her mind."

"So, there's a reason she's kept her identity a secret, and a reason she does not want a connection with you."

"Besides the fact that she abhors my presence?" Jonathan asked.

"Don't be an idiot, old chap," David said, draping one arm around Jonathan as they strolled near the park. "It's as clear as day to anyone seeing you together that there's definitely something there. The question you're asking is why does she try to deny it?"

"Yes, exactly."

"My question for you, then. Why are you so intent upon finding it out?"

Jonathan was subdued into silence for a moment by that question. For the second time in as many days, his brother had asked aloud the question plaguing his own mind. Why *was* it so important for him to know?

"Wouldn't you want to know?" He asked. "She may be a by-blow, a merchant's daughter, any number of things."

"Indeed," David said, leaning in. "And knowledge of any such fact in her past would change the way you feel when you're around her?"

"No, of course not, but it would change our prospect for marriage."

"But she is the ward of the Earl of Norwich," David argued. "And he has settled a living on her to boot. Surely such a match would be looked upon as anything but unsavory, even for the great Duke of Sutcliffe."

Something in Jonathan told him David was right, that perhaps it did not matter what deep, dark secret Anne carried. It was likely she was a by-blow, but she was under Norwich's protection now, and no one would dare question his protection aloud. There may be unsavory gossip surrounding their connection, but it would probably not be worse than any gossip surrounding his betrothal to anyone. The real question that would not let him rest was, why would she not just tell him the truth? And what had she been doing working as a nurse at Chelsea Hospital? He knew many genteel women had done so, but no one of noble birth would have been nursing there, at the pensioners' home, administering to the common masses.

"What is it?" David asked as he stopped walking and turned to look at his brother.

"I'm afraid," Jonathan said before he even realized the words had formed in his mind.

"Afraid of what?"

"That I am not the only man she's dallied with. That she makes a practice of it. That I am setting myself up for a disappointment, or worse."

"When you are with her, does she seem to be a practiced flirt?"

"Not at all," Jonathan said. "In fact, she has a purely artless way about her that I find charming. Tonight, we engaged in light flirtation at the soiree and I actually *liked* it," he said.

David laughed. "Will wonders never cease?"

They were both quiet for a moment, and they continued strolling back toward Sutcliffe House. After a length of several minutes, David said, "So?"

"So what?"

"Remember what I said?" David asked, "About the bull and the horns and all that?"

Jonathan only nodded. "Yes," he said.

"What do you think?"

His voice was barely audible when he murmured, "I think it may be time to start my campaign in earnest."

Chapter Eight

Anne yawned as she stretched and opened one eye to the blazing sun shining through her bedroom windows and reflecting off the bright walls and linens that surrounded her. It really was a lovely room, she thought as she yanked the bell pull. She swung her legs around and sat up with great effort, for some reason feeling ill-prepared to start her day. She refused to believe, she thought, that her discomfort had anything to do with the handsome face and piercing gray eyes that had haunted her dreams and plopped right back into her mind first thing this morning. One could not control one's subconscious, could one? Of course not. The dream world was filled with random images and meant nothing more than that the mind was at rest. It was only natural that she should dream of the duke after speaking with him at length at last night's musicale. Of course, in her dreams, they had not been at a musicale, indeed they had not been clothed. She covered her face with her hands as she felt the tell-tale heat of a blush creep up her cheeks. She stood up and pulled the drapes even wider, throwing up the sash and breathing in the morning air. She just needed to wake up, that was all.

After a soft knock at the door, Millie entered with a steaming pot of coffee.

"Good morning, Millie," Anne said with a cheerful tone. "Coffee. Just what I needed today. Thank you."

"You're welcome, Miss Anne," Millie drawled, eyeing her mistress and slowly setting the brew on a side table.

"What do we have for today?" Anne asked as she poured herself a cup and sat down at her nightstand. When Millie grabbed a brush and began to pull it through her hair, Anne sighed. "That feels wonderful."

"Well, Miss," Millie began, seeming to time her words with the strokes of her brush. "There are some flowers for you, Miss."

"Are there?" Anne asked. "From whom?"

"There are roses, lilies, daisies, hydrangeas, violets, and even *orchids,*" Millie exclaimed.

"And whom are these beautiful varietals from, may I inquire?" Anne clipped out as she grabbed the brush from Millie's hand and turned around.

Millie swallowed, and Anne knew she was remembering her tantrum from the day before. Dash it all, she'd never had such a display in her life, and now her own maid, best friend even, one might say, was afraid of her.

"Go ahead, Mildred," she said, her shoulders slumping. "I promise I won't throw anything at you."

"Well, Miss," Millie said, pausing. "They're from the Duke of Sutcliffe."

"Which ones?"

"Why, all of them, Miss," Millie exclaimed, "Filling the entire entry hall, they are."

Anne could not understand the exact physiology of it, but her heart seemed to soar and sink at the exact same time. She tried to hide her emotion from Millie as she said, "How lovely. I'll have to go down and look."

"Pardon me for asking, Miss Anne, but . . ." Millie began.

"Yes?" Anne said, encouraging her maid. "It will never do for you to keep acting so mousy around me, you know."

Millie smiled. "Don't think I was ever afraid of you, Miss Anne," she said, "Just concerned for my own welfare was all."

Anne laughed. "Indeed. So, what should I pardon you for saying?"

"Just that yesterday you did not find the duke's attentions so welcome."

"You're right," Anne said, turning in her chair again and looking at her maid in the mirror as she resumed brushing her hair. "I'm so confused. I'm not sure how to feel."

"I wasn't aware we got to choose how to feel," Millie said,

Anne frowned as she glared at Millie in the mirror. "You are too fresh by half, young lady." The rest of the morning passed in a blur as Anne hastened to get ready for the morning tea Sarah Marksbury had invited her to the evening prior. She was seated in the parlor of Sutcliffe House, trying to deflect the too-knowing gaze of her friend before the midmorning bells had even rung.

Sarah leaned forward in her chair, holding her tea saucer poised as if it were a flying projectile she had to balance in her grasp. "So," she asked, "What's going on between you and my brother?"

Anne took a sip of her own tea and smiled. "Why, David and I are becoming fast friends, why do you ask?" she said.

Sarah leaned back in her chair and threw her head against the cushion. "You know," she said, "I believe the two of you are making me old before my time."

"Such a thing should never be allowed to happen," Anne said. "David would find it positively disheartening to flirt with all your friends if they were dowagers and old maids."

Sarah laughed aloud. "Just for that, it might all be worth it."

"In all honesty," Anne said, leaning forward and trying to lend an air of gravity to what she was about to say. "I'm not sure what's going on between Jonathan and myself, but I do know that, no matter what happens, I hope our friendship will not suffer. I do not wish to involve you over much in my own affairs. I'd hate for you to have to feel like you had to choose one side or another."

Sarah tried to hide her smile. "You make it sound rather more like war than love," she said pointedly.

Anne sighed. "Who said anything about love?"

Sarah cocked her head to one side. "Nobody, to be sure."

"What's that supposed to mean?" Anne asked in mock outrage.

"Just that perhaps we should talk about bonnets or slippers or lace or something."

"All very safe subjects," Anne agreed, nodding, though she could not hide the laughter in her voice.

"By the way," Sarah said, "do you attend the opera tomorrow night?"

Anne sighed. "No, the earl had lent his box out for this performance to a cousin coming in from the country."

"Do you wish to attend?" Sarah asked.

"Of course," Anne said, "You know how I love music. But there will be other performances." She waved her hand.

"We have a seat in our box," Sarah said.

"Does your brother attend?" Anne asked, narrowing her eyes.

"David?" Sarah asked. "He adores the opera. Indeed, he never misses a performance."

"Touché, my lady," Anne said, conceding the point. "Do you wish for me to attend?"

Sarah took her hand and squeezed it, giving Anne such a warm smile, she almost felt overwhelmed. "Yes, of course, I do." Her friend said. "You are becoming like a sister to me."

"Very well," Anne replied as she clasped Sarah's hand in her own. "I will go."

Jonathan arrived at the opera with his sister Sarah on his arm. They nodded at different groups of acquaintances here and there among the teeming throng of audience members who gathered in the foyer of the grand theater before the performance began, stopping here and there to chat with particular friends or relatives. His Aunt Margaret and David were to follow them later, along with their guest. Sarah had said it just that way, *our guest,* but the smirk on her face had betrayed her, and Jonathan felt a thrill of anticipation at seeing Anne Batten once again.

Jonathan was startled out of his reverie by a loud whack and stinging pain in his elbow. He grabbed his arm, which smarted at the blow from his Aunt Margaret's fan. "What the devil?" He exclaimed as he spun around to face her.

"You're not a loon, boy," Margaret hissed in his ear when he leaned down at her insistence. "Stop poking your head all around. She's right behind you."

Though on the verge of a snappy retort of some kind, Jonathan's mouth snapped shut when he turned to see Anne walking toward him on David's arm. She was an absolute vision. Tonight, she wore blue, and Jonathan noted that there seemed to be no color in existence that did not complement her features in some new way. Somehow the deep sapphire color she wore tonight set off the darkness of her brown eyes and the luster of her soft hair. Her gown was, again, minimal in its adornment, but perfect in its fit around her torso and its enticing flow down across the full curve of her hip and to the floor. He took her in as he nodded politely, murmuring "Miss Batten," and reaching to take her gloved hand. As he lifted it to his lips, his eyes looked back up to meet hers. His fingers felt searing hot where they held hers, and he saw by her blush that even this small touch affected her as well. He smiled at her and shocked her with a slight wink, so subtle that no one else would notice.

Anne performed a shallow, yet graceful, curtsy as he dropped her hand, and she looked away. "Your Grace, how wonderful to see you again," she said, all politeness, and then the niceties were over. Though Jonathan repeated this sort of ritual with several beautiful women in any given night, he had never felt the occasion to be as momentous, or even as memorable. In fact, he could hardly remember to breathe now, so taken was he with the sight of Miss Batten's hips swaying, the soft rustle of the deep blue silk of her gown like a siren's song beckoning him as she again took his brother's arm and started off toward their box, her head bent toward Sarah in what looked, for all the world, like a sisterly chat.

"Well, shall we, my boy?" Aunt Margaret asked, this time with no hint of sarcasm or her usual biting wit in her demeanor. Jonathan looked at his wizened old aunt with narrowed eyes as he pondered her question, the same one he had heard so many times, this time delivered with—gentleness?

"Of course, Aunt," Jonathan said as he held out his arm for her. "Let us take our seats."

"About that, I cannot bear to sit in the front tonight, my boy. My rheumatism, you know. I need to be where I can make an easy escape for a quick stroll if I start to become stiff," Margaret said. He should have known his tricky aunt would make some sort of move.

"Naturally," he replied through gritted teeth, though he was making every effort to sound accommodating. "Let me hazard a guess that Miss Batten will *need* the front seat, next to mine."

"How did you know, boy?" His aunt's smile was mischievous beneath her old fashion feathered plumage as she looked up at him.

"What makes you all think I'm so incapable of wooing a woman on my own?" He hissed as he leaned down close to her ear so their conversation might not be overheard.

"We think you're capable enough, lad," Margaret's voice was barely a whisper. "It's just that you are even more capable with our help."

"Yes, well, it's been going swimmingly so far, you must agree," he bit off between gritted teeth.

"I'd say it's progressed further than it might have without our intervention."

"And *I'd* say if you left well enough alone, the chit and I might be obtaining a special license by now."

"Are you saying our kindly meddling has hampered you in any way?" His aunt asked, batting her eyelashes.

He stifled a groan. "Devil take you all," he hissed out the expletive as they arrived at his box and he handed her into her seat.

"Don't think I didn't hear that my boy," Aunt Margaret chortled, but he could swear he heard her add under her breath, "That's more the spirit."

Anne laughed at another of David's lighthearted witticisms as he handed her down to the seat at the front of the luxurious box. Sarah took her place next to Anne, and, to her surprise and extreme discomfort, Jonathan settled in on her other side. Though he took up his quizzing glass and made a great show of looking over the crowd, Anne could think of nothing but his presence so near to her, their legs were almost touching, with nothing but the thin lawn of his breeches and the whispery silk of her skirt separating them. She sighed, then turned to face Sarah, who was chattering away about the opera.

"Have you seen *Il Nozze de Figaro* before, Anne?"

Anne had not only seen Mozart's famous opera several times, from the sides of a few different stages, but she had heard the entirety of the piece more times than she could count. It was one of her fondest memories of her mother, practicing the part of the countess at all hours of the day and night, sometimes just singing it idly as she went about other business. Her mother had loved all of Mozart's works, but this comic opera, with its mockery of convention and nobility, had been her very favorite. She dared not say any of this now to Sarah, though, and it felt almost a betrayal of her mother's memory when she said only,

"I have seen it performed on one occasion."

"Have you?" Sarah put her hand to her chest. "This is my first time, and I am ever so excited. I have heard it is a comedy, but the arias I've seen have been very moving. Do you find the piece more comical or moving, Anne?"

Cocking her head to one side to think upon it, Anne answered, "I believe tragedy and comedy are not so very far apart, and the greatest artists never choose only one or the other."

Sarah's eyes widened. "Indeed. Look at the drunken porter in *Macbeth,* or the gravedigger in *Hamlet.*"

"Is tragedy always so very close to us?" Anne stiffened as she heard Jonathan's deep drawl behind her, and she fancied she could feel his breath on the back of her neck.

"Is happiness?" She countered as she turned to allow him into the conversation.

David leaned forward from his seat behind them. "This conversation is becoming much too philosophical for my tastes," he said, snapping open his quizzing glass. "Come now, we should not even be worrying about the imminent drama appearing on stage. There is drama enough in the seats around us."

Anne turned to follow David's glance and saw that the whole theater was, indeed, taken with the activity of staring at one another and whispering behind elegant gloved hands. Though she had been to the opera many times, she had never once thought to glance out at the audience and observe their behavior during the performance. She had been too engrossed in the drama to care, and she had been raised not to give two figs about the goings-on of the people who populated the *ton*. She had to admit she found herself very amused now at these people and their petty lives. Though she had grown to care for her father and Aunt Harriet, and she had found real friendship with Sarah, she could also better understand her mother's aversion to the nobility now that she had lived among them.

"Five quid for your thoughts," Jonathan said, glancing at her sideways.

"Isn't it a penny?" Sarah asked.

"You will find, sister," Jonathan replied, though he never took his eyes of Anne, "Miss Batten's thoughts are considerably too pricey for that sort of bidding."

Anne could not help the smile that sprang to her lips. "Well, Your Grace, if you must know, I was just thinking how silly and inconsequential these people's lives must be, and yet they appear to be so engrossed in gossip."

Jonathan's eyes narrowed, and Anne worried that, though she had kept her tone light, she may have offended the duke in some way. Her fears were soon put to rest, however, as a slow smile spread across his face, starting at the corner of his beautifully chiseled lips, and finally reaching those gray eyes. She realized with a sudden lightness in her head that he had a singularly lovely smile. She felt giddy with the knowledge that she had been the one to cause its appearance.

"Is *that* what you were thinking, Miss Batten?"

Sarah and David both laughed. David leaned forward again. "Truer words have never been spoken inside the hallowed halls of the Royal Opera House."

Anne sighed. "Thank goodness you all did not take offense to my forward comment," she said. "I'm afraid I still do not have London etiquette mastered."

"I am sure I speak for all of us," Jonathan began, and, though he claimed to express the feelings of those around him, she felt as if they were the only two people in the world when he leaned toward her, "when I say that I hope you never do."

She smiled. Jonathan continued to surprise her. Though he had been so solicitous and kind in the hospital, had been so agonized over the distinctions of rank the hospital represented, she had expected that now, as he had resumed his life as the great Duke of Sutcliffe, he would have thrown off those radical notions and easily wear the mantle of disinterested and self-absorbed nobility. She chastised herself for this idea; there was nothing in either Jonathan's behavior or the behavior of his family to warrant such judgment, but there it was nonetheless. She realized that, though she had so often bristled at the possibility that others might judge her mother or their life in Bloomsbury as inappropriate, lascivious, or worse, she herself had been at least as judgmental as all those tongue-wagging prattlers had been in her lively imagination.

The thought of her mother drew her back to reality as a hush fell over the crowd. These people would swoon over a soprano's voice easily enough, she thought with disdain, but they would never be caught dead speaking to the woman herself. Unless they were rakish men who were interested only in the woman's outward charms. Even the Earl of Norwich, her own father, who was a kind and gentle man, had only dallied with her mother, despite his claims of love. She steeled herself as the overture began. She wanted to enjoy it, but the bitterness she still felt toward her mother's life and the whole host of memories this evening awakened had taken the charm out of the outing. What would this wonderful, kind family think of her if they knew the truth? She could not help snorting to herself. She knew, unfortunately, despite all their kindness to her, what the answer to that question was. They might be unconventional, but they were still members of one of the most powerful families in all England. Even if they would want to accept her, their duty to their family would prevent them from doing so. She knew the *ton* well enough.

Anne forcefully shook her head to try and rid herself of the thoughts that were threatening to ruin the evening for her. Never in her life had she had such a wonderful vantage point from which to view any opera, much less her favorite one by Mozart. As if reading her thoughts, Jonathan leaned in toward her once more.

"I hope you enjoy it," he whispered. "I've heard the man playing Count Almaviva is riotous fun."

She lifted her opera glass and leaned forward. She recognized the man, but she had never heard him sing. "It should be delightful," she said. She *was* still looking forward to the performance, after all.

Anne was captivated by the actors but couldn't help but feel the duke's eyes on her person through the majority of the opera. The feel on them on her skin burned low and deep, and out of the corner of her eye, she saw Jonathan shift in his seat. She resolved to pay the man beside her as little attention as she could and allowed herself to be lost in the music and comedy playing below.

As intermission neared the music swelled and left the audience hanging on the very real question of whether love would conquer all, and Anne wiped the tear from her eye as the lamps were turned up and the audience applause rang out. Next to her Jonathan stood and offered his hand. "Would you care for a lemonade, Miss Batten?"

She nodded and stood. "Thank you, Your Grace." They all turned and made their way into the crushing crowd outside their box and down into the foyer. Several would-be hostesses left at the intermission so as to prepare their homes for after-opera soirees, and a few of the older gentlemen and ladies took their leave, but by and large, the entirety of the audience had spilled into the reception hall to gawk at one another and pretend to sip at refreshments. Though Anne sat in judgment of these people and their gossip, she felt the tug of the fairy tale princess inside her as she looked about at the bright colors and refined elegance that flowed around her with such ease.

Sarah came up and took her arm. "Oh, Anne, isn't it beautiful?" she gushed. "I declare, I cried three times already during the play, and now *look* at all this." She gestured around her. "I thought Lady Weatherby's ball was the very picture of elegance," she sighed, "but I didn't expect the opera to be so glamorous."

"I was thinking the same thing," Anne said. Sarah's enthusiasm was rather contagious, she realized and talking to her friend helped her throw off most of her maudlin mood from inside the theater. "And, might I say, you fit in quite well among them, my lady," she added.

Sarah blushed. "Oh, pish," she said, patting Anne's arm. "I am nothing next to you. What I wouldn't give for such beautiful hair."

"Don't be ridiculous," Anne said. "You know blonde is all the rage right now, and so are you."

"What's this," David asked as he brought them each a lemonade, "a mutual admiration society?"

"Yes, that's splendid," Sarah exclaimed. "What shall we admire about you, dear brother? Your knack for breaking into private conversations?"

Even as Sarah and David sparred with one another, Anne found herself looking around for Jonathan. He had just been with her, but now she could not see him. She smiled back at Sarah and David, hoping they hadn't seen her looking for him. She was having enough problems trying to quell her attraction to the duke without his entire family's efforts at matchmaking thrown in. The less she encouraged them, the better, she thought. In fact, she was feeling a little lightheaded right now, her mind a whirl of emotions and contradictions.

"Do you mind if I take a little air?" she asked Sarah, nodding upwards in the direction of the ladies' retiring room.

"Of course not," Sarah said. "Would you like me to accompany you?"

"No, that won't be necessary," she said. "Enjoy your lemonade. I'll meet you back in the box." She squeezed Sarah's hand, nodded at David, and made her way through the crowd. She did her best to politely avoid getting entangled in conversation, but even still it was several minutes before she finally arrived in the ladies' retiring room, where a few other women had gathered about. She made a pretense of looking over herself in the mirror and straightening her hair before she ducked back out. Wasn't there anywhere she could just be alone and think for a minute?

At just that moment, she felt a hand upon her shoulder and whirled around to come face to chest with Jonathan. She looked up at him. "Your Grace," she said, sucking in a breath, "You startled me."

"Terribly sorry," he said brusquely as he laid her hand over his arm and began walking quickly down the carpeted corridor. "Ah, here we go," he said and before she knew it, he had disappeared behind a red velvet drapery. She stood there, staring before a strong arm covered in black superfine shot out and grabbed her elbow.

"Well, aren't you coming?" he hissed.

"Your Grace?" She ducked behind the curtain and let her eyes adjust to the dusky light.

"Please, Anne, call me Jonathan for God's sake."

He leaned back against the wall in what was a small alcove cleverly created by the curtains and a curving corner of the corridor. There was a dim lamp lit in the alcove, and Anne wondered if this was a locale created for secret assignations.

"Jonathan," she whispered, "I do not think this is appropriate."

"Of course, it's not," he said, still against the wall and not making a move toward her. "If we were to be seen here together, you would be ruined, and I would be forced to make you my duchess."

Anne jumped back a pace at his words. "Your Grace," she said, "I really should get back to my seat. There is still time to escape. If we leave separately, no one will be the wiser."

"Who says I want to escape?" Jonathan asked, his gray eyes half-lidded and dark.

"Surely you do not wish to be trapped into marriage with a young woman of unknown origins and no interest in you," she snapped.

"You are correct on one point," he said, pushing his large from off from against the wall and moving a step toward her. "I do not wish to be *trapped* into marriage with anyone."

"You see, Your Grace," she said, "We really should be going."

"Why do you not leave, then?" He asked.

She realized belatedly that, despite all her protestations and her words of shock and indecency, she had not only made no move back toward the corridor but had indeed moved deeper into the curtained recess, so they now stood no more than two paces apart. At his question, she found herself speechless. Why *hadn't* she left? What had come over her?

"This is madness," she stammered, looking up at him.

"Is that what it is?" He asked as stepped forward and pulled her into his arms. "No wonder the mad reject society's attempts at curing them."

Her knees went weak as his lips met her own, this time more urgently than they had at the musicale. There was no sighing or gentleness now, only hard, raw need, and she could not say she did not feel it as well. Their tongues darted in and out as they each tried to devour the other. Anne felt herself grasping his lapels, almost as if she was afraid he would disappear from the spot without warning. After what seemed like an eternity of wanting, Jonathan's head lifted for a moment as he started showering kisses all over her face, neck, and shoulders, his hands roaming over the back of her dress and the curve of her hips.

"Jonathan, please," she sighed, pausing between the words only so he could bring his mouth to her own again.

"Hush," he whispered, his breath ragged and near as he nipped her earlobe and then seared her neck with more hot kisses. When his mouth dragged its wet trail down the top edge of her gown, across her collarbone, and down into the chasm between her breasts, she felt a tiny little moan escape the back of her throat.

Jonathan looked up, and she was surprised to see him smiling, though his gaze was still intense. "I thought we were to be quiet," he said, tugging the top of her bodice down to expose her breast.

"I'm trying," she panted.

"We'll be missed soon," he said just before his mouth covered her nipple and drew it in, suckling and teasing. A white-hot bolt of lightning went down her spine and seemed to settle into her belly, tingling and working her into a frenzy of passion.

Anne's mind could barely make out his words, but some sensible part of her still existed, and, though she melted back against the wall in complete helplessness, she did manage to squeak out, "We have to stop."

Jonathan's hand covered her other breast through her gown as he continued suckling the exposed nipple. Through the soft muslin of her gown and the chemise underneath, she could feel every exquisite sensation of his fingers kneading and then pinching. She wanted—oh, God, she wanted what they'd done in the hospital. She wanted more than that, but how much, she didn't know.

"Jonathan," she whispered, placing her hands on each side of his face to pull him up. "You know we have to stop."

He pulled back, and she tried to steady her breathing. She could feel the hot flush in her face and she seemed to notice her exposed nipple and the curls that had fallen from her hair at the same time. She pulled her bodice back up in one sharp motion, then tried to smooth the hair back into place, all the while avoiding his face. She was trying to smooth her gown back down when she felt his finger under her chin. He lifted her face to his again and dropped the lightest kiss on her forehead.

"I don't regret it," he whispered. "In fact, I would very much regret it if I had not found a way to pull you into my arms again." He ran his hands down the length of her sides and hips, smoothing her gown and leaving her one last caress to savor.

"I'll go back to the box now," he said as he tugged on his own waistcoat and ran a hand through his hair. "You go to the retiring room, fix your hair and compose yourself, then return to the box when you're ready."

She frowned when she looked up at him. "You sound like

you've done this before, Your Grace."

He smiled back at her. "Not like that, I haven't."

Anne's mind was in such an uproar she barely registered walking to the ladies' retiring room. She fidgeted with her hair and smoothed her gown for what must be the twentieth time. Surely nothing good could come of this, she admonished herself. What she was doing was worse than any of her mother's behavior. At least her mother's profession had been honest and straightforward, a business transaction. In her dalliance with the duke, she was not only being dishonest with Jonathan by behaving in a manner that directly contradicted her feelings and intentions but dishonest with his family and her new one. She was deceiving all of them about the extent of her relationship with the duke and by sneaking around behind their backs like this. She gave herself one more critical glance in the mirror and turned to go.

She sincerely hoped she hadn't missed any of the resumed performance, and she was relieved when she could just hear the strains of the orchestra beginning as she lifted the curtain to step back down into the box.

"There you are," Sarah exclaimed in a loud whisper, reaching out her hand, "I was worried you'd fallen asleep or something."

Anne's laugh sounded so nervous and forced, even to her, that she almost winced. She tried to avoid thinking about Jonathan's hulking presence on her other side. It took all of her willpower not to look over at him. "I just needed to get away from the crowd," she tried to sound as casual as possible. "These crushes are still so overwhelming to me."

"Well, I'm just glad you're back now," Sarah said. "I can't wait for the second half."

"Yes," the deep voice came from just over her right shoulder, "I hear love triumphs in the end." Her heart skipped a beat, but she took a deep breath and lifted her quizzing glass to peer down at the stage.

Chapter Nine

Jonathan felt light on his feet as he made his way back to the mews. "Good morning, Jeffries," he said to the footman. "Saddle Percy for me, will you?"

"Of course, Your Grace," the man nodded and disappeared into the stable.

Jonathan pulled on his riding gloves and took a deep breath of the fresh late morning air. Though it was still warm, there was a cooling breeze, and the whole world seemed to open up before him. The sky seemed brighter somehow, each cloud seemed more exquisite in its airy lightness, and each leaf on the birch tree that grew near the stable seemed a deeper and more striking hue of green. London seemed alive today, he thought to himself. And why shouldn't it? He was a man in love, about to start his whole life over again. After last night at the opera, he knew Anne cared about him, felt passion for him. He wasn't sure she loved him yet, but he knew that if, with patience and time, she could grow to feel for him even half of what he felt for her, they would be happy together. He didn't care what her past was. David had been right; it was truly of no importance. She could learn to love him. In fact, she might even one day tell him herself. But until then, he cared not a whit. All he cared about was that she would be his wife, and he would take her back to the country in Sutcliffe, show her the pool he and his brother and sister swam in, the trees he'd climbed, the old trick closet in the library where he and David used to hide from Sarah. She would be a member of his family, and they would all love her, just as he did.

"Here you are, Your Grace," Jeffries said, leading Percy out into the courtyard.

"Thank you, Jeffries," Jonathan replied as he leaped up into the saddle. He nodded at the little, wizened stable man and threw him a silver guinea. His mount pranced and sidestepped beneath him as he told a stunned Jeffries, "Buy something special for your wife today, old man. Enjoy it." He turned Percival around and trotted off to meet his destiny.

The short ride over to Norwich House seemed to go by in a flash before he was standing at the front door, hat in hand, and more nervous than he could ever remember being in his life. He tried to quell his roiling stomach by telling himself the deed was practically a given. A woman in Anne's position did not spurn the attentions of a duke, and there was no reason to believe she might want to, given her behavior with him last night. No, he told himself, of course she would say yes.

The butler opened the door, and Jonathan almost felt he might be expected, so unsurprised was the little man to see him there. He led him wordlessly into the salon to wait for Anne.

He sat there for an eternity, nervously tossing his hat from one hand to the other and looking up at the clock every fifteen seconds with what proved to be an uncanny precision. When ten minutes had passed, he stood and began to pace. He supposed this was what ladies did, all a part of the *ton*'s ridiculous mating ritual, keeping a man waiting downstairs, as punishment, it would seem, for his having had the courage to come and call upon her. But Anne wasn't like that. Was she so happy to see him that she was taking extra care with her toilette before she came down to present herself? Or was she stalling for time to avoid him? He could not help a smile of pleasure at the idea of the first possibility.

When he heard footsteps in the hall outside the door, he whirled around and then looked down at his hat, trying to think where he could hold or place it and look the most casual. As the light clack of a lady's slippers grew nearer, he shifted it from one hand to the other, then held it in front of him in both hands, and, just before Anne walked into the door, he threw it on the sofa and leaned his elbow against the mantle, pasting a lazy smile on his face.

"Good morning, Your Grace," Anne said with a shallow curtsy. She looked over at the maid who followed her. "Some tea and biscuits, please."

Though she was dressed in the same shabby morning gown she had worn when he'd taken her for the drive in the park, Jonathan couldn't help thinking that Anne had never looked lovelier. The only image he could conjure that could top this one was of her naked on his bed, but he pushed those thoughts away. There would be time for all that later.

Anne gestured to the sofa. "Won't you please sit down, Your Grace?"

"Thank you," he said, feeling foolish now that he would have to push his hat out of the way.

Anne sat in a chair opposite him. "So, what brings you here this morning, if I may ask?"

"I wanted to see you," he replied, looking straight at her. She squirmed and looked away as if meeting his direct gaze was difficult for her. Again, a whole range of possible reasons for her behavior swam through Jonathan's mind. It was deuced difficult dealing with other people and their feelings, he thought. Why did anyone put themselves through this torture? But he knew why. Even with all the confusion, excitement, and anxiety he felt, he also knew her presence made him happier than he'd been since he'd regained his memory. Just being around her was enough to completely change his mood.

Anne shifted in her seat again, and he realized he'd left a considerable silence hanging between them. She smiled and raised her eyebrows. "Is the weather fine this morning? I haven't yet gone out."

"It's a beautiful day," he said, gesturing above his head. "The sky is this perfect shade of blue. And the trees, have you noticed—" He broke off, feeling, if it was possible, even more foolish than he'd felt before.

He sighed with relief when the maid arrived with the tea service just then. He sat silent as Anne went through the motions of serving them both, speaking only when prompted about sugar, lemon, and milk.

"So, you were saying about the trees?" Anne finally broke the silence.

"Damn it all," he replied, and he raised his eyes to meet hers. "I came to ask if you'd marry me. Will you?"

Jonathan waited for agonizing seconds before she replied, "That's some proposal."

In only the blink of an eye, he was right beside her chair, kneeling, with both her hands in his own. "I'm sorry, Anne," he said, "I'm not very good at this sort of thing, having had no practice at it. It all seemed so simple in my head. Indeed, it still is. I'm an excellent catch, you're here for the season to make a match, and we obviously have a tremendous attraction for one another. There is simply no reason not to marry."

"Except that I do not wish it," she said, and he felt his chest seize up.

He pulled away from her and stood up, and he was aware of every sound in the room. The clock ticking, her soft breathing, and the wild beating of his broken heart.

"Why?" He finally asked.

"I wish I could tell you," she said, shaking her head and

looking down at her hands, "I wish you could understand."

"I'm sorry, I do not," his voice was clipped with anger as he turned to pace the room. "If you knew all along that nothing could come of our dalliance, why did you continue it?"

Anne closed her eyes to blink back tears. "I don't know," she said, and he knew she was telling the truth. "I did not wish to hurt you."

"Well," Jonathan replied as he turned around and then became very still. "You've done a fine job."

She looked away again, and he knew he should go, but he felt rooted to the spot where he stood across the room from her. "I don't know what to say," she said, and her voice sounded very small and distant.

"Why not, 'Yes, I'll marry you?'" he asked.

"Jonathan," she said, and he winced at the sound of her voice breaking. "Why make this harder than it already is?"

"It seems to me that is all your doing," he said. "It's still rather simple in my mind."

"It's only simple to you because you don't know what you're talking about."

"I know my own heart."

Anne laughed. "You think you do, I'm sure."

His eyes narrowed as he glowered at her. "Now you're telling me how I feel?"

After what seemed like an eternity of silence, during which neither dropped the other's gaze, he finally said, "I know you're hiding something." When she opened her mouth to protest, he raised his palm to silence her objections. "I also know that, whatever this secret is, you feel it's impeding our ability to marry. I'm telling you right now, Miss Batten, I have no need to find out your secret. I'll stop asking and prove to you how very unimportant it is to me. I'm a powerful man. I'm an influential man. Whatever it is, my title will take away from almost all scandal. I won't take no for an answer."

"You're very arrogant," Anne said.

"Perhaps."

"You're very confident," she said.

"Only when I truly want something," he said.

"Jonathan, I can't stop you."

"No, you cannot."

"But I can warn you that you will be wasting your time."

"You may be wasting our time, right now, Anne, by not just telling me the problem so I can fix it."

"You can't fix everything."

"Why won't you let me try?" He could feel his voice starting to break as well, the arrogance and confidence he'd had just a few moments before, draining from him like air from a balloon.

"I just can't," Anne finally said. "Please go now. I will speak to Sarah about the events you'll be attending so we will not be forced to see one another about town."

Jonathan retrieved his hat from the sofa and put it on. "Don't think this is over, Anne," he said, pulling on his gloves. "You make a mistake to underestimate me."

"Perhaps you make the opposite mistake," she said as she rose to nod her goodbyes.

"Oh, no, Miss Batten," his voice was like a razor as it cut across the room to her. "Something tells me there's much more to you than I can even imagine." His gaze smoldered as he looked her up and down. "Though I can imagine quite a lot."

She inhaled, and he gave her one last look, waiting for her to change her mind, but it was for naught. He strode from the room and out into the street, where the bright sunshine nearly blinded him and caused an almost immediate aching in his head.

Jonathan again felt clarity on his way home to Sutcliffe House, but it wasn't the same kind he'd felt when he'd left. It wasn't born of surety about his own feelings and about the rightness of the world. Now it was the clarity of anger and grim determination. He'd gotten past his own difficulties in imagining a future with Anne Batten, and he found it almost inconceivable that she could not do the same. As ridiculous as it had seemed this morning, she had denied him, despite his own willingness to put her past aside, despite his own offer to accept her, marry her, and give her a comfortable future. What could possibly have happened to her to set her so vehemently against marriage? And why *had* she dallied with him? Could it be she had been toying with him? As unbelievable as it was to him now, he could do naught but doubt himself after what had happened during their visit.

A niggling voice in the back of his mind told him to give up. Maybe she was right, and he wouldn't like what he found if he delved into her past. He should perhaps find another nice girl to marry. There certainly had to be easier women to court. He was the Duke of Sutcliffe, after all. He could have his pick of any fine debutantes with large dowries and impressive pedigrees. It was pure foolishness to stay fixated on this mysterious woman. But even as his mind repeated this litany of reason and logic, he could feel his heart pulling him in the other direction. No, he thought, there was something special about Anne Batten. He'd met hundreds of beautiful, charming women in his time, had even shared some of their beds, and enjoyed the experience, but none of them had ever occupied his thoughts and dreams the way Anne had. It wasn't just lust, he knew, for his appetite for her seemed only to increase with each encounter they'd shared.

His thoughts were so consumed as he traveled back across Mayfair this bright morning that he barely even noticed his horse turning into the drive at Sutcliffe House. As he dismounted and handed Percy over to the groom, he could hear David's voice behind him. He spun around and saw his brother leaning against the door of the stable, smoking a cheroot. Jonathan rolled his eyes as David pushed himself away from the door and began strolling toward him.

"Not now, David," Jonathan said, pinching his nose with his thumb and forefinger, and was both surprised and relieved to find that his brother heeded the warning in his voice.

"What happened?" David asked.

"I don't really want to talk about it right now."

"I am going to assume it didn't go well."

"That's a safe assumption."

"So, what are you going to do now?" David had reached Jonathan's side, and they began to walk toward the house. "And how can I help?"

Jonathan stopped walking and looked up. "Are you sure you want to offer?"

"I haven't seen you so animated since before the war," David said. "I had begun to despair that you would ever return to normal. Now, look at you. Yes, I want to help."

"I need to know who she is, David."

"What difference will it make?"

"I want to prove to her how little it matters."

Out of the corner of his eye, Jonathan saw David smile. He allowed himself a quick moment to feel gratitude for his brother's love and to feel a tiny bit of hope that they might be successful, then he quickened his stride, grim determination dogging his steps.

The next morning, Jonathan glared at David and Sarah over breakfast. They had both wisely refrained from asking any more questions about his visit with Anne, and Jonathan was grateful his brother had been circumspect about what he knew in front of the rest of the family. Still, Sarah's mouth would twitch at the corners, Aunt Margaret's eyebrows would lift, and all of them would make ridiculous references to the weather and the price of horses, barely concealing their curiosity or their amusement.

Jonathan didn't feel amused. Though he was determined to find out more about Anne, he was still reeling from her words and demeanor in that fateful conversation. He couldn't stop replaying it in his mind. And to make matters worse, his nightmares had returned. He felt suffocated by the city, trapped in his home, in the park, even riding his horse alone. It all seemed so false, so pointless, so deeply and utterly without meaning.

"Hello?" Sarah was snapping her fingers in front of his face when he finally looked up. He forced a smile.

"Sorry, sister," he said as he pushed his chair back away from the table and laid his napkin next to his untouched plate of food. "If you'll all excuse me, I believe I'll go for a short ride."

He winced at how heavy his footsteps seemed to fall as he all but ran out of the room, barely hearing Sarah's remark about the rain behind him. He did allow a moment's pause for her words to sink in and to grab his greatcoat from the rack in the foyer on his way out. Pulling his collar up around his neck, Jonathan stepped out into the bleak gray chill of the morning and was grateful for the melancholy day. He realized he didn't need to subject Percy to this weather and strode down the street, jamming his hands in his pockets and drawing further and further into himself as he walked. The rain began to pool at the back of his neck even with the collar of his greatcoat pulled up, and he could feel small rivulets running down under his shirt. He shook his head several times to get his dripping hair out of his face and ran a hand through the strands to smooth it back. The bracing feeling of the rain fit his mood, and his pace quickened. He took a moment to thank the heavens that the weather kept all the rest of fashionable London indoors. He wasn't quite sure what he'd do if he ran into someone and had to muster the usual pleasantries.

He had no sense of purpose or destination, and that also suited him. Every time the image of Anne Batten rose in his mind, he blanked it out, like dropping a cloth over a painting. He turned his attention to something else. Would Percy need shoeing again this week? Had Aunt Margaret properly notified the staff at Sutcliffe Manor about the date of their return to the country, or would he need to attend to it? From whom were the flowers that had arrived this morning for Sarah? Was David really going to court one of the Weatherby sisters, and, if so, which would be better suited to him?

So lost was he in his thoughts that he did not notice he had turned toward the park. As he ambled in through the gate, a thunderous clap of sound boomed behind him, and he dove to the ground without thinking. Scenes from that ditch outside Hougoumont flashed through his mind with the lightning above, and he felt as if he were falling down a well, where reality was a circular light above him that kept receding farther and farther into the darkness. He smelled the blood and fear, the horse dung and the scorched earth, he heard the cannon fire, the musket fire, and the thundering of cavalry hooves. He heard the tortured screams of men and horses, and he could see clearly the mud, the blood, the gashed wounds, the anguished faces of the fallen, and the tattered flags flying and falling as the battle raged around him. He could hear his men calling for him, but he was frozen, unable to speak. He could hear them still, now farther away, now closer, wavering like screaming through glass or water.

"Your Grace," now the voice came solid, clear, and real as his own hand. Jonathan looked up and saw his footman standing over him where he lay on the ground, near the entrance to Hyde Park, the rain puddling beneath him.

"Your Grace," the footman said again, holding his hand out. Jonathan grasped it and rose to his feet, dusting off the slick of rainwater from his trousers, pulling the lapels of his greatcoat back up, and running a hand through his soaked hair.

"Thank you," he finally said, as he looked around and continued to get his bearings. "Thank you."

"Your Grace," the footman said again, this time more gently, "you forgot your hat when you left, and Miss Sarah sent me out after you."

"Ah, yes," Jonathan replied. He looked around once more in some confusion, then back at the footman, and he took the hat, though it would be useless to put it on his drenched head. "Thank you so much and," he hesitated, not sure exactly how to frame what he wanted to say next, "I'd appreciate it if you did not mention my—fall—to my sister."

"Of course, Your Grace," the footman nodded.

"You are dismissed," Jonathan replied with a grateful nod of his own. "I believe I'll finish my stroll now."

The footman nodded and ducked away, and Jonathan again looked around himself. How much time had passed? It felt like he had been "gone" for hours, but the footman had reached him so quickly. It couldn't have been more than five minutes since he'd left the house.

Jonathan remembered those months after coming home when he hadn't really remembered who he was. That had been disorienting, confusing, and difficult, but it had been nothing at all like what he'd just experienced. He realized now, not for the first time, that his lack of memory may have been a blessing. Though he'd gradually regained all his memories of home, family, his own experiences, the three days of Waterloo had remained foggy, cloudy. He could glimpse bits and pieces here and there, but never a true clear picture, never a sensory image of what it had really been like. He had, of course, since read the accounts of the battle, the glory and heroism, and the great Duke of Wellington's ultimate defeat of Napoleon. But it had seemed as distant to him, who had actually been there, as it was to David or Sarah or anyone else: a factual account of what was already a great historical moment. Nothing more, nothing less. He knew, of course, that he had been there, but his actual physical experience of the battle continued to evade him.

Until today. He hadn't just remembered the battle just now at the entrance to the park. He had *been* there. He tried to trace back in his mind what had caused the episode. He had been walking toward the park, feeling braced and invigorated by the rain, matching his bleak mood, thinking about Anne, when . . . His thoughts trailed off as another peal of thunder rang out, this time much further away. Yes, the thunder. It had transformed in his mind almost immediately and had become cannon fire.

Jonathan looked around again. He was completely alone in the park, and he watched as some ducks played in the Serpentine, dipping under the water then shaking their feathers as a spray of droplets fell around them. His immediate and most pressing thought was about how to avoid experiencing such an episode ever again. Would he need to stay indoors every time a thunderstorm popped up? Would he need to avoid shouting? Why had this happened today, of all days, over a year after his return from Waterloo? He ran a hand through his wet hair again and shook the water off as best he could, a decision beginning to form in his mind.

Chapter Ten

"I'm not sure about this one, Millie," Anne said, holding up a light chapeau she had gotten before coming to town, but she had never worn. She didn't see how it would be useful back at Norwich Grange. In fact, she didn't see how any of the vast wardrobe she'd amassed since coming into her father's house would be of any use to her in the country. She looked around at the various gowns, bonnets, spencer jackets, parasols, and shawls spread around her room and sighed. It was such a waste, she thought, not for the last time. These people dressed themselves as peacocks, paraded around, greeted each other with niceties, then gossiped about them behind their backs. It was an elaborate ritual about nothing, in the end, it seemed. Though her father had promised her London season was not for the purpose of marrying her off, she knew that part of his feeling of "getting her settled" would rely on making a good match for her and that her desire to flee before Parliament adjourned in July was cutting that dream short and would almost certainly be a disappointment to him. She sighed again.

Millie looked up at the sigh, and Anne could see her maid employing a great effort not to roll her eyes. Anne felt the edges of her mouth twitch into a smile. She tossed the chapeau on the pile and turned back to their work. "Millie," she said, "I believe I just want to bring my old wardrobe from Heathermere. I can't see any use for these frills and furbelows in the country."

"Yes, ma'am," Millie replied with a nod, and she began clearing and piling the dresses to be put away.

Anne walked to her writing desk and sat down. She stared at the sheet in front of her.

Your Grace,

Yes, that was all she'd been able to come up with in the two days since Jonathan's proposal. She knew she would not change her mind, that she needed to flee town, and it was better to leave without saying goodbye and make a clean break to avoid any further embarrassment on either of their parts, but she could not shake the niggling feeling that she owed him more than that. She had busied herself with the preparations to leave to Norwich Grange. Her father and Aunt Harriet had been accommodating and more than willing to take the trip and escape the heat of the city for a while, and they had even been tactful and sensitive enough to avoid asking too many questions, though their knowing glances to each other had betrayed their curiosity clearly enough.

The plans and preparations for their departure had gone smoothly, but here this letter sat, with nothing written on it but a formal address, and even that had been written over and over again. *Dear Jonathan, Your Grace, Lord Marksbury*—she'd tried them all and none were quite right. In fact, she wasn't even sure writing a letter to a duke was even possible. Would the post actually deliver it? Would she send a footman over? Would anyone at Sutcliffe House accept it? She sighed again before being startled out of her reverie at the hat that came flying across the room.

"I'm sorry, Miss," Millie said, throwing her hands up, "I

can't take it any longer. The sighs, the sitting, the writing, the erasing. You're going to have to make up your mind."

"Have I mentioned lately that this move to the houses of the nobility has increased your insolence by half?" Anne teased.

"Yes, Miss, every day," Millie retorted with a wink.

Anne opened her bleary eyes one at a time in the intense sunshine of the open carriage door. She hadn't remembered dozing off, but the drive to Norwich Hall had been an easy several hours, and she must have been lulled to sleep by the gentle movement of the carriage. She heard the footman clear his throat and realized her father and aunt were still fast asleep. Anne felt her heart swell as she looked at them, both leaning against the side of the carriage with open mouths, Aunt Harriet faintly snoring, though Anne would never tell her so. She smiled, let out a small sigh, then turned to face the open carriage door.

The footman held his hand out to assist her down out of the carriage, but she was so excited she jumped without even looking. The smell of the country overwhelmed her. Having lived in London all her life, she had not really known how clear, crisp, and fresh everything would smell out here. She closed her eyes and turned around, taking a deep breath, and heard nothing. As she stood still, completely silent, she realized it wasn't *nothing*—it was birds, crickets, some rustling in the underbrush near the drive. She imagined such things must also make noise in London, but she had never noticed them. Yes, she thought to herself, this trip would be good for her.

"Fine day, isn't it?" Her father was stepping from the carriage, stretching his legs one by one before he climbed down, looking around him with his hand shading his eyes. "Always wonderful to return to the ancestral seat."

Aunt Harriet swatted a fly from her face as she peered out the carriage door behind him. "Is it?" The footman offered his hand, and Harriet frowned at him, batting him out of her way before she grabbed the door frame with both hands and let herself down. She landed heavily on the soft gravel of the drive and surveyed the scene. "The place does look well. Glad to see they keep it in shape when we're away." She then looked at Anne and her father, shrugged, and said, "Well, what are we waiting for?" before trudging up the steps to the front door.

Anne and her father stole a glance behind the old woman's back and the Earl of Norwich winked as he offered his arm to his daughter and led her into her family's home. A contingent of maids ushered her through the lavish yet tasteful foyer and upstairs to a room she assumed was to be hers. Anne surveyed the territory.

"Millie this is far too big." She sighed, turning to her maid who'd arrived soon after with some of the other London servants.

"You should see my room. They've private chambers for all the maids, a gathering room for meals and play. I've never seen so much space," Millie said, a bit breathless from lifting a hatbox to the bed.

Anne touched her chin. "It's unnerving," she said, trying to pitch upon just the right word. "It's lovely, but," she paused again. "The silence, the air, the largeness of all the rooms . . ."

"You're just not used to it, is all," Millie replied. "Give it a few days and you'll be strolling the grounds, swinging your arms, and taking up all the space you need."

Anne threw out her arms and twirled. "Maybe you're right," she said, laughing. "Here, let me help you with that." And she and Millie got to work unpacking her hats.

Jonathan Marksbury, Duke of Sutcliffe, stepped out of his carriage and heard the crunch of stone under his boots as they landed on the gleaming white gravel drive of Sutcliffe Manor. He had spent the greater portion of the past year here, convalescing, or, as his Aunt Margaret would say, hiding. He would have been content to stay in the country forever if it weren't for David and

Sarah's excitement about the season, and his duty to help Sarah come out in London. After his disastrous proposal to Anne Batten and his episode in the park, he had been especially eager to get back here, but now that he stood looking at the house, on a gorgeous June day, the sunlight glancing off the white sandstone of his ancestral hall, he felt unnerved by the silence.

"Penny for your thoughts?" Sarah asked as she jumped out behind him.

"I've never come out ahead in that bargain," he said, turning to his sister and shoving his hands in his pockets. Sarah laughed and put her arm through his, though he did not move his hands.

"Brother," she said, squeezing his arm, "I'll steal them if I have to."

Jonathan laughed out loud at that, and Sarah tugged him forward. He pulled his left hand from his pocket and patted his sister's where it rested on his other arm. "Don't worry, Pet," he said. "I have a feeling there will be plenty of time to talk." They both looked up the steps on the wide portico of the manor house as the butler swung open the door.

"Your Grace, my lord, my ladies, so wonderful to have you back."

Jonathan nodded and said a curt, "Thank you," but Sarah ran up to Grimes and enveloped the stiff old man in a warm hug. Grimes bent his head down and whispered something to her, and Jonathan's mouth twitched at the corners as he saw the quick pass of candy between the two hands. Sarah, hiding her contraband in the folds of her wide skirt, ran inside and did a twirl in the hall before Jonathan heard her light footsteps fading up the grand stair.

A low whistle behind him prompted Jonathan out of his reverie, and he turned to see David leaning against the frame of the doorway while Aunt Margaret was led up the stairs by the footman behind him.

"You let that go without so much as a word," David said, pushing himself from the doorframe and walking in, shaking his head with mock ruefulness. "There was a time little Sarah never could have sneaked a treat past you before dinnertime." David smiled as he walked toward his older brother, and Jonathan just laughed.

"You know, I wanted to get out to the country to escape everyone's scrutiny," he said.

"There's no escape from me," David replied, the heels of his Hessians clicking on the polished marble of the grand hall.

Jonathan followed his brother through the hall and into the front parlor, where Grimes and the staff had laid out a quick tea and coffee service for the weary travelers. Jonathan walked along the walls, running his fingers along the spines of books arranged in shelves from floor to ceiling. As he reached the Roman histories, he cursed softly under his breath. David appeared right at his side as if by magic.

"What is it? Still mourning Caesar?"

"No, I just realized I forgot to bring back the volumes I took with me to town."

David sauntered over to the escritoire and lay his hand atop a pile of books. "You mean these?" His eyes sparkled.

Jonathan smiled and perched himself on the edge of the settle. He turned over a teacup and filled it with steaming hot coffee from the samovar. "How did I ever have the luck to end up with you two as my siblings?" he said. "You are always one step ahead."

"You'd do well to remember it, too," David replied as he took another cup from Jonathan and dropped a lump of sugar in it. "Sarah's probably *two* steps."

Jonathan laughed. "Too true. Too true."

David leaned back, took a sip from his coffee, and sighed. "So, what next?"

"Well, I thought I'd take a turn around the stables and check on the horses, then maybe go for a ride before the sun sets."

David leaned forward again and set his coffee on its saucer. He folded his hands between his knees and peered into

Jonathan's face. "I think you know that's not what I meant."

Jonathan realized that his dark moods, his lack of candor, his avoidance of the topic, was not going to do anyone any good, least of all him. "I don't know," he said, finally looking into his brother's eyes. "I am not giving up on Miss Batten if that's what you're really asking. On the other hand, I am also not going to try to force a woman into marriage with me. I want to take a good long rest, clear my head, and see if some answers come."

David nodded, and his dark eyes narrowed as he responded, "Well, then that's what we'll do." He swigged the final sips of his coffee and stood up, dusting off his trousers. "I believe I'll head upstairs and look over my riding clothes if my valet has them ready. Meet you at the stables in half an hour?"

Jonathan nodded and rose as David left the room. He walked over to the table with the pile of books and began to arrange them back on the shelf in their proper place, leaving the volume he hadn't finished out near the tea service. He sat and poured himself another cup, opened Volume III to page twenty, and began to read where he'd left off back in town. So engrossed did he become that he did not hear the soft step on the carpeted floor behind him, and not until he felt the breath on the back of his neck did he realize his Aunt Margaret was bending over his shoulder, reading along. Jonathan closed the book with one finger still in place and turned to his old dragon of an aunt.

"Yes?" he asked.

"Don't close it there—it was just getting good." She humphed.

"The Council of Constantinople?" Jonathan asked, raising one eyebrow.

"Sure," his aunt replied as she came around the corner of the settle and established herself in a large armchair around the same table. "Theodosius was quite a man," she nodded. She leaned forward and poured herself a cup of coffee, but not before sloshing the liquid in the nearly empty samovar a bit. "Glad you could save me some," she said, frowning.

"Isn't tea more to your liking?" Jonathan asked.

"No, my boy, now that I know what I'm up against, I'm going to have to start fortifying myself much more heavily." She took a long sip of the steaming hot liquid, then rested the warm cup in her bony hands and let out a very long sigh.

"Up against?" Jonathan asked. "I thought we came to the country to rest, to be up against nothing. Isn't that the idea?"

"Certainly, that's the *idea,* my boy," his aunt replied, taking another sip of her coffee. "But something tells me we bring our sorrows wherever we go."

"Sorrows?" Jonathan said. "Aunt Margaret, my dear, what's giving you sorrow? You're the most formidable woman I know."

His aunt frowned at him and leaned forward, her keen gaze sharp, but curious.

"You really are that dense, aren't you?" she said. "My boy, I had hoped to see you married, settled—"

Jonathan frowned. "Yes, yes, everyone is very concerned with how I'll settle myself." He looked up at the ceiling and prayed for patience.

"You didn't let me finish," his aunt said, clucking her tongue.

That surprised Jonathan. He looked back at her, meeting her gaze and seeing the love there.

"While I had hoped to see you married and settled, more for my own selfish desire for little ones running around to spoil than anything," she began, "My real desire has always been, first and foremost, your happiness."

"Yes, I know that, Auntie," Jonathan said, reaching across the table and placing his hand on hers.

"When you came back from the war, I could see how hard it must have been for you. Not just losing your memory, but what you had gone through. It almost seemed like the more you remembered, the worse it was."

Jonathan lowered his gaze and pulled his hand away, embarrassed now.

Aunt Margaret snatched his hand as it retreated and pulled it back to hold it between her own two papery palms. "When I saw how changed you'd become, and how serene you managed to make yourself here at Sutcliffe Manor as the months went on, I realized that perhaps marriage and children wasn't what would make you happiest. Perhaps you'd be happiest here, doting on your sister and brother and their families."

"Not such a bad life," Jonathan said.

"No, it's not," his aunt replied. "The closer I get to the end of this life, the more I have come to appreciate it."

"So, what's making you sorrowful now, then?" Jonathan asked.

"Well, my dear, as we took to London and I saw you taking an interest in David and Sarah, my suspicions were all but confirmed. You'd be the doting old uncle, moldering away happily on the estate, coming to town to do your duties in Parliament and attend the theater. It all seemed so settled, until . . ."

Jonathan frowned. "Until the night of the Weatherby ball," he said, understanding his aunt for the first time.

Aunt Margaret sighed. "Yes, until that night," she said. "At first, I thought you'd simply admired this new great beauty, and had indulged in a little flirtation. But every day I saw you stiffen and color ever so slightly when she was mentioned. I saw your entire face brighten up like a July dawn when she walked into a room."

Jonathan laughed. "I had no idea I was so transparent."

"My dear, I have watched your face change since the day you were born. Perhaps it wasn't as obvious to others, or perhaps not as serious, even to Sarah or David." She sighed, leaning back again and taking another sip of her coffee. "I knew that day you returned from calling on her what must have happened. I'm not the doddering old fool everyone thinks."

At that Jonathan had to laugh out loud. "I'd like to see one person ever attempt calling you doddering."

His aunt smiled. "Yes, and perhaps you think I'm not as observant as I used to be, but my dear boy, your happiness, and David's and Sarah's have been all I've thought of since my brother and your dearest mother passed on. When I saw the look on your face that day . . ." she trailed off, and Jonathan was dismayed to see real tears welling in her rheumy eyes.

He stood and went to her, kneeling next to the chair she sat in. He rested his head on her shoulder, and she stroked his hair. "What happened the next day, when it rained and you took your walk to the park?" She asked.

Jonathan bent his head and took a deep breath. "I'm not sure I'm ready to talk about it," he said.

He could feel his aunt's shoulder rise and fall with her deep sigh. "Then I won't ask again," she said.

He leaned back and took her hand. "Can I ask you something, Auntie?"

"Of course."

"Why did you never remarry when Uncle died? You were so young. You could have had a family of your own."

His aunt pursed her lips in a wan smile and the tears that had welled in the corners of her eyes fell. "I'm not sure I'm ready to talk about it," she said, almost in a whisper. Jonathan nodded and pulled her in for a tight embrace. He held her there for long moments before he pulled back and said, "Then I won't ask again."

Chapter Eleven

Though it was a warm July day, the wind was whipping violently through Anne's long hair as she urged the horse into a canter. Anne clung to the reins so tightly that her knuckles began to turn white. *Easy, easy,* she whispered to herself, trying to remember what the riding instructor had taught her. *The horse can feel your anxiety. Hold the reins with ease. Don't tense up.* She took a deep breath and tried to relax her arms and legs, letting the balance of the saddle hold her upright, and moving along with the horse rather than fighting him. She took a moment to look around and savor the day. Bright, sunny, warm, but with a strong breeze that intimated a storm might be coming. She turned her head over her shoulder to see her father trotting around the edge of the field on his own mount, probably looking for evidence of fox for the hunt he had planned for the following week. Anne noticed that her father seemed more at ease out here in the country, and it occurred to her that he had sacrificed that peace to come to town and offer her a London season. She smiled. Being away from London had also done wonders for her own mood.

Anne looked ahead of her again. The wide-open expanse was the perfect place to practice the canter, and her horse was used to the terrain in the area, so she felt safe nudging him to a faster gallop. The horse responded, and Anne caught her breath as they lurched forward. The feeling was both terrifying and exhilarating. She had left her hair down under the tight hat, though it was pinned to keep strands from flying in her face. Still, she felt it whip around behind her, and she breathed deeply again and closed her eyes for a moment. When she opened them, she realized she had covered almost the whole distance of the wide clearing and was nearing the tree line on the other side.

"Good boy," she said as she slowed the horse down to a walk and leaned forward to pat him on the side of his strong neck. She straightened and was a little startled to see another horse and rider coming from the wood. The figure who sat upon the gray mare was dressed all in yellow, with blonde hair streaming out behind her. The rider raised a hand in greeting, and Anne returned it. She hadn't known of any other young ladies staying nearby, but she would be glad of some company her own age. She nudged her horse forward toward the rider.

"Hello," the girl called, and Anne froze. It couldn't be. It simply was not possible. Her happiness at the possibility of seeing her friend fought with her dismay. She groaned.

"Anne? It can't be," Anne heard as the young woman approached. Indeed, it was Sarah Marksbury in the flesh. Anne didn't need to force a smile—she was genuinely happy to see Sarah again, but her stomach felt tied in knots nonetheless.

"Sarah? How is it possible?" Their horses neared each other, and Anne and Sarah shook hands.

"We've come to the country for a while. Jonathan needed . . . " Sarah paused, looked up, and chewed her lip. "Well, we all needed a little break from town," she continued. "We've been at Sutcliffe Manor, but our cousins the Westchesters live near here in Crosswood Grange so I'm here for a little visit."

"How wonderful," Anne said. Sarah's use of "I" instead of "we" put her a bit more at ease. If she could see Sarah without having to see Jonathan, things might not be as bad as she feared. At just that moment, however, they both turned at hearing a voice coming from the wood.

"Sarah, blast it all. I asked you not to canter through the trees. You take such unnecessary risks."

Anne's heart raced, and she could feel her palms becoming clammy as she tightened her grip on the reins. The voice was unmistakable. She heard it every night in her dreams. Jonathan Marksbury, the Duke of Sutcliffe was just about to emerge from the wood.

Sarah turned toward Anne, her mouth downturned and eyebrows raised. She mouthed an apology and grimaced. She motioned for Anne to ride away in the other direction, flapping her hand and nodding her head. Anne didn't have time to think, she simply nodded, mouthed her thanks, and turned her mount back toward her father, who was still walking the tree line toward home. As she galloped away, she could hear behind her, "Who was that," and Sarah's breezy, dismissive answer, "Must be the vicar's daughter. Come, let's head home for tea."

When Anne and her father sat down to tea with Aunt Harriet, the sharp old woman's eyes missed nothing.

"Quite a ride you must have had," she said, looking sideways at Anne.

"Bracing," her father replied. "The wind has picked up considerably. A storm is coming. Saw some pigeon remains at the tree line, so there should be good hunting Tuesday."

His sister gave a soft cackle. "I see," she said, staring at Anne. "And what did *you* see, my dear?"

Anne tried to keep her tone even and light as she responded, "Strangely enough, I did see something unusual, though I don't think it will help with the hunt."

Aunt Harriet raised her eyebrows.

"I saw Sarah Marksbury," Anne continued, feeling the heat

of color rising to her cheeks to betray her. "Apparently she's visiting with cousins at their estate. Thrushcross Grange?"

"Crosswood Grange," Aunt Harriet corrected her. "Yes, I had forgotten the cousin had married a Westchester." Aunt Harriet leaned back in her chair. "I suppose we ought to invite them for a dinner."

"They didn't seem like they were staying long," Anne said.

"Well, we could at least have Sarah over for tea," her aunt said.

"Yes, I would like that," Anne replied. She really would like to see her friend again. She hoped the time away from Jonathan might heal some of her heartache, and her dearest wish was that she and Sarah could maintain their friendship as the wounds began to scar over and become less immediate. But she had to admit to herself, she'd been here at Norwich Grange for almost three weeks, and the wounds were if at all possible, sharper than ever. She'd experienced many genuine moments of happiness, and she did feel more serene than she had before leaving town, but whenever she thought of Jonathan, and nowhere was this more apparent than when she'd heard his voice earlier today, her heart physically ached as if he'd just turned on his heel that day in the parlor.

Anne sighed. Aunt Harriet looked up with her keen eyes and said, "My dear, if you're afraid of telling me the truth, don't be." She laid her hand on Anne's, and Anne was surprised to see tears starting to form in the older woman's eyes as Harriet spoke. "I want you to be happy, and I trust your heart. Whatever happened between you and the duke, I won't pry or persist. I can see you're suffering."

Anne laid her other hand atop her aunt's and responded, "Thank you for that."

In the armchair across from them, Lord Norwich looked up from his newspaper and gave them a quizzical look. "What are you all gossiping about over there?"

Aunt Harriet turned to the tea service and poured him

another cup. He set the newspaper down on his knee and took the cup in both hands.

"Don't worry your head about it," she said. "Tell me about the hunt. Are the vicar and his brother both joining you?"

"Yes, of course." The earl chuckled. "They never miss a chance to miss a shot."

"They only make you look the better," Aunt Harriet said, laughing. "I think that's why you continue to invite them."

Anne's father lifted his cup to his pursed lips but then winked.

In spite of herself and her melancholy mood, Anne giggled. Maybe time really did heal all wounds, she thought.

Time most certainly did not heal all wounds, Jonathan thought to himself as he and Sarah rode through the wood back to their cousins' home. He had thought a little change of scenery would lift his spirits, and the country around Crosswood Grange *was* beautiful, but he had not been able to shake his melancholy or his worry about the episode he'd had in the park. He looked at the sky, starting to gray over now and keep the promise the winds of the morning had made. A storm was coming. After what had happened that day in the thunderstorm, Jonathan was determined never to be in public or around anyone else during a storm again. He could still not explain what had happened to himself, let alone attempt an explanation with another person, and especially a person as close to him, as perceptive, as irritatingly caring, as his sister. As they neared the drive leading to the country home, he winced as he heard a peal of very distant thunder. He nudged Percy into a trot, prompting Sarah to shout, "What's the hurry?"

"Can't you see it's going to storm?" he said, starting to worry his lower lip with his teeth. "I'd rather not get soaked, would you?"

Sarah nodded and cantered up alongside him before taking

the lead.

Jonathan had to laugh. "You think we're racing back now, eh?"

"Are we?" Sarah threw behind her as her horse took off in an all-out gallop.

Jonathan leaned forward and whispered to Percy. The horse almost jumped to chase Sarah and her mount. Their laughter rang out as they rounded a turn in the drive, and even the sound of the thunder drawing nearer didn't dampen Jonathan's pure enjoyment at that moment. Maybe healing could be found, he thought. Maybe his family, being away from town, breathing the fresh air—maybe that would be enough. Maybe he'd end up like his Aunt Margaret, a doting uncle, tottering around in the country, tending to the estate and reading all the books he might want. As they neared the stable, they both slowed to a walk, and he shouted, "I call a tie."

"Of course, you do—*I* won," Sarah replied, laughing. They dismounted and led the horses to the stable boy, who took both the mounts to cool down while Jonathan and Sarah both peeled off their gloves and walked across the drive back to the Grange together.

To their surprise, David was standing in the parlor door, leaning on the door frame, and appearing for all the world as if he'd been waiting there for hours.

"Enjoy your ride?" he asked with a smirk.

"Yes," Sarah said, "I won the race back home. Now, where is that tea cousin Martha promised?" She started to brush past her brother into the parlor, but David held an arm out.

"Not so fast," he said, teasing. Jonathan narrowed his eyes at his brother. What mischief was he into now?

"A little birdie told me that we've been invited to a country dance."

"Is that so?" Sarah asked, rolling her eyes.

"Indeed, and imagine the host's surprise at your not telling me that you had already declined the invitation, especially seeing as how it was on account of my illness."

Sarah backed up and chewed her lip. Jonathan laughed.

"I'd think you'd be thrilled to get out a little and see people," David said, a little more serious now.

"Some people," Sarah nodded in agreement. "Sure. But Sir Godfrey . . ." She grimaced. "He's sure to be there, especially if he knows I will be there, and I don't know how to tell him 'no' in any other language he might understand. The man has not gotten the hint."

Jonathan's eyebrows came together. "He hasn't tried to force his attentions, has he?"

"Goodness no," Sarah laughed, "He's not capable enough for that. He just follows me around like a lost puppy." She sighed. "I try to be kind, but I've gotten progressively less kind, and he still—"

"Say no more," Jonathan said, "I can plainly see you're not feeling so well now," his eyebrows raised as he nodded to exaggerate. "No possible way you can attend this dance."

Sarah hugged him, then looked at David. "There, now you may make a sudden recovery and go yourself if you feel like it," she teased.

"I believe I will," David said, finally moving from the doorway. "Not nearly enough Weatherby girls out here to keep me entertained. Besides, I'll need to help Jonathan navigate the Mamas." He strolled away whistling while Sarah and Jonathan went into the parlor for their promised tea.

At that exact moment, only a few miles away, Anne was sitting down to write an invitation for Sarah to come to tea, just as her aunt had suggested. She sat at the beautiful little escritoire in the parlor and pulled one drawer open. Instead of the creamy linen paper she had expected, though, she found a familiar, bound bundle of letters. She immediately recognized them as the letters her father had saved from her mother for all those years and had brought with him that fateful day in London. Anne wondered with a start how they could have found their way here to Norwich Grange. She lifted her head and looked around her as if she expected to see the culprit standing nearby to catch her expression. She sighed. Of course, the whole house was busy today, with the earl out on his hunt and Aunt Harriet meeting with the milliner in the village. The old lady was just as dowdy and irascible as Aunt Harriet, but Harriet had insisted that she had hats made by one woman, and one woman only. Anne's lips had twitched. Aunt Harriet hadn't worn a hat in years as far as she could tell. She felt sure her aunt just wanted a bit of village gossip.

And Anne was pleased to finally be alone. She had been startled by her reaction to seeing Jonathan yesterday. She wasn't surprised she'd felt taken aback—that would have been true of anyone she'd met in London and not expected to see here. It was the reaction of her body that had shocked her. Even after several weeks of not seeing him, her pulsed had quickened and the heat had risen to her face as quickly as it ever had.

She did *not* want to see him again, she told herself. But she did miss Sarah. Still, it had taken her a full day to make the decision to finally sit down and write to Sarah, only to find this bundle of letters. It was almost as if someone were trying to rattle her composure. She shoved the drawer shut with a bang and pulled open the second drawer where she found the perfectly stacked paper she had sat down to look for. Sighing, she pulled out a fresh sheet, dipped her pen in the inkwell, and began.

It only took a few moments to write the invitation, call the footman, and send it off to Crosswood Grange. Anne looked around her, a little lost, wondering what to do next. She felt such a weight lifted from that simple small action that she now felt adrift, like a boat that had hauled in anchor but not set sail. She wasn't sure what she had expected, that Sarah would magically receive her invitation and show up on the doorstep, or that she would immediately have the promised tea right then. She laughed to herself, shook her head to clear her thoughts, and stood. She had been promising herself *Much Ado About Nothing* since she'd finished *Othello,* and now was as good a time as any to begin. She was on her way through the front hall to the library when the footman cleared his throat.

"Miss Anne," he began.

"Yes, Peter?"

"It's Miss Sarah. She's stopped in to visit." He turned to look over his shoulder and there, standing in the hall near the door was Sarah Marksbury, looking disheveled, but as dear as ever. Though Anne was shocked to see her, she felt a wide smile spread across her cheeks.

"Sarah," she said, making her way across the hall and taking her friend's hands in her own. "Peter, take Miss Sarah's coat and see to some tea in the parlor if you wouldn't mind?"

"Of course, Miss," the young footman replied, complying with the request and backing out of the room.

"Come in, come in," Anne said, gesturing to the parlor. "I just sent Peter with an invitation for you to join me for tea."

Sarah laughed. "I know. I seem to have befuddled him when I arrived on the doorstep just as he was headed out. He looked at the envelope, then at me, then at the envelope." Sarah held out the offending piece of correspondence. "He finally gave it to me, but stood there as if I had grown three heads."

"Well, I'm glad I could save you then," Anne responded, laughing along with her friend.

Sarah leaned forward. "I'm so sorry about yesterday," she began.

"Please, think no more of it," Anne said. "I appreciate your allowing my escape," she said with a slight grimace, a little embarrassed at how that sounded.

But Sarah nodded. "Now that I have had to jilt a suitor, I feel much more sympathy for you," she said with her own frown.

"Truly?" Anne asked, wincing a little at Sarah's

characterization of her behavior toward Jonathan. "But who could be pursuing you here?"

Sarah rolled her eyes. "If only you knew the notions these country gentlemen get into their heads."

Just then the tea arrived and for a moment both ladies were concerned with the positioning of the tray, the necessity for one lump or two, the squeeze of lemon, but soon they were settling back into the settee.

"Sir Godfrey Broadbent," Sarah said. "He's a local squire, newly gifted with a baronetcy, and anxious to start his filial line." She shook her head. "Two country dances at the party last weekend, and now he considers us as good as engaged."

Anne laughed.

Sarah looked up, "I'm sure it does sound funny, but wait until you've had to live it."

Anne felt terrible. "I'm so sorry," she said. "It must be awful to have to hurt his feelings."

Sarah looked up and smiled. "Honestly, it would be more awful if I thought his *feelings* were involved in any way." She sighed. "I suppose it's our lot as women to never know when we're just objects to gaze upon or vessels for children or—"

"Actual human beings?" Anne finished.

Sarah nodded and leaned back into the settee. "You know," she said, "I'd been waiting for my introduction to society since I was a little girl. Dressing up in mother's pearls, watching her get her hair powdered, and lying on the floor of the nursery with my ear to the wood to try and hear the music from parties downstairs."

Anne smiled. "Sounds familiar," she said, smiling

"As I got older, it got even more exciting," Sarah continued, sipping her tea as she went along, musing, "I met some of my brothers' friends, I realized how good-looking men could be, I enjoyed being flirted with, and I became very excited about gowns and bonnets." She laughed. "But now, after my first season . . ."

"You feel like a piece of meat hanging in the butcher's window?" Anne said with a frown.

Sarah laughed at that. "Yes, I believe you've hit it spot on."

They both laughed together and then sat in comfortable silence for a moment. Anne, of course, knew what Sarah felt, but she also felt so much more that she could never tell Sarah about. Watching her own mother getting ready for parties, yes, but also much more sordid occasions. Never knowing when the men who came to call were friends or something else, learning the truth slowly as she grew older, never feeling the emphasis her mother had put on the "freedom" their life had afforded her. But here was Sarah, who had been given the most traditional, comfortable, safe, and accepted lifestyle imaginable, and who still felt that sting of dehumanization, that feeling that as a woman, she never would really be in control of her own destiny. The thought was sobering.

"There's one way out of this, you know," Sarah said, looking up and meeting Anne's eyes. Anne raised one eyebrow in question. "One of us could meet an acceptable man, fall in love, and fulfill society's expectations as well as our own." She shrugged and then added, with a sarcastic shrug, "Just a suggestion."

"Yes, I suppose that's what everyone wants us to believe we're doing," Anne said.

"Some of us could," Sarah replied.

"Yes, some of us."

Two hours later, after a much more lighthearted round of various topics, from the weather to the books they were reading, Sarah had taken her leave and Anne allowed herself to lean all the way back into the cushions of the settee, emitting a deep and exhausted sigh. Why had she thought it would be easy to continue her friendship with Sarah? There was so much she couldn't tell her friend, so many misunderstandings and hidden motives. It was clear Sarah knew there was more to Jonathan and Anne's leaving off, but also clear she was too polite and too sincere of a friend to pry. The fact that Sarah hadn't come right out and asked her about it made it even harder to keep things from her friend. *And why was she keeping the secret at all?* She asked herself for the hundredth time.

The answer was complicated. She knew in her heart she had done the right thing in turning Jonathan away that day, but she also knew lying about it was wrong. It felt dishonorable to her mother's memory, it felt unfair to her father, and most of all it felt unfair to Jonathan himself, a man who had done nothing wrong save lust after the wrong woman, and of course, he couldn't have been the first man to do so.

Not for the first time, Anne wondered if telling the truth might be an option. But where would that leave her? A satisfied conscience and even more of a broken heart? Once the Duke of Sutcliffe knew about her parentage, what would stop the entire *ton* from finding out? Her father had reassured her more than once that his title protected them from the worst gossip, but only as long as they kept up appearances. The *ton* loved talking around an issue, but parading it in front of them all was anathema. Lord only knew she wasn't the first bastard to be claimed and introduced to society, but nobody would ever dare utter those words out loud, let alone countenance a duke marrying one. What kind of position would she be putting Jonathan's family in by telling them the truth? What about her father? No, she thought, even though her conscience pricked every time she thought of it, even though her heart felt like it was breaking all over again every time she thought of Jonathan's face that day in the parlor, it still would not compare to the pain of telling the truth.

And what about the truth, after all? She hated that her mother's memory was dishonorable, but hadn't she always had that twinge of shame her whole life, even while loving and appreciating her mother with her whole heart? Hadn't she always longed for a normal, respectable family? Hadn't she shunned all her mother's attempts at prodding her to her own freedom, preferring instead to study, learn, manage the household, and stay in the background? She hadn't even allowed herself to continue piano lessons, afraid that the love of music might lead her to follow in her mother's footsteps.

What was it that actually frightened her? The idea of letting herself go, of giving in to the temptation of what she felt in Jonathan's arms, filled her with dread, shame, trepidation, and something else. Excitement? Wasn't that the most tempting part of it all, that sense of freedom and abandon, the very thing she'd guarded against her whole life? Though her mother claimed to enjoy her life, to feel free of the yoke of society, and to be able to pursue her passions and interests, hadn't she really always depended upon the attention of men for her very livelihood? Anne had no romantic notions of her mother's life. She had been a courtesan. She had made monetary transactions with her body. She had sung and acted all over Europe, yes, but she had also dallied with men when the performance money ran dry. Anne heard a distant door open and close, and she sat up and smoothed her skirts, her mind brought right back to the present. And wasn't that the worst part of it all, that her father, the loving and kind man she'd come to know, had been one of those transactions?

Anne stood up, cleared her throat, and began to clear the things from tea. No, she thought to herself, she would not fall into the same life as her mother. She was here now, she had found a family and a home, and she would while away all her days caring for them, reading, wandering the woods, and doing all the things she most liked. The rest was behind her.

Jonathan came in from the country dance and slammed the door behind him with a huge exhale. Thank God that was behind him. He had never seen so many fawning chits, and that was saying something after the past season in London. He handed his coat and hat to the footman and strode into the parlor. He stopped in front of the beveled glass decanter, poured himself a generous swig of brandy, and swallowed it, almost in one continuous motion. He sat the glass back down on the sideboard and rubbed his temples, closing his eyes and trying to breathe.

"You look great," he heard from behind him, and he was so startled he nearly fell backward.

Jonathan turned to face his sister with a scowl. She was seated with her legs curled up under her on the settee, her slippers thrown on the floor nearby. She, too, had a glass of brandy, but hers looked barely touched. On her lap lay an open book.

"Well, I'm glad to see you're recovering from your brief and convenient illness," Jonathan said as he poured himself another drink and walked over to sit next to his sister.

"Yes, it's remarkable what a quiet evening can do for one's spirits," Anne replied. Her smile turned to a frown as she asked, eyebrows drawn together in concern, "How's Sir Godfrey?"

Jonathan laughed. "He's devastated. He spent five full minutes mourning you before making his way down the prettiest and richest girls there."

Sarah chuckled. "Yes, that sounds about right."

"Well, he had some competition," Jonathan said, sitting forward and resting his elbows on his knees, brandy glass dangling in his hands. "You see, all the richest and prettiest girls had their eyes on someone else." He brought the glass to his lips and took another long swig.

"Poor Sir Godfrey—he'll never be a duke." Sarah laughed out loud.

"And I'll never just be Jonathan."

"You never were."

He stared at her, eyes narrowing. He said, his voice just above a whisper, "I was when I met Anne."

Sarah sat up and closed her book. He knew his sister was eager for the gossip, but her furrowed brow betrayed her concern as well. He wanted so desperately to tell someone, anyone, the whole story of his meeting Anne Batten, but he didn't know if it was fair to burden her with that, especially given her own friendship with Anne.

Sarah stood and walked over to where Jonathan sat. She leaned over and laid a hand on his shoulder, kissing his forehead. Jonathan closed his eyes and tried to steady his breathing. Sarah stood up and went back to her seat on the settee.

"You don't have to—" she began, but her words were cut short when the footman, red-faced and short-of-breath, burst into the room, a man running behind him, holding his hat and fumbling with it.

"My God," Jonathan exclaimed, standing. "What is the meaning of this?"

The footman stammered. "I tried to tell him it was too late for visitors, Your Grace."

The stranger came forward and bowed. He was a middle-aged man with wrinkles around his eyes from a life spent laughing, a bushy mustache resting above his wide, expressive mouth. Jonathan recognized him but couldn't quite place him. "Your Grace, I am truly sorry to disturb you, but—"

Jonathan cut him off, remembering. "You're the blacksmith from Sutcliffe, are you not?"

The man sighed, "Yes, Your Grace, my name's Tobin. I thank you for rememberin' me."

"What's the matter, Tobin?" Jonathan said, feeling a heaviness in the pit of his stomach.

"It's the pox, Your Grace," Tobin said. "It's spreadin' through the village like wildfire. Some up at the big house are falling ill, too."

Jonathan stood up. "Sarah, will you make my apologies to our hosts?"

Sarah stood as well. "Of course—I'll help you prepare." They both rushed off into action as Tobin and the footman went to see about his horse.

As Jonathan and Tobin rode in silence on the main road,

Jonathan realized he hadn't thought about Anne in over two hours, since that first rushed announcement. In a way, it felt good to be needed, to be jumping into action, and to be making decisions. He realized that, after the war, he'd felt purposeless. Courting Anne had given him a new sense of urgency and occupied much of his thoughts. But he'd imagined that would end happily, with marriage and children, and retiring in the country with the love of his life. He'd never imagined what would happen once that was accomplished. Of course, it was a moot point now, but for the first time since his failed proposal, he began to see a glimmer of the life he could lead without Anne, and it felt good. As Jonathan pulled himself back to reality from his musings, he realized the forest around them had gone strangely still.

"Look lively, Tobin," he warned, afraid of highwaymen, or even wolves.

"Yes, Your Grace, storm's a-comin,'" Tobin replied over his shoulder.

Of course, what could be worse for the Duke of Sutcliffe, riding alone in the forest with a blacksmith, than highwaymen or wolves? *A thunderstorm,* Jonathan thought wryly. It was almost comical, in a way, the idea that he had felt so driven and filled with purpose a moment ago, and now he was cowering at the idea of a thunderclap. He shook his head and nudged his horse forward.

"Is there anywhere nearby we could take shelter," he asked Tobin, trying to sound casual, "should the lightning get too close?"

"Not really, Your Grace," Tobin said, shaking his head and pulling his collar up around his ears. "We're only an hour out from Sutcliffe, anyway."

Jonathan just nodded, his lips a grim line, and pulled his own collar up.

Just as the pair came to a clearing in the woods, the sky opened up with a sudden downpour of rain. Both men nudged their horses again and they quickened to a trot. The rain was thick, heavy, and loud as it whipped on the wind through the trees and slanted sideways to pour in right over Jonathan's raised collar. But it was a warm night, and his physical discomfort was nothing compared to the increasing anxiety he felt as he leaned down and tried to shelter his face with his hat. Rivulets of water fell from the hat's brim and down to the saddle, but his faithful horse Percy trotted forward.

After several minutes, Jonathan heard Tobin speaking, but could not make out his words over the unrelenting rain. He called out for Tobin to repeat himself, but before the other man could respond, lightning coursed its way across the sky, seemingly from one side to the other in a ragged, brilliant spike. Jonathan held his breath, but soon enough the thunderclap roared around him. He leaned forward and held his face close to Percy's mane, whispering to himself to hold it together. He kept the horse trotting but trusted Percy to see the way as he cowered and pulled himself inward as much as possible while staying on the saddle.

"Your Grace?" Tobin shouted behind him. "I said the horses can't keep a trot for long."

Jonathan inhaled. He knew he wasn't lost the way he'd been that day at the park. He assumed it was because this time he knew the thunder was coming and knew what to expect, but he was still in no shape to converse with the blacksmith. He remained bent over and tried nodding so Tobin could see he had heard him.

"Your Grace? Are you all right?"

Again, Jonathan nodded but still could not speak. Tobin had slowed his own horse and come up alongside Percy. Soon, Jonathan could feel Percy's reins being gently tugged and he felt himself slow down, though the rain was still hard as ever.

He felt a hand on his elbow.

"Try a deep breath in, Your Grace," Tobin said, "then let it out slowly."

Jonathan had no choice but to try what the man said. His mind felt entirely frozen, but he gulped a breath and could almost hear his whole body shaking.

"That's it, Your Grace, but slowly, slowly." The man's voice was so soothing. Keeping his eyes shut, Jonathan slowed down his breath and tried to fill his lungs. He could hear Tobin inhaling along with him.

"Now let it out, sir," Tobin said, releasing his own breath by example.

Jonathan did as he was told and he felt his grip on the reins slackening just a bit. He raised his head and looked over at Tobin, a comical sight with his hat dripping and even the ends of his mustache leading rivulets of rain down his cheeks.

"Thank you, Tobin," Jonathan said.

"You were in the war, Your Grace?"

Jonathan looked up in shock. "Well, of course," he replied, "I thought everyone knew my story from Waterloo."

"Sure, Your Grace," Tobin replied, "Begging your pardon, sir, but when I was over on the continent, though I was told there were plenty over there givin' the orders, I never saw any noblemen *in the war* if you get my meaning."

Jonathan frowned. "I do indeed get your meaning, Tobin."

"But you was," Tobin said, nodding. "You know what gets me? The smell."

Jonathan looked over at the blacksmith. "You saw things, too, eh Tobin?"

"Saw them, smelled them, heard them," Tobin said. "I have three cats, Your Grace. I wanted to be sure they'd catch every mouse and get rid of it. I want to be sure I never smell a dead thing lying around my shop as long as I live."

Jonathan nodded. "Ay. It's amazing what a man can't forget, isn't it?"

"Yes, it is, sir," Tobin said. "That's why I came to get you as soon as I realized the pox was breaking out. I can't stand any more death."

Jonathan looked up to see the moon peeking from behind a cloud. Sure enough, the rain had slowed. He turned to Tobin, they both nodded, and they urged their horses on toward Sutcliffe.

Chapter Twelve

It was sun-up by the time Jonathan and Tobin strode into Tobin's blacksmith shop. The smell struck him even from outside the door, but once they entered and his eyes adjusted to the darkness and gloom in the larger room, Jonathan stopped short. Even in the war, even at Chelsea, he hadn't seen anything so grotesque. Children, women, men, all lay in agony, strewn about the floor, drenched in sweat and moaning. Some of them were so swollen around the eyes that they appeared sightless. They looked like monstrous creatures rather than humans, with boils over every inch of skin he could see. There were several young women moving around amongst the sick, giving water, wiping feverish foreheads, and holding pock-marked hands. Even though he was appalled, he also couldn't stop his thoughts from wandering to Anne, thinking of her desire to help the sick, and her experience in Chelsea. He realized she had probably seen horrors he hadn't imagined.

Jonathan pulled Tobin back out into the street. "How long has this been happening?"

"We had the first hint of fever last week, Your Grace, but many came down with the rash just in the past few days."

Jonathan's lips came together and his forehead furrowed. "Haven't the villagers been using the cowpox method?" Dr. Jenner's inoculation against the smallpox through exposure to cowpox had proven so effective that its use had spread throughout London as well as all the small villages and towns.

"Yes, Your Grace, some had started asking after the local physician whenever he was in the village." Tobin nodded, but then he stopped and looked around before leaning in and adding, "Until *he* started spreading the rumors around."

Jonathan's eyes narrowed. "What sort of rumors?"

"Oh, you know, that the cowpox was dangerous, that the inoculation made people sick, that it was against God's will, that it came from an animal and was unclean. The usual tripe."

Jonathan grunted. "I think you'll have to take me to him. Who is he?"

"The vicar from Northridge, Your Grace."

Jonathan rolled his eyes and took a deep breath. "The vicar?" he mumbled. "Truly?"

"Aye, sir, he comes in every few weeks or so and riles everyone up. Most of us who were here before have taken the cure, but these youngers, Your Grace, have been driven away from it."

"What about these young women tending to the sick?"

"The milkmaids, Your Grace. They've all had the cowpox, so they're protected."

Jonathan nodded. "What about accommodations? Why the blacksmith shop?"

"I had the space here when I cleared out the stores," Tobin said, looking around, "And, well, Your Grace, to be frank—"

Jonathan looked the man in the eyes. "Be frank, Tobin, from now on."

"Well, Your Grace, there wasn't anyone else willing to take 'em."

"What about the church?"

"The vicar, Your Grace . . ."

Jonathan frowned. "Very well, I will stop at the house and wash up, then pay a visit to this vicar."

"I'm not sure it'll help, Your Grace," Tobin said.

Jonathan raised an eyebrow. "I'm the Duke of Sutcliffe. He'll have to do what I tell him."

"Aye, sir, that's true enough," Tobin continued, "But without the vaccine, I don't know as what anyone can do."

"Without the vaccine?" Jonathan's worked to keep his voice calm. "Explain."

Tobin looked at the ground and nudged a rock with his foot. "He destroyed the town's supply, Your Grace."

Jonathan's jaw tightened. He could feel his fingernails digging into his palms as he struggled to maintain his composure. "Very well. What are the alternatives?"

Tobin took a deep breath. "I've heard tell of taking an infected cow and doing it that way, Your Grace, but I don't know nothing about the particulars. And we haven't had a proper physician in the village for years now."

"What about the Northridge physician?"

"Driven out by that vicar, Your Grace."

Jonathan closed his eyes and rubbed his brow. He opened them and, through the darkened doorway, saw the eyes of a child, no more than seven or eight years old, peer out at him from beneath a shock of unruly hair. He was responsible for these people. If he hadn't been so preoccupied with his heartache and his own problems, he might have been more involved. He made a note to have words with his steward, but in the meantime, something had to be done. He watched as one of the milkmaids leaned down with a ladle of water for the child. She smoothed the boy's hair back from his forehead so tenderly. In a flash, he was back at Chelsea, watching Anne in the hall tending to wounded soldiers.

Anne.

"Tobin, keep an eye on things here," Jonathan said, standing up and turning back to his horse. "I'm going to the main house for supplies and to send out a few messages. I'll return posthaste. Have one of the maids send a list of what the village needs."

"Aye, Your Grace," Tobin said, nodding. He started to walk through the doorway but turned on his heel abruptly. "Your Grace?"

"Yes?" Jonathan muttered as he tightened the strap on his saddlebag.

"They're lucky to have you here, Your Grace."

Jonathan turned around to look the older man in the eye. "Not as lucky as they are to have you, Tobin," he said.

Tobin nodded and went in to tend the sick.

Anne closed her eyes and just smelled the air. There was nothing like a morning in the country after a rainstorm. The sky was clear blue, there was a light breeze that fluttered the thick leaves of the trees, and the entire world smelled fresh. The green of the leaves seemed more intense, and everything looked crisper and cleaner. She had sneaked out before breakfast to go for a ride. She still wasn't entirely sure of herself on the horse, but she had improved much since coming out to Norwich Hall.

She'd decided this morning that she needed to shake some of the cobwebs out of her mind. She'd spent so much time trying not to think about Jonathan, trying to keep her composure with Sarah, with her father, with her aunt, and it was exhausting. Even her beloved Shakespeare was not helping. So, she'd run out, asked a stable boy to saddle the gentlest mare and come to the meadow. Once she reached the vast expanse, she had the urge to gallop. The feeling of the wind through her hair and the horse's strong muscles moving in time beneath her made her feel as peaceful and free as she had since her mother had died. It wasn't long, though, before she reached the edge of the clearing and was instantly transported back to that day she'd glimpsed

Jonathan here. She slowed the horse to a stop and turned around slowly, taking in the wide field in front of her. It seemed no matter where she went, she could not escape thinking of the Duke of Sutcliffe.

Anne nudged the horse back to a walk, and they crossed the field more slowly this time. As she neared the road back to Norwich Hall, she spied a figure standing there. She urged the horse forward into a canter and pulled up short when she reached the footman, who looked very nervous indeed.

"My lady," he nodded and handed her a note. "This came for you a few minutes ago," he said, out of breath.

"Thank you," Anne nodded, and the man turned and hurried back toward the house.

Anne opened the note and felt her heart seize when she recognized Jonathan's strong hand. *I need you in Sutcliffe,* the note began, and Anne caught her breath. But the missive finished with *medical emergency.* Anne closed her eyes and bowed her head, trying to gain her composure. Damn him, she thought, damn him to hell. As she nudged her horse forward, her fingers relaxed, and the little slip of white paper blew away on the breeze. She rode to the house as quickly as she could and explained to her father and Aunt Harriet.

Without delay, the earl ordered the carriage and Harriet helped Anne gather the few things she would need right away. She was grateful neither of them made a fuss about a chaperone, agreeing that sending Millie along with the rest of her things as soon as they could be packed provided enough propriety. It was clear Harriet was worried, and they all hoped it wasn't Lady Margaret. It seemed Anne had no sooner received the note than she was sitting in the carriage as it rolled along the road toward Sutcliffe, Anne looked out the window, surveying the wide expanse of lawns and manicured gardens that swept up to a clear view of the imposing manor house, seen even from half a mile away as they approached the little village that had once served as the feudal seat of the house. Even after the opulence of a London season, Anne was still struck by the grandiosity of it all, and the inherent unfairness of the system, despite all their talk of democracy and The House of Commons. She realized she was thinking more and more like her mother had, in spite of herself. She had to smile.

As the carriage turned on to the drive toward the house itself, Anne tried not to think too much about her worry over Margaret, or whoever was in trouble, but she knew her heart beat faster at the other thought that she tried to combat. Seeing Jonathan again went against every plan, every instinct, every feeling she knew to be right, but the prospect excited her. Her stomach felt tied in knots as the carriage slowed and came to a stop on the wide expansive drive in front of the stately and imposing home.

The footman gave his hand to Anne as she stepped out, and she was again struck by the blinding whiteness of the drive and the exact precise trimming of each hedge. It was a grandiose property. She made her way up the steps and through the front door, held by another footman, who bowed as she passed. In the front hall, with columns reaching three stories to a domed entrance, her eyes adjusted to the dimness after the bright sunshine and she heard, rather than saw, Jonathan approaching, his step unmistakable even after the time they'd spent apart. He stopped in front of her, reached for her hand, and gave a slight bow.

"Thank you for coming," he said.

"Of course, Your Grace," Anne croaked out, almost forgetting to curtsy in return. Anne closed her eyes and braced herself, but even still, the shock of Jonathan's touch, when he took her hand in a simple polite greeting, sent a thrill through her entire body. She looked up and met his eyes, and it was almost as though a thunderbolt passed between them. For all her mental preparation, her self-assurance that she had made the right decision, her consistent attempt for nearly a month to put the Duke of Sutcliffe out of her mind, she felt the thrill of his presence as if their dalliance in the Chelsea Hospital were just yesterday. That pang in her heart was still there when she thought of it, how simple it had been when they could just be humans with each other. She steadied herself. "Thank you for having me," she managed, with only the slightest tremor in her voice. "How can I be of assistance?"

"It's the smallpox," Jonathan said, dropping her hand and stepping back and looking away from her. She was disturbed, but also gratified, to see a flush rise just above his cravat, their handshake seeming to have affected him as much as it did her. But now he was composing himself as he began to explain the outbreak.

Anne listened as she gave her outer coat and bonnet to another waiting footman, and Jonathan led her into the front parlor. They sat and yet another footman brought a tea service.

They looked up when Margaret entered, her voice loud and angry as she said, "Well, the first order of business ought to be a horsewhipping for this so-called vicar." She sat and motioned to Jonathan to pour her a cup of tea. "A man of God who cares not for the children of God." She shook her head.

"I found it hard to believe myself," Jonathan said with a sigh, leaning back against the cushion of the chair he sat in. "Dr. Jenner's inoculations have been in use for almost two decades now. I had no idea anyone would *choose* not to get them."

"Only those who never saw the horror of a smallpox outbreak," Aunt Margaret replied. "This is what happens when people forget their history."

Jonathan nodded.

"At any rate," he said, "The doctor left in outrage at this vicar's intrusions, and now we've got the milkmaids nursing the sick, and the only thing I could think to do was call you."

Margaret's eyebrows raised just the tiniest fraction of an inch, and Anne caught her expression with an inward groan. He had shown that he knew more about her past than her blood relatives, and the perceptive old woman had noticed. Anne didn't have time to think of that, though. She stood. "I think you'd best get me to the sickroom as quickly as possible."

"Of course," Jonathan stood and bowed.

Jonathan felt unmoored. That was the simplest way to put it. He had just started to finally feel as though some semblance of calm had settled upon his life and, even if he wouldn't ever be happy with the way things turned out with Anne, at least he could be at peace.

Now, though, after just the briefest touch of her hand, his thoughts were a complete scramble. He knew the top priority was helping those who had fallen ill and protecting the rest of the village, but he could not keep that goal in his mind for more than a few seconds while in the presence of Anne Batten. She was even more beautiful than he remembered, but the fact that she was here, that he had risked even his own heartache to bring her here because he knew her to be so capable, was itself like a dash of cold water. It was the sudden reiteration that it was not her beauty he most loved, but the plain fact that what he most loved about her was what would make it the most difficult to ever get over her—she was the only person in the world he could have called in a time of crisis like this. He loved, admired, and respected many people, his own siblings very much included, but none of them had her sense of calm, her sense of duty. As he walked behind her out to the waiting carriage, he blinked, realizing tears were stinging the corners of his eyes. He knew the days ahead would be the hardest of his life, but he steeled himself against these thoughts and memories. He had called her here for a reason, and lives were on the line. He would see himself through it, he thought, or die trying.

He stepped aside and tried to compose himself as the footman helped Anne into the carriage first, then shook his head, straightened his cravat, and stepped in behind her. He settled into the seat across from her and watched as she leaned forward and peered through the window.

"You had an easy journey, I trust?" he asked, trying to make his voice light and wincing when he heard a small break in it.

"Yes," she said without looking at him, "The weather is perfect and the road quite good."

"And you've had a nice time in the country?"

She turned and looked at him then, he felt almost lost in the depths of her brown eyes. "It might be easier," she began without breaking his gaze, "if we just stick to the task at hand."

Her words cut him like a knife. He dropped his eyes and nodded. "Yes, very well," he said, then turned to look out the other window. They sat in pained silence as the carriage made the short trip to town before stopping in front of the blacksmith's shop.

Jonathan hopped out first and was greeted right away by Tobin. He helped hand Anne out of the carriage and introduced the two to each other. Anne smiled and took Tobin's hand. "Pleased to meet you, Tobin," she said, and the older man blushed.

"Not as pleased as I am to meet you," Tobin said, nodding over Anne's hand. "I hear you've got nursing experience?"

"I do," Anne said, "Though not much with the pox, I must admit. However, I have read Dr. Jenner's work and was inoculated myself before volunteering at Chelsea."

"Aye, His Grace here and I were both inoculated in the army, as well," Tobin said, motioning them into the shop. Jonathan and Tobin bent to cross the low doorway, and Tobin continued, "We've got several milkmaids immune here from the cowpox and a few of the older people who were inoculated before the vicar came."

"Do you have any vaccine?" Anne asked.

Tobin shook his head and spit. "All destroyed by that son of—"

Jonathan cleared his throat.

Anne looked at both of them in turn. "No need to refrain

on my account. This man has endangered the lives of all these children. If he is not a son of a bitch, I don't know who is."

Tobin laughed out loud, and a few of the nearby milkmaids giggled before pursing their lips and turning away.

Anne bent over a child who was turning fitfully in a restless sleep. Jonathan watched as she placed the back of her hand on his forehead then bent down to hear his breathing. She stood up, wiping the sweat from the child's brow on her voluminous skirt.

"The first thing we need to do is triage."

Tobin and Jonathan looked at her with blank expressions.

"Assess them by severity, separate them, and allocate resources according to need," Anne explained.

Both men nodded and motioned to the milkmaids to come forward. Anne extended her hand to them one at a time. "I'm Anne. What are your names, girls?"

"Betty, my lady," said the oldest, clearly a *de facto* leader of the group, a plump and commanding presence. "Then this here's Jane, my sister," she said, putting her hand on the shoulder of the petite blonde beside her, "and on my other side is Lydia."

"Betty, Jane, Lydia," Anne said, squeezing each of their hands. "You've done wonderful work here already, but we're going to need you to stay on and help a little longer. Can you do that?"

"Aye, my lady," all three said in unison, nodding.

"Now, how many head of dairy cows do we have here in the village?" Anne asked.

Jonathan just stood, amazed. That she was able to come into an unknown situation, take charge, and show not only competence but also compassion, was incredible to him. He had seen many a nobleman throw orders around, but most of them never took the time to understand what they were doing or to do it with such warmth and sincerity. They loved to delegate the real work and then play the magnanimous leader, but he realized as he watched Anne that he was actually witnessing real leadership. She talked with the dairymaids, her head nodding, cocked a bit to the side as she listened and thought about what they were saying. He knew he'd never met another woman like her, but it was even more apparent to him now how special she was. And how wrong he'd been to try and push her into something she didn't want. This wasn't a woman to be ordered around or led by the promise of money and title. As he stood watching her, he was amazed that he had ever found her so beautiful before, because now she radiated goodness, light, and empathy. She was simply the most breathtaking woman he'd ever seen.

"Your Grace?" Tobin's voice broke into his thoughts. Jonathan looked down at the older man, embarrassed to show how little he had been paying attention to the conversation.

"Yes, Tobin," Jonathan said, looking up and shaking off his reverie.

"We need you to go around to the farmers and ask if any cows have the pox, Your Grace."

"Of course," Jonathan said. Grateful for a concrete task he could complete, he nodded at Anne and the dairymaids and made his way into the street.

Anne's eyes followed Jonathan as he strode out into the street, his large frame darkening the doorway. She hadn't realized she'd been holding her breath until he was gone and she felt herself exhale. She closed her eyes, took another deep breath in, then opened them, wiped her hands on her skirt, and moving to help the girls give water to the patients.

"Is there another area we could use so these people aren't so cramped together in here like this?" Anne asked.

Tobin shook his head as he held his hat in his hands. "No, Miss. The rest of the village is either holed up hoping to avoid the sickness or helping out in their own way. Every storefront's been shuttered, and this is the only place with any space anyhow."

"Is it?" Anne said, raising an eyebrow and inclining her head toward the manor house.

Tobin laughed out loud, then coughed a bit to cover it, ashamed to show humor in the sick house. "Aye, Miss, to be sure there's plenty of space up at Sutcliffe if you're speaking strictly in square footage. 'Tis only the duke and his aunt here in residence now. The brother and sister are over at a friend's house."

Anne nodded, "Yes, I know."

"Not that there wasn't room for a hundred more people if they wanted to have 'em."

Anne set her lips in a grim frown. "Yes, I know that, too." She'd have to talk to Jonathan, and soon. This place was enough to make even the inoculated feel ill. Not only were the conditions unsanitary, but the darkness, the heat, and the closeness would aid in the despair that so often claimed those who were gravely sick long before the illness could. Anne had seen it many times over.

In the meantime, she began assessing the patients and helping the girls triage. She soon learned that Betty, Jane, and Lydia were all capable, cheerful girls. They had done an incredible job assessing and assisting the patients already but hadn't had much experience with serious illnesses. She observed their shoulders relaxing and their laughter coming a bit more easily now that they had someone more knowledgeable there to tell them what to do.

"First," Anne said, holding up the ladle. "We'll need more fresh, clean, cool water. Is there an icehouse in the village?"

"Of course, Miss," Lydia responded. "But it's for the manor house's kitchen."

Anne laughed. "Not anymore," she said and added another thing to her list of discussion points for Jonathan.

She didn't have to wait long, for at that moment, Jonathan returned, his shadow darkening the doorway.

"Back so soon?" she asked, a little afraid his errand had been unsuccessful.

"It only took two quick conversations to learn they've got the cowpox over at Findlay's," Jonathan said. "What's next?"

Anne sighed with great relief. "I've only read about Dr. Jenner's initial methods in random papers and books," Anne said, "but the basic gist of it is that we need to take pus from the pox on the cows, and put it into an open wound on everyone who hasn't come down with smallpox."

Anne was talking as she felt the forehead of a child who lay motionless on the floor, and didn't notice the whole room had gone quiet for several seconds before she looked up. Jonathan, Tobin, Lydia, Betty, and Jane all stared at her, their mouths agape.

Anne shrugged. "I don't know what to tell you. That's how it was done. Once Dr. Jenner realized the cowpox inoculated from the smallpox, he just intentionally spread it. That's it." She nodded at the girls. "It's why you're immune. You had mild cowpox from your work long ago, I'd presume."

The three dairy maids nodded.

"Tobin and His Grace were inoculated in the army." She said it as a statement of fact, and both men nodded their assent.

"And I was inoculated before working in Chelsea," Anne finished. "But these people have not had the fortune to live near an educated vicar, and here we are."

Several people in the room coughed and looked away, possibly ashamed of themselves for having listened to the vicar, or offended by Anne's blasphemy. She wasn't bothered. "Since we don't have any proper inoculant, and no way of getting any quickly, we're going to have to do this the old-fashioned way."

Tobin stepped forward, hat in hand. "Begging your pardon, Miss," he began, obviously choosing his words with care, "but if these people wouldn't get a proper inoculation, what makes you think the rest of the village will get such a crude one?"

Anne nodded. She'd wondered that herself. "They'll come and see their family, friends, and neighbors suffering, and realize the error of their ways?"

Tobin cocked his head and raised his eyebrows, "Might be," he said, "God willing."

Anne nodded but left the rest unsaid. Once the deaths began, more would surely change their minds.

Chapter Thirteen

Jonathan wiped sweat from his forehead and stole a glance over at Anne. They were walking in silence back to Sutcliffe Manor along the village road. Tobin was with them, discussing the next day's work. All three had spent the afternoon helping the dairymaids care for the sick, changing bedclothes, bringing water, and just generally trying to brighten the mood with their presence. Tomorrow would be a long day, and Tobin was discussing the best way of beginning their inoculations. Once again, though, Jonathan felt his attention only on Anne, and not in a professional way. As they walked, he watched her from the corner of his eye, making it look like he was looking at Tobin, who walked on Anne's other side. Once, when the cobblestone dipped and Anne tripped a little, he grabbed her arm to steady her, and it was as if he had been struck by lightning, his fingertips almost glowing with heat when he released her bare arm. She lowered her eyelashes and murmured her thanks, and Jonathan had no way of knowing if she also felt it.

Soon they were at the end of the village road, and Tobin

turned to say goodnight. He tipped his hat to both of them and made his way up the small side street to his home.

Anne and Jonathan strode forward in silence until Anne cleared her throat. Jonathan turned to look at her.

"A penny for your thoughts?" he said, unthinking.

Anne sighed. "Please don't."

Jonathan felt himself blush. "I'm sorry. Please, were you going to say something?"

"Yes, but," Anne began, hesitating. "I'm not exactly sure how to broach it."

Jonathan stopped and turned toward her. "I know this is not easy."

Anne laughed and again her eyelashes lowered as she looked to the ground, then off in the distance to her right. "Yes."

"There's too much between us, and too much at stake now, to be circumspect with me."

Anne looked up then and met his gaze. Jonathan was surprised to see that her eyes were shimmering with tears.

He dropped his own eyes and began walking again. Anne cleared her throat once more, and then said, "I think we need to use part of the manor house as a makeshift hospital."

Jonathan nodded. "I had the same thought."

At that, Anne grabbed his arm, peering up at his face. "You did?"

"Of course. That blacksmith shop is no place to nurse the ill."

Anne continued, "We'll also need to requisition ice from the icehouse."

"That can be easily managed."

Jonathan watched her as she looked up at him with slightly narrowed eyes. "Aren't there ices or glacés you'll need to make?"

Jonathan sighed and stopped walking. "Anne," he said, reaching for her hand. To his surprise, she did not immediately pull it away. "Anne," he said again, "What can I do? What can I do to make you see me as a man, and not just a duke?" He felt his voice catch and become huskier than he would have liked.

"But you *are* a duke," she said, plainly.

"If it's any consolation, I never asked for it, and have no taste for it," Jonathan said with a mirthless laugh. "I joined right up to the army just out of Eton, trying to get away from it."

Anne laughed at that. "It worked," she said. "You weren't a duke for several weeks if I recall."

He watched the corners of her eyes crinkle as she smiled, the edges of her full lips turning up, her hand still settled in his. He squeezed her hand before saying, "The best day of my life was the day I woke up in Chelsea and saw you standing there."

Jonathan's heart seized as Anne drew her hand away from his. She gulped. "It was a good day for me, too," she said, and Jonathan felt as if the earth was swaying beneath them both.

"But," she continued, and with this she began walking forward again, looking as if she was choosing each step with care, "we have something greater than both of us to work for right now."

Jonathan nodded in agreement. He felt ashamed that he had been drawn back into his lust for her amid all this turmoil and sadness. He cleared his throat.

"All right, let's discuss using the manor over dinner. I know Aunt Margaret is eager to visit with you."

Anne smiled. "It will be so pleasant to see her."

Jonathan laughed. "I believe you may be the only person in the world to say that."

"Except you," Anne said, cocking her head to one side.

"Except me," he agreed. "I've never been afraid of her."

They hadn't realized they had gotten so near to the house until they heard an emphatic throat clearing from the wide portico. Aunt Margaret stood there with her cane, and she rapped it three times on the porch floor. "Just afraid of me *enough*," she said, then she waved her cane toward the door being held for them, and they all went inside.

Margaret took one look at Anne and began barking orders.

"You're a fright, dear," she said, almost at the same time as she pointed her cane at one of the housemaids scurrying about. "She'll need a room, a bath, and some fresh clothes immediately."

Jonathan watched with amusement as Anne tried to protest. "Oh, no," she said, "My day dresses will be brought over tomorrow."

Margaret frowned. "Yes, I'm sure," she said, "but we have dinner to eat tonight, correct?"

Anne laughed and threw one last pleading look behind her as Margaret led her up the stairs. Jonathan shook his head, knowing he couldn't save her now. "Until dinner, then, ladies," he said.

Anne settled back into the warmth of the bath and sighed. Her hair, which had been pulled back into a utilitarian knot, coated with sweat and dust from the road and the blacksmith shop, now spread across the surface of the water in undulating waves. She reached up and massaged her scalp, feeling the stress and tension of the day melting away. As she reached for the cloth and began to wipe her arms with the soapy water, her thoughts turned from the sickroom and its grime to the far more difficult feelings she had about Jonathan. Her breasts peeked just above the water and, to her shame, she both felt and saw her nipples harden at the thought of him. Even his slightest touch, as they walked near each other in that darkened room, or when he had taken her arm to steady her on the rough cobblestones of the street, had elicited much the same response in her all throughout that day—a tightness in her nipples, a warmth between her legs, and a blush on her face. Thank God only one was visible to anyone else, and that could be chalked up to shyness at the touch of any man.

But Jonathan wasn't just any man. She had to admit it to herself. He wasn't just any man, and he wasn't just any duke, either. Maybe in his preoccupation with his own recovery after

Waterloo, he had neglected the village, but his commitment now belied her previous unfair characterizations of the nobility. His willingness to help, as well as his apparent unwillingness to be in charge in the first place, showed the humility with which he saw himself, and his discomfort with his class in general.

Her original ideas about him had perhaps been mistaken, but as she felt the heat rise in her again at the memory of his touch, and the way she saw her own naked body with new eyes thanks to the awakening he had brought about within her, she knew her ideas about herself were not mistaken at all. There was, inside her, not just the memory of her mother, but the shame of what her mother had been, and the fear—nay, the certainty—that the wantonness which had been her mother's downfall had been handed down as a legacy to Anne herself. Anne drew her forearms over her breasts and brought her knees up close. She rested her forehead on her arms and tried to keep from crying. She was startled from this moment of weakness by a sharp rap at the door. She started to respond, but before she could, Margaret barged in, two maids scurrying behind her.

The water in the tub splashed up the sides as Anne made quick movements to cover herself. Margaret rapped her cane on the floor and waved her other hand in the air. "Please, my dear," she said, dismissing Anne's attempts at modesty. "It's nothing I haven't seen before."

Anne frowned but felt the corners of her mouth quivering as she tried to hide her smile watching the old lady move. Margaret flew around the room, picking up the dresses the maids were laying out, inspecting them, then throwing them back down. Anne cleared her throat. "Excuse me, ma'am, but there's no need to—"

"Posh," Margaret said, without turning around. "Of course, there's no need. There are sick people down in the village, and you'll do all you can for them tomorrow. You could just go right to bed."

Anne sighed with relief. "Yes, that's what I was thinking, a quick dinner here in my room, and I'll get some much-needed re—"

Margaret waved a hand at Anne, and she couldn't tell if it was in amusement or annoyance. "You *could* just go right to bed," she went on, "*or* you can enjoy the evening, pass the time with good company, and restore yourself a bit before you get back to work tomorrow."

Anne could tell she was no match for Margaret, so she sighed and sank back into the water. "I suppose that would be all right," she said.

For the next hour, Anne gave in to Margaret's every whim. A light silk frock in cobalt blue, a matching ribbon in her hair, a just-this-side-of-elaborate updo fixed with a diamond comb. But when the old dragon tried to tie an ostentatious string of pearls around her neck, Anne brought her hands to her collarbone and shook her head. "Only the ruby from my father, please," she said, and Margaret nodded, smiling. Anne took the case from her reticule and handed it to the maid, who fastened the necklace while Anne held the ruby pendant in front.

She turned and Margaret smiled. "You're a vision, my dear," she said. "An absolute vision."

Anne chuckled. "It appears everyone in my life over the age of forty gets great pleasure out of playing dress-up with me," she said.

"I'm old," Margaret retorted, "not blind." Then she muttered under her breath, "And neither is my nephew."

Anne turned on her heel and marched up to the old woman. "That's his business," she said.

Margaret raised her eyebrows. "Indeed, it is," she responded. Then she rapped her cane on the floor once more and proceeded toward the door. "Shall we?"

Anne nodded, laughing, and took the old woman's arm. "We shall."

As they proceeded down the grand staircase to the main hall, Anne couldn't help but mull over what Margaret had said. There was a part of her that was thrilled with the idea of Jonathan finding her attractive, and then another part that was ashamed of being thrilled by a man's attention. Then there was the whole complicated feeling she had for him that appeared to be unrelated to attraction or that heat she felt. There was the honest and genuine respect for him, as a person, as a brother, and now she was starting to see how much she admired him even as a duke, the very thing that was standing in the way of her accepting his proposal in the first place.

She sighed. Margaret flung her a glance through narrowed eyes but said nothing. Anne was grateful.

As they approached the dining room, a footman held the door for them as they made their way to the table, where Jonathan already sat reading a London paper. At their arrival, he stood and gave a small bow. "Ladies," he said, nodding and holding his hand to their seats, just to the left and to the right of his at the head of the table.

"Your Grace," Anne said, as she sat down in the chair offered by a servant. Margaret went right past the other footman and planted a kiss on her nephew's cheek. She patted his shoulder before moving toward her own chair.

"Well, you two have certainly riled up the village," Margaret said, dispensing with any niceties. Not that Anne had expected them.

Jonathan frowned. "I'd say that vicar did quite enough damage," he said. "This is what happens when I neglect my duties here at the estate."

Margaret's head snapped up. "Neglect your duties?" she cried. "As if finding a duchess and producing an heir weren't one of your duties, or securing a suitable future for your sister and brother weren't duties?"

Anne kept her head down, but she could feel the heat rising all the way to her hairline. Not only was she embarrassed at the reference to Jonathan's courtships, which everyone knew included her, but she was also embarrassed to be sitting in the middle of such an intimate family conversation. She cleared her throat.

"Please, my dear," Margaret said, waving a bejeweled hand. "Even if you won't marry my son, you're here now. If we can't speak frankly it's going to be uncomfortable going indeed."

Anne had to smile at that, though she knew her face must resemble a tomato. She looked up and into the old woman's eyes. "You're right," she said, keeping her voice steady. "We've got so much more to worry about with this smallpox outbreak."

"Quite right, my dear, quite right." Margaret turned to Jonathan as the maid brought in the soup tureens. "What's the next step?"

Anne enjoyed a satisfying meal as she and Jonathan filled Margaret in on the details of the inoculation, the preparations for the makeshift hospital in the manor house, and the use of the ice house. Margaret seemed years younger when, by the end of the meal, she declared she would be taking charge of the east wing of Sutcliffe Manor and supervising the care of the quarantined ill. Anne was surprised to hear that Margaret had been inoculated, but the old lady regaled her with the tale of her own intrepid grandmother having caught the craze when Lady Montagu had returned from Turkey with the variolation method. Anne was fascinated. She had read of Lady Montagu, of course, but she had never given much thought to how brave the original patients must have been.

As they finished dessert, Anne stifled a yawn. "It seems we have the plans for tomorrow well in hand," she said.

"Indeed," Margaret nodded and folded her napkin next to her plate as she rose. "Much to do, and much rest needed. Will I see you both for breakfast in the morning?"

Anne nodded and began to rise with Margaret, but Margaret dismissed her, shaking her head. "I'll be all right. You two should retire to the parlor and play cards, or piano, or whatever it is the young people do after dinner now."

Anne looked over at Jonathan, his face lit up with a half-amused, half-exasperated frown. She smiled and looked back to Margaret. "I used to love listening to my mother play piano after dinner," she said, "but I myself never learned to do it very well."

One of Margaret's eyebrows rose at the mention of Anne's mother, and Anne cursed under her breath. The old lady probably saw the look of dismay on Anne's face, and she said, much more gently, "Rest well children," but as she walked toward the door, she leaned down toward Anne and said, her voice very quiet, "I'd love to hear more about her someday."

"As would I," Jonathan said. Anne's head snapped back to meet his gaze, expecting a challenge in his eyes, but she saw no such thing. He was looking at her without the hint of a smile, a frown, or any bitterness. There wasn't a trace of teasing, questioning, or even that veiled heat that so often passed between them. The result was unsettling for her. She had just started to reconcile herself to the turmoil of being with him again, the heartache, the shame, the excitement—it was painful, but she had gotten somewhat used to it in the past year, and then again in the past day. For him to change course this way was new and it startled her.

"You look shocked," he said, as if he could read her thoughts.

She was speechless. How should she respond? "I am," she said.

Jonathan sighed and it was a long exhale. "Why don't you believe how ardently I care for you? Why is it so hard for you? I'm taking your no for an answer, despite all my avowals to the contrary. I'm not a man to give up so easily, nonetheless I've determined not to push you any further, but why can't you understand how much I want to know you more, to know you every day, to see you every day—" his words trailed off, and Anne was shocked to see a tear glistening in the corner of his eye. She stood so abruptly that she knocked the chair against the table leg.

"I'm sorry," she said, and she meant it, "I am. I am so sorry." She ran from the room, dashing tears from her cheeks as soon as she turned the corner on the staircase landing. When she reached her room, she leaned against her closed door, struggling to catch her breath in her stays and fine silk before she began tearing the finery off herself.

"Aye, only a year of nobility, and here you are destroying perfectly good silk."

Anne almost screamed in surprise that there was someone in her room, but when she turned and saw Millie there, she almost collapsed in her maid's arms. "When did you get here?"

Millie frowned and rolled her eyes. "You thought I wouldn't set out as soon as your things were packed?"

"I guess I hadn't thought much about it at all," Anne said.

"Well, it feels wonderful to hear that," Millie said, running around gathering up the things Anne had already discarded.

Anne rushed over to grab Millie's hand. "Of course, I didn't mean I hadn't thought of *you*," she said, then she pulled back. "Have you been inoculated against the smallpox?"

"No, Miss," Millie said, shrinking back at the tone in Anne's voice. She dropped Anne's hands.

Anne grew concerned. "Have you had it? Ever? Even as a child?"

"No, Miss," Millie said.

"What about the cowpox?" Anne asked, dreading the answer.

"No, Miss," Millie said, "I wasn't ever really around no farms."

Anne pulled back. "Millie, I don't want to frighten you, but you've got to get back to Norwich House."

Millie drew her eyebrows together. "I've only been in the coach and here in the manor," she said.

"Yes, you're probably not too exposed yet," Anne agreed, "and I could really use your help here, but without inoculation, you're in grave danger anywhere near this village. There's no telling who or what could be carrying the pox."

"Well, can't you inoculate me?" Millie asked.

"I could, but it won't be pleasant."

Millie laughed. "Posh, as unpleasant as repairing this fine silk dress?"

Anne smiled. "Quite so," she responded.

Millie turned around and cleared her throat. "May I ask you something, Miss Anne?"

Anne nodded.

"Why won't you marry him?"

Anne felt like screaming. "Why must everyone constantly concern themselves with my affairs?" She sat at her vanity and began pulling pins from her hair, one by one, and slamming down on the marble top. With each pin that clanged to the surface, she punctuated the sound with a name. "My father. Aunt Harriet. Margaret. Sarah. You. Even Tobin was looking at us funny today."

Millie came toward Anne, and it was clear her glower was not holding the maid away. Though she was approaching somewhat cautiously, she did not stop until she came behind Anne and began removing the pins from the back of her head.

"I notice something about that list," Millie said, pulling Anne's curls down and using the brush to smooth the tangles. "That's a long list of people who care about you."

Anne turned around and looked at her maid square in the eyes. "If all of you care about me so much," she said, "Why can't you let me make my own decisions?"

"You're free to make them," Millie said, grabbing Anne by the shoulders and turning her back around so she could continue brushing her hair. "But I'm free to notice if they're not the right ones."

Anne lowered her forehead to her arms resting on the vanity in front of her. "How do you know what's right, Millie?"

"I think usually our hearts will tell us," Millie said, rubbing Anne's shoulder.

"Mother made every decision with her heart," Anne replied, lifting her head to look in the mirror. She saw so much of her mother in her own face. The expressive eyes, the stern and determined set of her nose. "I'm resolved to use my head."

"That doesn't keep the heart from hurting, does it?" Millie asked, and instead of the frustration Anne had been feeling with everyone's meddling, she only felt a deep sense of gratitude that someone understood her. She shook her head. "No, it doesn't."

Anne stood and turned to embrace Millie. "I'm so glad you're here," she whispered.

"So am I," Millie responded.

Chapter Fourteen

The next morning Jonathan would not have known it was morning if it were not for the insistence of his valet, who had also arrived the night before. Jonathan opened one eye to find the room just as dark as it had been all night when he had tossed and turned restlessly. "Is something wrong? Why are you waking me in the middle of the night?" he mumbled.

"I'm sorry, Your Grace," the valet threw behind his shoulder as he laid out Jonathan's clothing. "It's a bleak one, it is, but I assure you it is morning."

Jonathan rubbed his eyes and yawned. *Good,* he thought to himself, *a day to match my mood.*

As he went about his morning ablutions, his thoughts, as usual, turned to Anne. He was as confounded by their relationship as ever, perhaps more so. He had just begun to accept the idea that she truly did not want to marry him, had just started to get used to the idea that he would not see her again except in large crowded ballrooms, where she could be avoided. He had even started to reconcile himself to the idea that next season he might try to look for a more suitable wife. Now, though, not only had he come face to face with his own failures as a duke and landlord, but he had also come face to face with the idea that he could not imagine any part of his future life without this woman, this woman who remained as stubborn as ever in her refusal of his advances, all while being completely honest that she reciprocated his feelings. He remembered his determination in London, to woo her, to convince her to marry him. He thought about his methods now and regretted them. She wasn't a prize to be won or a fish to be lured. She was a thinking, feeling, complicated human being.

He sighed as he made his way down the stairs. Margaret and Anne were already in the dining room, chatting as they awaited him. He sat down and bid good morning to them both, then began to work at cracking the coddled egg in front of him.

"A dreadful morning," Margaret said, sipping her coffee. "Just dreadful."

"Hopefully it'll at least mean a break in the heat," Anne said, "though it'll complicate the move of the quarantined up here to the house, that's sure."

"The stable men will know how to navigate the mud," Margaret said. Jonathan watched them both talking, though he had nothing to add to the conversation. He was again amazed at the ease with which Anne assumed responsibility. He was also amazed at the kindness and gentleness of his old aunt's demeanor around the young woman. He'd only ever seen her soften this way around himself, his sister, and occasionally, David.

"What's first on the agenda?" he asked when there was finally a lull in the conversation.

"Aunt Margaret has agreed to prepare the east wing and welcome the invalids here."

"East wing is ready," Margaret said, taking another proper bite of her egg. Jonathan turned to stare at her. He and Anne waited for the old woman to finish chewing. Finally, she looked up at them. "Well, close your mouths before flies start nesting," she said. "You think I'm incapable of doing things because I'm old?"

Anne and Jonathan laughed. "Of course not, Aunt," Jonathan said, hesitating, "It's just that—"

"I needed rest?" Margaret said, taking another bite and chewing. "I rested, and I also did what I do best—I ordered a team of servants to prepare the east wing."

Jonathan and Anne looked at each other, smiling. "Yes, of course, you did."

"It didn't take much planning. I simply told the servants to move everything fancy and unnecessary out of the way, and make beds for fifty people."

"Yes, of course, you did," Jonathan repeated, shaking his head and pursing his lips while looking sidelong at Anne. Her cheeks were bright with pent-up laughter. It made her even more beautiful. He cleared his throat.

"So, Miss Batten," he began, turning toward her and trying to shake the vision of himself tenderly cupping one of those cheeks in his palm. "Where does that leave the two of us?"

"Well," Anne said, apparently unaware of Jonathan's thoughts, "I had the good fortune of having my maid, Millie, arrive last night, and she has no immunity to the pox."

Jonathan was shocked at Anne's casual tone but said nothing. However, Margaret's eyes narrowed, and she almost growled. "Good fortune, girl? You may be new to the *ton,* but we still do believe our servants are people."

Anne nodded. "Millie is eager to be inoculated," she continued. "And it seems a perfect opportunity to demonstrate to the villagers the safety and efficacy of the procedure."

Margaret and Jonathan looked at each other, their glances echoing their thoughts: *how could you have doubted her?* They both laughed.

"And me, please," Jonathan said. "Everyone's been given a task, it seems, but me."

Anne turned to him. "I'll need you for backup," she said.

Jonathan raised his eyebrows.

"In case my demonstration does not have enough of a convincing effect," she began, "we may need your lordly command."

Jonathan felt his stomach drop at the idea that he would be commanding these people to do anything. He sincerely hoped it would not come to that. Would they even listen to him? He had never been an interested landlord, and certainly never a commanding one. It wasn't even in his nature.

"I know you think it's not in your nature," Anne said. Jonathan's head shot up to look her in the eyes. How had she known what he was thinking?

"But," she continued, a bit hesitant but pressing on, "didn't you command all those men at Waterloo?"

Jonathan frowned. "That was completely different. I had earned their respect and worked alongside them. They followed me because we had a duty, a mission to complete together."

"Yes," Anne said. "But did you think of the army as a *duty*? Did you have to do it?"

"Of course not," Jonathan said.

"Maybe a duty is not really a duty unless some part of you dislikes it," Anne said.

Margaret laughed. "She's got you there, my boy. You always loved the army."

Jonathan couldn't help but smile. If this woman would continue besting him at every turn, maybe it would be easier to get over her not marrying him. Imagine a lifetime of being known better than you knew yourself. He laughed.

"Very well," he said. "I shall fulfill my duties to the best of my ability." His voice sounded resolute, but his stomach began to tighten at the idea of spending the whole day with Anne. He had both hoped for and dreaded the possibility. In fact, he'd spent all night thinking about it. The closeness of her shoulder near him as they walked, the faint scent of citrus in her hair as she turned in the breeze, that pink glow in her cheeks as the day grew warmer. It would have been so much easier to be apart from her today, he thought, but his whole being longed to be near her nonetheless.

He was drawn from his reverie by Margaret tapping on her water glass. "A toast, then," she said. They all raised their coffee cups. "To doctoring, and to our duties," Margaret said, downing the last of her coffee in a very unladylike gulp.

"To duty," Anne and Jonathan replied in unison.

"Shall we?" he said as he stood and offered Anne his arm.

"We shall," she replied, and as she looked up at him, he felt a tingle in his chest again. She was smiling and there was something in her eyes that gave him hope, though he had no right to expect it.

They waited at the bottom of the staircase in the grand hall for Millie, who soon arrived with a far livelier step than Jonathan had expected. A small, dark, sprightly creature—Millie seemed like something out of the faerie stories of his youth. Her mop of dark curls was tied up under a smart little cap, and she wore a plain traveling dress and sturdy shoes. She did not look like a noble lady, but she also did not look like a servant.

"Miss?" Jonathan began as he gave a slight bow and offered Millie his hand down the last few steps of the staircase. Millie laughed and swatted his hand away. "Call me Millie, Your Grace," she said, "Everyone does."

"Very well, and I am Jonathan."

"Yes, I know."

Jonathan met Anne's eyes over Millie's head as the maid marched toward the door on her own. Anne shrugged, then motioned to him to follow.

They were all quiet on the walk down the drive toward the village road. It was an oppressive morning. The rain had slowed to a drizzle, but the air felt thick and hot, hanging there as if just waiting to open up again. The frogs croaked in the wetlands nearby and the birds chirped just as cheerfully as if the sun were shining. It was a strange feeling, the gray air and the brightness of that song. Suddenly, Millie began to sing.

What's this dull town to me? Robin's not nearby:

Jonathan walked a little behind the two women and raised his head in awe at the clarity, strength, and sweetness of the little maid's voice. She continued through the first verse, which he had heard a million times at musicales and in his own drawing room as Sarah practiced and practiced it over and over. But he had never heard it quite this way. Something about the dark wood, the gray sky, the peeping of the frogs, and the whistling of the birds made the tune sadder and more melancholy than he'd ever realized. Just then, Anne's voice joined Millie's, and though she was a less confident and skillful singer, the emotion he heard more than made up for her lack of traditional talent.

Yet him I loved so well,
Still in my heart shall dwell;
Oh! I can ne'er forget
My Robin Adair.

The two women held the last notes of the song in a soft harmony and Jonathan was surprised to feel tears stinging the corners of his eyelids. He blinked several times and looked at Anne.

"That was beautiful," he said. He watched as Anne and Millie smiled at each other, and Anne wiped a single tear from her own cheek.

"One of my mother's favorites," Anne said with a smile before turning back away from him to train her eyes on the road before them.

"That it was, my lady," Millie said. "That and 'Watkins Ale,'" and with that, the little maid launched right into possibly the bawdiest song Jonathan had ever heard outside a gaming hell. He blushed to his hair as Millie warbled on.

He took this maiden then aside,
And led her where she was not spied.

Anne cleared her throat, but Millie did not stop until Anne

clapped the younger woman's shoulders and nodded back toward Jonathan.

"I'm sure he's heard it, Miss," Millie said, turning back and winking at him. This saucy maid was going to make the day much more interesting, he had to admit. He said nothing but moved forward to walk abreast of the two women.

"So, Millie," he said, glad to change the subject, "What has Anne told you about this procedure?"

"Sounds right scary, don't it?" Millie said, but her voice was light.

"I have to say, yes, it does," Jonathan said.

"Well, Your Grace," Millie replied, "I'm not sure how many people you've seen die, but I have seen a few, and that's always the scarier option."

"A few," Jonathan said, looking Millie in the eyes. "I was in the war. I was at Waterloo. So, a few. I've seen a few people die."

"Well, I suppose I should say thank you for your service to Lady Britannia, this sceptered isle," Millie said, and Jonathan was surprised to hear her voice lilt into sarcasm.

"But?" he said, hearing the rest in the girl's trailing off.

"But I don't really like congratulating anyone on killing people," she said, and again Jonathan was shocked, but pleased, by the maid's frankness. He'd never met a servant who wasn't intimidated by the nobility, at least in front of their faces.

"Nor should you," he said, and Millie's head snapped up to look him in the eye again.

"I like you, duke," she said, then looked ahead of her again to begin humming another song.

The rain had just begun to fall again when they met Tobin at the bottom of the manor drive as it merged with the village road.

"I wasn't sure you'd be out so early," he said them.

"We're anxious to get started," Anne replied, and she introduced Millie and explained the plan. To their great relief, Tobin informed them that he'd already gathered a crowd at the church.

"I think some of them are there out of curiosity," he said, "and some maybe to gloat if you fail. But I think most are scared of the pox now—scared enough to try anything."

Millie snorted. "Too bad they weren't so scared months ago or years ago." She couldn't hide her disdain for the people who had refused inoculation, and Jonathan couldn't blame her.

But Tobin's reply was soft and gentle. "These aren't educated people, Miss. Most of them have never traveled five miles beyond this very street we walk on. When the vicar comes from London and 'teaches' them, they listen. I wouldn't be too hard on the lot."

Millie frowned at that, but she nodded. "Fair enough."

As they walked up the steps to the old stone church, it was clear that even more people had gathered in the time Tobin had taken to go and meet them. There were several women with small children in arms, some tugging at skirts, some playing little games with each other in the vestibule, where people had come to take refuge from the rain.

It was hot and close in the crowded room, but Jonathan moved forward and people parted to give way. Anne, Millie, and Tobin followed close behind as a hush fell over the gathered townsfolk. Jonathan went to the heavy oak door of the sanctuary and pulled it open. It seemed even in the vicar's absence people were afraid of crossing that threshold. Jonathan used the heavy metal door stop to leave the doors wide open and motioned for the gathered crowd to follow him and take their seats in pews. As Jonathan walked down the center aisle of the church toward the nave, he himself felt a trepidation about crossing to the pulpit. Not much of a churchgoer himself, and feeling extremely blasphemous thoughts about this particular vicar, he nonetheless felt a certain respect for the faith of others and for the meaning with which so many people imbued this building. He stopped short of the pulpit and turned around in front of it on the top step instead.

"Please," he said, motioning to the empty rows in front of them. "Please come in and be comfortable."

He waited for the villagers to file in and be seated. Millie and Tobin flanked him to his left, and Anne on his right, and he felt almost as much trepidation as he had before riding into battle. Except in battle he knew his training, and he knew his value. Here he only knew that the accident of birth gave him authority, something he hadn't asked for and did not relish. Once the vestibule seemed empty and people had taken their places, he cleared his throat.

"I've returned to Sutcliffe because of a crisis," he said.

A few people in the crowd murmured, and Jonathan looked at Anne, who nodded, encouraging him to continue.

"The smallpox, which has not been seen in years, has shown its ugly head here in our village. Our children and neighbors are afflicted. I must do what I can to help."

There was a more approving murmur at that and a few nods.

"I know the vicar frightened you," he said, trying hard not to sound judgmental. "But the inoculation methods of Dr. Jenner have been tested and proven by science, and the best proof of their efficacy is the vastly lowered rates of pox in London."

There were some grudging nods and some disbelieving frowns.

"Now we have come to this moment," Jonathan went on, starting to feel more confident, "and it is too late for those who've already taken ill. We will make them as comfortable as possible. I've opened my home as a makeshift hospital, and my Aunt Margaret, whom many of you have known for decades, will be in charge of caring for them. We hope, with clean beds, clean cold water, and capable nursing, we can save as many of them as possible."

"Thank you, Your Grace," shouted a few of the villagers from the pews.

"But we've gathered you here to accomplish something much bigger—the protection of the rest of the village."

The people in the pews looked around at each other as if trying to gauge the reaction of their friends and neighbors.

"I've brought to Sutcliffe a woman who's a trained nurse. She worked at Chelsea Hospital in London, helping to care for the sick and wounded returning from the war. She's been inoculated, helped with inoculations, and read Dr. Jenner's work herself. This is Miss Anne Batten."

Anne nodded to the crowd.

"Her maid accompanied her here, and unbeknownst to Anne, this young woman, Mildred, was not inoculated. She stands here in our village in danger of contracting the pox, just as many of you do."

Millie nodded to them as well.

"Miss Batten has written and pleaded for a new supply of inoculant, but it could take weeks to arrive. So, she has studied Dr. Jenner's earlier methods, and we have been fortunate enough to find a cow in the village who has the pox." At that, Jonathan nodded to Tobin, who went to the door behind the pulpit and shoved it open, showing the vestry and a large, docile cow, chewing a mouthful of the hay that had been strewn upon the floor in front of her. Some of the villagers gasped, and some laughed outright.

"It's a comical sight, I know," Jonathan acknowledged, "But the science has shown that if a human is exposed to the cowpox, they will become mildly sick, then be immune from the smallpox. It is a small price to pay for saving your lives."

"*This is madness*," someone shouted from the back. "It's unnatural. I don't want my child being turned into a *cow* baby."

Again, there were some murmurs of agreement and some laughter. Jonathan could not tell from the reaction of the crowd how many people were being swayed. He looked to Anne once more, and the encouragement in her eyes gave him hope.

"In the history of inoculation and vaccination, in many countries around the world," he said, "No human has ever been turned into a cow or experienced any cow-like characteristics."

It took every bit of strength he had not to scoff at the idea. He remembered what Tobin had said on the road. It was not these people's fault they had been so misled. "Do we not eat cows?" he asked.

Some of the men laughed. "When we can," one of them said.

"And yet none of us are cows now, are we?" Jonathan asked. "I just ate venison last night, but I have not sprouted hooves," he looked down at his feet, "So far as I know." The crowd laughed heartily at that.

"At any rate," he went on, "I know some of you are scared. I know you are afraid for your children. You're afraid of what the vicar told you, but now you're also afraid of the smallpox." He paused. "I know with all my heart which is the real terror," he said, "but I am also determined to show you the inoculation is safe and is our best hope right now." He nodded at Millie and Anne, who both came forward. Tobin pulled a chair from the back of the nave, and Millie sat.

"Mildred," Jonathan asked the little maid, "Are you prepared to be inoculated by purposeful infection with the cowpox?"

"I am, Your Grace," she said, her chin high.

"Have you been informed of the risks and what the cowpox illness is likely to entail?"

"I have."

"Are you afraid?"

"Yes," Millie said, startling Jonathan, Anne, and Tobin, who all looked up at her unexpected answer.

But she continued, her black curls escaping from under her cap as she leaned forward and moved her head from side to side, surveying the crowd. "I'm afraid," she said, pausing for effect, "of dying from smallpox out of stupidity." Then she leaned back in her chair. Jonathan fought to hide his smile, but one look at Tobin's frown sobered him. They couldn't afford to lose the crowd to pride or shame. However, Millie's vehemence had seemed to have some effect on the crowd, many of whom responded with eyebrows raised in grudging nods, though their arms remained crossed.

"Very well, then," Jonathan said, nodding to Anne, "Shall we begin?"

He watched as Anne opened the satchel Tobin had brought from the doctor's house. She removed a few lancets, a small vial, and several strips of cotton. She nodded at Tobin and he led the cow through the vestry door. As the large animal lumbered its way through the space, Jonathan could clearly see the pustules all over its udders. He only hoped it would be enough. Anne worked quickly. Again, he just stood in amazement at her competence. She was so sure of herself, so focused, so capable. She used one lancet to open a small wound on Millie's arm. The crowd gasped, and Millie winced a bit, but then she looked up and smiled, giving a wink to the masses. Anne used another lancet to poke a boil on the cow's udder, and Jonathan could see that she was scooping up a small bit of pus. This she applied directly to the small wound on Millie's arm, scraping both sides of the blade over it to ensure direct contact. She tied a small strip of cotton around the wound and pronounced, "That's it."

The crowd looked around. Even Jonathan was surprised that all this drama had been over such a small act. Millie rubbed her arm near where the bandage was tied and stood. "Thank you, my lady," she said, "Now, I've got to get back to work if you don't mind." Anne and Jonathan again shared a look of amusement over Millie's head.

"Not so fast, Miss," Jonathan said. "You may relax here and chat with the villagers so they may see how the wound progresses and how you feel today as the infection takes hold."

"I don't need to wait," one woman said from the crowd. "I'm ready to inoculate me and my babies right now." Jonathan watched as Anne breathed a sigh of accomplishment.

"Very well," she said, "step right this way." Soon a queue was forming, and Anne set to work taking care of the willing villagers. But the vast majority of people still sat in the pews, eyeing both Millie and Anne warily.

Jonathan pulled Tobin aside. "It looks to me like things are well in hand here for now," he said quietly.

"Yes, Your Grace," Tobin said. "She's incredible, isn't she?"

"That she is," Jonathan said.

"She'd make a fine duchess, she would," Tobin said, looking Jonathan right in the eyes.

"Don't think I don't know."

At that, Tobin frowned, but continued on a different note, "Where are you going?"

"I'm going to check in at the house to see how Margaret's getting on, and then I'm going to pay a visit to a vicar," he continued, his tone sharp like a steel blade.

Tobin's face was grave. "I think you're needed here, Your Grace," he started.

"I won't be needed until tomorrow when we see who the holdouts are."

Tobin nodded in agreement. "That's true, but . . ."

"Spit it out," Jonathan said.

"I don't think *she'll* like it much," Tobin said.

"I know," Jonathan said. "Her mind is on her duty—the village and saving as many lives as possible. Mine is on my duty—the very future of Sutcliffe."

Tobin nodded. "It's about time," he said.

Jonathan frowned at the man but bent his head in a small nod. "I know."

Chapter Fifteen

Anne worked through the morning, inoculating fifteen families in all. She felt tremendous pride in what they had accomplished, but her sense of fulfillment slackened as she looked at the room where so many more still sat, unsure of what they were doing. It would be a very long day, indeed. She looked over at Millie, playing with children, telling stories and jokes, and she realized it was truly her maid who had been the hero of the day. Well, her and Jonathan. Anne recalled Jonathan's speech that morning. So much of the time she had spent with him was alone, just the two of them, and she had judged him based on his station in life, had placed him only in the privileged position of duke at the ball or the club, driving his phaeton near the Serpentine in Hyde park, and had completely dismissed the general, the patriarch, and the landlord. She'd been attracted to *the man,* and that had meant a great deal, but now it was the duke who was garnering her respect.

As the time for luncheon grew nearer, Anne began to wonder where that duke was. Millie assisted her, and Tobin ran back and forth for water, more cotton bandages, and other items they needed. But Jonatan was nowhere to be found.

Finally, they finished inoculating the last person who was willing that day, and she stood, wiping the sweat from her brow. It was humid and oppressive in the church, though not too warm, thank God. The rain outside and the damp stone space made for an uncomfortable workplace. When Anne stood, Millie did as well, and Tobin came to join them. "I believe Millie and I should head back to the manor for luncheon," Anne said.

"Of course, Miss," Tobin said.

"I'm sure Jonathan will be here to accompany us at any moment?" Anne asked.

"About that, Miss, he went to see the vicar."

Anne frowned. She cursed under her breath, eliciting a gasp from Tobin and a snort of laughter from Millie.

"I *told* him not to do that," Anne said.

"He's the duke, Miss, he doesn't have to listen to you," Millie said, her lips pursed into an almost-smile.

Tobin paused. "Miss, I understand you feel you need him here, but . . ."

Anne looked at the man, whom she had begun to admire a great deal. "Go on, Tobin."

"Well, I am not sure he's wrong, my lady."

Millie smiled and nodded, impressed at the man's audacity.

"This problem is a crisis right now, but it'll be a crisis for decades, and not just here in Sutcliffe, if that vicar's not taken care of."

Anne knew Tobin was right. She was also surprised Jonathan had taken it upon himself to try and remedy the situation on his own. She wondered if part of her disappointment at his having left had more to do with the realization that she might not see him the rest of that day, might not feel his nearness or be able to look over and find reassurance in his eyes. She had become all too accustomed to his presence in just the past day. Even though it made every cell in her body feel like it was smoldering, even though it confused her and worried her, and even though she felt entirely conflicted by it, she had to admit she enjoyed it very much. She enjoyed just being with him. And this time was so different than it had been before, without the heat and flirtation of Chelsea, without the passion and intensity of London. This was different, but it was no less affecting.

"Very well," she finally said, as she saw Tobin and Millie both looking at her. "Will you accompany us to the end of the village road? We can make our way up the drive ourselves."

"I can bring you all the way to the house. Never you mind that," Tobin said.

"We appreciate it very much," Anne said. She turned to the still assembled crowd. "Since those of you who wished to be inoculated have been taken care of today, and we will not see Millie's illness manifest until tomorrow, we will retire to the manor house to care for the ill now. Does anyone have any questions or concerns?"

"Will ye back tomorrow, Miss?" a dirty-faced boy asked. He looked to be no older than eight.

Anne bent down to speak to him. "We will be right back here after breakfast in the morning."

"I think I want the in-toc—"

"In-oc-u-la-tion," Anne helped him.

"Yes, Miss," the boy replied. "I think I want it."

"Then you shall have it," Anne said, her hand on the boy's shoulder. "Where are your parents?"

"Both in the sick ward with my baby sister," the boy replied.

"Have you no other family? Who's taking care of you?"

"I'm getting food myself mostly, trying to keep up the shop as best I can."

"What shop? What's your name?"

The boy looked taken aback at the questioning, and Tobin stepped in. "This is Oliver. His father is the butcher."

Anne took a deep breath and knelt to take the boy's hands. "Well, Oliver, you can get the treatment now, if you like."

The boy shook his head. "Miss, I'm afraid." He gestured to Millie. "I'll wait to see what happens if it's all the same to you."

Anne smiled. "Of course. Go home, get some rest, eat something, and we will see you tomorrow morning. Good?"

The boy flashed a happy smile. "Good," then he ran off out the vestibule with his hat in his hand.

Anne and Tobin looked at each other, each allowing a small sigh of hope. "Maybe this will work after all," Tobin said under his breath as they made their way to the manor house.

The sky was clearing as they made their way back through the wood, and again Anne felt like singing. As she and Millie began "Robin Adair" once more, they were both surprised to hear Tobin enter with a beautiful tenor harmony. They all three sang loud into the empty forest, enjoying the time together and the melancholy tune. When they finished, Millie clapped her hands. "Tobin," she began. "What a beautiful voice you have."

"I sing all day long in the blacksmith shop, lady," he said, blushing, "Just usually no one there to hear it but my poor wife."

Anne smiled. "I'm quite sure she doesn't mind."

"That's probably true," Tobin said in agreement, "I'm sure if she did, I'd have heard of it by now."

Both women laughed.

They all three walked up the wide white portico of Sutcliffe Manor, and as they approached the big door swung wide. A footman bowed and said, "This way, Miss."

The ladies each took Tobin's hand and wished him farewell for the day, but the footman said, "No, Miss, 'tis all three of you Lady Margaret is wanting."

Tobin raised his eyebrows at that but said nothing and walked inside the door, removing his cap. He stood in the foyer shifting his weight from foot to foot, wondering exactly what to do. Millie remained still, only her eyes darting from Tobin to the room and back to Tobin.

The footman looked from one to the other, then said, "Here, I'll take your caps." He took their things, and Anne's reticule then called another servant to take them away. He led all three of them to the dining room, where Margaret sat waiting.

Anne was once again surprised by the old dragon's fortitude, but she was starting to wonder why. Nothing this woman did was ordinary. They stood at the doorway and just stared. Margaret had laid out a veritable feast. There were joints of meat, delicate-looking fish, and more cakes, pastries, glacés, and ices than Anne had ever seen at once.

"My goodness," Millie said, whistling.

"Posh," Margaret said, standing with considerable care. "When we started using the ice, we realized we'd also have to eat the sweets cook had been keeping in the icehouse. We are the lucky recipients of a smallpox feast."

Anne smiled and nodded her head. "Sounds reasonable."

"This isn't even near all of it," Margaret said, chuckling. "You should have seen the way the children in the east wing brightened when the servants started bringing in trays of ice pops, shaved ice with syrup, and every other damned thing."

"I bet there were some heads that perked up, indeed," Anne replied, laughing. She made eye contact with Margaret, then raised her eyebrows and shook her head toward Millie and Tobin.

Margaret came forward and took Millie's hands. Millie blushed a little but met the older woman eye to eye. Margaret's eyes narrowed as she looked at Millie, but Anne saw her squeeze the little maid's hands in her own and then lead her to a chair near the head of the table. She laid her hand on the place next to Millie, and said, "Please, Mister—"

Anne turned, startled, as Tobin replied, "Smith, ma'am, Tobin Smith." How had she never found out Tobin's full name? She wondered if her time with the *ton* really had changed her.

"Yes, Mr. Smith," Margaret said, "Please, sit."

Tobin took the seat, then added, "But you can call me Tobin."

"Very well, Tobin," Margaret replied, pleased. "When will someone tell me how it went today?"

Anne spoke warmly of the way Jonathan had engaged with the community, then praised Millie and Tobin for their parts. They described every detail of the morning for the old dragon and she sat, lifting her soup spoon from the tureen in front of her and pausing to ask a question here or there as she listened.

"You only inoculated fifteen-odd people today, then?" She finally said, laying the spoon next to the soup and signaling to the footman that she was done. All the servants moved forward to remove the tureens, then brought the fish course around, filleting a cod at the table and delivering the portions.

Anne had to admit she was taken aback at the old lady's questioning. She had felt so accomplished this morning, as she'd just returned from a victorious battle, and Margaret's skepticism made it feel as if she'd done nothing at all. Heat rose to her cheeks, but she remained silent. Unfortunately, Millie had no such compunctions.

"*Only* fifteen?" Millie cried, incredulous. "Fifteen more people who won't die now on account of Miss Anne's knowledge, courage, and wherewithal."

Anne grimaced and sent a sharp look to her maid, whose curls were further escaping from their pins as her whole body seemed to vibrate. Anne made a cutting motion as if to tell Millie to stop, but it only seemed to anger her further.

"You want *me* to stop talking?" Millie asked, and even the mild and even-keeled Tobin couldn't hide his wide eyes and open mouth. Anne and Tobin both stared at Margaret, trying to gauge her reaction, but Millie just took another bite of fish and chewed it with vigor.

Margaret's gaze was hard and flinty as she stared at the smaller woman, but then the edges of her eyes began to crinkle as she nodded. "Quite right, and good for you for speaking up, my dear." Margaret turned her head to face Anne and said, "Forgive me."

As shocked as Anne had been at Millie's outburst, it was nothing compared to her shock at hearing the great Margaret

Marksbury, dragon of Hyde Park and terror of the ballroom, apologizing to *her*.

"Of course, my lady," Anne said, trying not to let her surprise show on her face as she bowed her head to acknowledge Margaret's apology.

Tobin cleared his throat and said, "This cod is delicious, Ma'am."

They all seemed to relax then, and fell into the easy pose of friends who'd known each other forever, though the situation was anything but easy, and the idea of Tobin and Millie eating in the dining room with the gentility almost unheard-of. Margaret asked genuine questions about their lives and interests, talked about the weather, and of course, gave lively and colorful updates about her patients in the east wing. The meal continued into dessert, and they all ate their fill of iced treats until Anne declared, "I could not possibly eat another bite."

Millie raised her eyebrows, said, "Speak for yourself," and grabbed another glace. Anne stared at the other woman, but she couldn't help but enjoy watching her maid's enjoyment of the rich desserts. She realized that even though she had known Millie for quite some time, she didn't really *know* her at all. She knew she sang beautifully, that Annelise had treated her like family, and she knew that she herself felt almost a kinship to Millie, but in the end, Millie still gathered her dirty clothes, did her hair, helped her with her bath, and all the other things a servant did. It had never occurred to Anne to ask her about her day, her interests, her family, or what she did when she wasn't working. She felt intense shame at the idea that she had never really considered Millie an equal, even though they were both human, and had so much in common. It was a sobering and disturbing thought.

Anne knew she was exhausted. She also suspected that Millie would probably soon be feeling ill from the cowpox inoculation, so she suggested they all retire and take some leisure time in the heat of the afternoon.

"Splendid idea," Margaret said, wasting no time in standing up and rapping her cane on the floor. "I'm old, so I always nap after luncheon," she said, "but you three should rest. Millie, Tobin, feel free to use any part of the house that suits you." With that, the old dragon took the arm of a footman who led her from the room.

Millie yawned and said, "I am feeling tired, Miss, if you don't mind."

"Of course, Millie," Anne replied. "I believe I'll take my book to the garden, but I'll come check on you in a little while. If you start feeling *very* poorly, send for me as soon as possible."

"I will, Miss," Millie said, looking down at the bandage. "Just tired and a little sore for now."

"With luck, that will be it, but you might expect a low fever. Thank you again for what you did today."

"Thank *me?*" Millie said. "You probably saved my life. Thank *you.*"

"Yes, and thank God, too," Tobin said, laughing. "Now if you all are done appreciating each other, I am going home to see the wife and rest." He bowed to the women and strode out.

After having grabbed *Love's Labor's Lost* from the shelf in the parlor, Anne found herself a lounging chair in a garden gazebo. Though the day had gotten warm, the humidity from the rain had not broken, but in the shade of the gazebo there was a breeze, and Anne felt like it might be the most heavenly place on earth. One of many structures on the meticulously tended grounds, it was tucked away past the orchard and contained just one lounging cushioned chair and a little side table. Anne removed her bonnet, looked around to be sure she was alone, then untied the ribbon at the top of her dress to let the breeze in a little more. She sank down on the cushion and soon lost herself in the play, which she hadn't read in years. She found herself laughing aloud at the antics, and she was relieved to feel that she was finally relaxing, even if just for an afternoon.

As Jonathan rode Percy back to the stable, dismounted, and handed the exhausted horse off to a stable hand, he realized that even in the heat and exhaustion he felt, he was finally relaxing for the first time in days. His visit with the vicar had been tense, but not terribly long. It didn't take much time to tell someone to get the hell out of the county and never show his face again. Once he had come face to face with the despicable man, his task had grown much easier. He could see immediately that the man cowered in his presence. He'd at least have had a grudging respect for the minister if he'd stuck by his convictions, but instead, the title of duke was intimidating enough for the man, and he agreed to leave with very little protestation and much sweating—though from the heat or from fear it had been hard to tell. Either way, it had been over almost as soon as it started, but the ride there and the return were both long and hot, and Jonathan was relieved to finally be back at Sutcliffe.

He knew he was too late for luncheon, but he popped his head into the kitchen and was relieved to find a plate had been left for him, covered with a towel. He grabbed it and a bottle of ale and headed out to the garden. As he approached his favorite gazebo, he groaned when he saw someone was already there. He began to turn away and look for another quiet place, but as he changed pace, he saw the figure in the wicker chair shift positions and realized with a start that it was Anne. He crept closer, not wishing to disturb her, but also hoping for a glimpse of her face. One of the things that had made his morning more difficult was the fact he had missed her. He had been back in her presence just for that day, and already he was hooked. He had actually felt bereft without her on the long ride to Northridge, and most looked forward to the opportunity to see her again, which he'd thought would come at dinner. Now, seeing those curls escaping their pins and her state of repose, and he could not help but want to drink in the sight just a bit longer.

She lay reclined, a book resting on her stomach, her eyes intent on the page. Her head lay on one arm, propped behind her, while her other hand held the top of the book with two fingers. As he got closer, he could see her facial expression changing with the plot of the story, which he could see was yet another Shakespeare play. When she laughed out loud, it startled him, and he rustled the lilies he'd been standing in.

"Who's there?" she asked, folding the book on her lap, sitting up, and looking around the gazebo. When she did so, the loosened neckline of her dress draped down, offering the most tantalizing expanse of bosom. Jonathan closed his eyes and took a deep breath before stepping forward.

"It's me," he said, feeling sheepish and wondering if she could tell how long he'd been standing there.

Anne sighed and fell backward upon the cushion; apparently thankful it wasn't someone else.

"I was worried Millie was feeling poorly," she said by way of explanation. "I am on edge, hoping she has no adverse effects from the inoculation."

"Just me," Jonathan said. "Mind if I join you?"

"Not at all," Anne replied, "Though I'm afraid there's not much room."

Jonathan placed the plate and the bottle of ale on the floor of the gazebo and folded his long legs under him as he sat. "Not a problem for me," he said, "after bouncing around on that horse through all that mud this morning, the solid ground feels like heaven."

"I'm surprised you're back so soon," Anne said, "I'm almost afraid to ask how it went."

Jonathan laughed and took a bite of cold chicken. "I can be very convincing when I want to be," he said. "I don't think we'll hear from him again, and hopefully neither will any other village. At least not on the subject of vaccination."

Anne smiled. "Sounds like it was almost fun."

Jonathan met her gaze. "It was," he said, smiling back. "How are things here?"

"We inoculated fifteen," she said, and he nodded. "But that's not the best thing that happened."

Jonathan raised his eyebrows, and Anne continued. "Margaret had all three of us for luncheon."

Jonathan was pleased, but not overly surprised. It was just the sort of thing his aunt would do.

"And since we're using so much ice from the ice house, she made us eat all the iced treats that had already been prepared."

Jonathan laughed. "I'm sorry I missed such an eventful meal," he said.

"I'm sorry, but there's none left for you," Anne said, laughing. "Millie made sure of that."

"She's quite something, isn't she?"

"Yes, she really is."

Jonathan looked up at Anne and could not help himself. "So are you, you know."

He watched the blush rise in Anne's cheeks. "I'm sorry if I embarrass you, but sometimes when I look at you, I just feel like I have to tell you. You were amazing today."

Anne looked down at her lap, where the book still lay closed. He held up the bottle of ale. "Want a sip?"

She looked up and smiled. "Yes, thank you." She took a long draught of the cold liquid and then wiped her mouth on the back of her hand like a stable boy. She handed the bottle back to him without breaking eye contact. "So were you, you know."

"Hmm?" he asked, taking the bottle back and setting it beside him.

"Amazing today," she said, and he snapped his gaze back up to hers. "You were. Your speech, going to see the vicar—all of it."

"We make a good team," he said, not caring how it sounded.

Anne whispered, "We do." She swung her legs to the side, moving them from the lounge to make room, placed the book on the table next to her, and patted the cushion by her side. He hesitated, not sure what to say.

"Are you sure?" he asked.

"Come sit next to me, Jonathan," she said, patting the cushion again. "Bring that bottle," she added.

He did as she asked, and when he sat near her, he could almost feel the heat coming off her body, though they were not touching. She held her hand out, asking for the ale again, and he gave it to her. Instead of bringing it to her lips, though, she brought the cold bottle, slick with sweat from the humidity, up to the side of his face.

"You must be so hot after your ride," she said. Jonathan almost groaned. Her voice was so gentle, so kind, so full of the feeling he'd been longing to hear. There was a long silence between them, and all he could hear was the faint tweeting of birds, the buzzing of insects in the garden, and the steady, fast beating of his own heart.

"Anne, I—" he began, but she cut him off by placing one finger on his lips.

"I know," she said. "Nothing has changed." She paused before adding, very quietly, "Except *everything* has changed." He felt tears forming in his eyes and cursed himself for his weakness. But he nodded and took the hand she held to his lips and turned her palm toward him. He bent forward and kissed her open palm, then her wrist, where he swore he could feel the fluttering of her heartbeat. She sighed. He shuddered, stopped, and looked back up.

"We're both exhausted," he said, trying to give her a way out, sending out feelers to be sure.

"Yes," she agreed. "I'm so tired." She laughed. "Tired of pretending I don't want this, most of all."

Jonathan closed his eyes and took a deep breath. Before he could open them again, he felt her soft lips against his own. He could hold back no longer. He slid one hand around her waist to the small of her back and pulled her to his lap, where he was already straining against his breeches in his need for her. She gasped with pleasure and writhed against him, and he felt her tongue dart inside his mouth, tentatively at first, then with confidence and brazen need.

Jonathan tried to maneuver Anne to the cushion, but she stopped him, pushing against his chest so he was lying back on the chaise. He looked up at her, astride him, the sunlight gleaming around her, her hair falling haphazardly from where it had been pinned, and that neckline draping open. He wasn't sure he'd ever felt anything like this in his life. She ran her hands up his chest and along his neck, then bent to kiss him where her hands had traveled, tickling his earlobes with her tongue. He heard her voice in a hoarse, raspy whisper.

"This feels so good."

He took her face back in his hands and kissed her again, wanting to taste every inch of her. "It does. It really does." She ground against him again, and he felt ready to explode. As if she sensed this, she raised herself to her knees and pulled his shirt from his breeches. She scooted back on his legs and started laying kisses all across his chest and stomach. She rubbed her palm across the hair growing on his abdomen, and it felt so much more intimate than the kisses had been. He leaned back and sighed when she kissed his belly button and moved lower. She had some trouble untying his breeches, so he reached down and yanked the cord, heard it rip, and they both laughed a little. She looked back up at him, her brown eyes soft and full of desire, but also so much more. He beckoned for her to come back and kiss him again, but she shook her head and kissed lower.

When she finally pulled him free, she wrapped her hand around his cock and looked up at him, her pupils were so wide and dark that her eyes had become almost black. He groaned as she moved her hand around him.

"That feels good?" she asked, but it was more like a statement. All he could do was nod. He closed his eyes and just enjoyed the feeling of her hand on him, but his eyes flew open in shock when she kissed him on the tip of his cock.

"Is this—" she began.

He cut her off. "Yes, God, yes, it is."

She responded by putting the tip of his cock in her mouth, and his whole body rocked up with the sensation. Slowly, she ran her tongue around the head then pulled all of him into her mouth, moaning as she did so. He could feel the reverberations down to the tips of his toes. He shuddered and asked her if she felt good. He knew she was inexperienced, but he also knew how her body had responded to him before. He wanted to make sure she was comfortable. She took his member out of her mouth and nodded and then licked it up and down exploring him. When her teeth raked him a little, he flinched and she drew back.

"No, no," he said, trying to reassure her and, most of all, trying to get her to continue. "That's normal." She smiled and put her head back down, circling her tongue around the head again, a caress to soothe where she'd hurt him before pulling him back in all the way. Only one or two of these and he knew he was done for.

"Anne," he said, "I'm going to—"

"Oh, God," she said, lifting her head. "I want you to. I want to give you this." She circled her hand around his shaft before taking the head back in her mouth, and he lost all control. His body exploded with the sensation, and he could feel his seed spilling all over her hand and his stomach as she lifted her head just at that moment. When he opened his eyes, he saw her kneeling over him, her hand still around him, those big brown eyes staring at him, dark with desire. She was breathing hard and fast, and her chest heaving from the effort. Lying there on his back, the hazy feeling of lust thick in the air around him, he pulled up her skirts and slid a hand up underneath the elastic of her pantaloons. She was slick and wet with need, and he only needed to circle his fingers around her folds a few times before she moaned and collapsed on him in her release. Careful not to let her dress fall in the mess he'd made, he gently moved to the side and pulled her down alongside him, her head falling on his shoulder and her fingers tracing patterns in the hair on his chest.

"It was as good as I remembered," she said. "I was afraid of that." She laughed.

He smiled and pulled her closer, kissing the top of her head. "All I can think about is when we can do it again," he said.

"Yes, I was afraid of that, too," she replied, and Jonathan's heart seized at the serious tone in her voice. Even though the insects were still buzzing, the birds were still chirping, and a light breeze rattled through the leaves in the garden, the world seemed to come to a halt while he waited for her to continue.

"I don't want to hurt you," she said.

At that, Jonathan could bear it no longer. He sat up in his exasperation, springing from the chaise and pulling his breeches up, trying his best to rig the broken cord to tie them back. "Too late for that, I'm afraid," he said, and he hated the meanness in his voice. "Several weeks too late, in fact."

"I know," her voice was very quiet, and she did not look up at him.

He didn't even know how to respond. Was she just using him? "We both wanted this, didn't we?" he asked, afraid of the answer.

"I know I did," she replied, and her voice was so flat, he knew she was telling the truth. "I didn't ask for it, or expect it, but when you showed up, I just couldn't help it. I wanted it so badly, have been thinking about it for so long."

"Then why does anyone need to get hurt?" Jonathan asked, and he heard his voice breaking. "Marry me. Marry me and we can do this every day. We can do it *twice* a day, and we don't have to worry about what anyone will say or think. In fact, my Aunt Margaret, my brother and sister, your father, Aunt Harriet—they'll all be ecstatic."

"You don't understand."

"You're right, I don't." He turned and picked up what was left of the lunch plate and the ale, and strode off without looking back. If he stayed, he wasn't sure what else he might say.

Anne watched Jonathan's purposeful gait as he walked out of the little glen where the gazebo sat and waited until his broad back disappeared into the lilies. How could she explain her fears to him? How could she explain about her mother? She felt ready to talk about her with him, but she wondered if he could ever understand, even if she told him everything. Her mother had been proud to be a free and independent spirit, beholden to no one. She had been unapologetic about the way she lived her life. She had been a loving, doting mother. But had she ever experienced real love, the kind that was supposed to make a marriage? Did it even exist? Her father had claimed to love Annelise Heatherington, but if that were so, why had they not married? Why had Annelise kept their daughter from him? Surely if the Earl of Norwich could announce a long-lost ward and introduce her to the *ton* with so little gossip, he could have found a way to marry an opera singer. Her mind wandered back to the bundle of letters in her bureau in the parlor at Norwich House. She wondered if it might be time to read them.

But what if they only confirmed her worst fears? That her mother hadn't been capable of love, and this wanton feeling Anne was experiencing had clouded her judgment and had taken priority over her life? Anne was afraid of the way Jonathan made her feel. She had tried so hard her whole life to be good, to be chaste, not to make a spectacle of herself. She would have been quite happy in Bloomsbury, living a quiet life in their comfortable house, volunteering as a nurse, and reading. She would have loved to have kept on as they had, with her caring for the house while her mother was away, and caring for her mother when she was home. But illness had taken Annelise from her, and there was nothing she could do about that. She missed her mother every day, but more so than ever now when she wasn't sure there was anyone else in the world she could confide these feelings to. She felt more alone than she had since that day the earl had shown up at her door.

Anne sat up and brushed off her dress. She pulled her pantaloons back in place and tightened the ribbon on her dress's neckline. She bent to pick up some of the pins that had fallen from her hair and tried to replace them in a way that would not betray what had happened here. She hoped the rest of the household would assume she'd fallen asleep while reading and not question her disheveled appearance. She straightened the cushions on the chase, picked up *Love's Labour's Lost,* and headed back to the house.

The moment she entered her bedroom, Millie popped up from the chaise. "You're back sooner than I expected," she said. The little maid's eyes were puffy with sleep, but they narrowed as they took in Anne's appearance.

"You look a fright," she said, her customary insolence still in place.

Anne frowned. "Go back to sleep," she said, laying the book on the bureau and staring at herself in the mirror. She had to admit, she *did* look a mess, but she didn't look a fright. She looked fully alive. There was color in her cheeks and wildness in her hair. She wasn't altogether displeased with the effect. It matched her mood.

Almost as if reading her mind, Millie said, "You look beautiful, though, Miss, if I do say."

Anne turned. "Thank you," she said, "but we do need to fix me back up before dinner, I suppose."

"Miss Anne, you didn't think I'd let you go to dinner with the same hair you had this morning, do you? I heard the duke is back."

"Millie, aren't you supposed to be resting?" Anne asked, both to change the subject and out of genuine concern.

"I slept ever so well," Millie responded, already throwing open the wardrobe and looking at the dresses Margaret had the staff bring up the day before. "It itches under the bandage, but I don't feel a bit sick."

Anne sighed with relief. "That's wonderful." Hopefully tomorrow Anne could bring Millie back to the church, show the small cowpox infection under the bandage, and convince more villagers to get the inoculation. She just hoped it wasn't too late. All they could do was wait and see now, though.

"I still want you to rest tonight," Anne said, in a maternal tone. "I can do my hair just fine on my own. In fact, I was thinking of taking my meal up here so I could watch over you."

"I'm sure it's your concern for me keepin' you away from the dinner table," Millie said, frowning. "Sounds very likely."

Anne walked over to where Millie was still standing in front of the open wardrobe. "I don't want to see him," she said. "I'm afraid."

Millie turned to face her, and Anne was surprised to see Millie's eyes wide with shock. "Yes, you must be," Millie said, for once without the usual lilt of sarcasm. "I can see that now. But what I can't understand is, why?"

Anne led Millie to the edge of the bed and sat. "I honestly don't know. I'm afraid of how I feel, I suppose, is the easiest answer."

"Afraid of being like your mother?" Millie asked, and once again Anne was both uncomfortable and grateful at the maid's penchant for getting right to the point.

"Yes," Anne responded.

"I know how you feel."

Anne turned to look at Millie. "You do?"

"My own mum was an opera singer you know."

"No, I did not know."

"Well, she was, that's how I came to be with Miss Heatherington. My mum was Italian, a great beauty by all accounts, but I never knew who my father was."

"How did I not know any of this?" Anne asked.

"I didn't want you to know," Millie said. "And when I don't want something, it won't happen, as you well know." They both laughed.

Anne sat enraptured as Millie continued her story. "My mother died of syphilis when I was but ten or eleven. She wasn't a good mother like yours was. She was mean, and she drank. Now that I'm older I can see she used laudanum too much, too." Millie stared past Anne, seeming deep in painful memories, but she continued. "There were different men in the house every day. By the time I was old enough to appreciate her voice, she barely sang anymore."

"Clearly you inherited your musical talent from her," Anne said.

"Yes, and I always loved to sing. It's the only good memories I have of her."

"But how did you meet my mother?" Anne asked, trying to piece it all together.

"She performed with Mum many times, and Mum always seemed jealous of how she had managed to keep her career and her *other* activities, and also raise you well. When Mum realized she was dying, she asked your mother to take me in, and your mother did it without hesitation."

Anne colored with shame at the idea that this woman had trusted her mother to care for Millie, and her mother had made her a servant instead.

"Don't even think it," Millie said, reading Anne's thoughts again. "When I came, I said, 'I'm no ward, and I'm not going to be a singer either.' I begged her to let me work, and your mum let me care for you instead."

In quick succession flashes of memories swam through Anne's head. Her mother singing with Millie, her mother cradling Millie in front of a fire when Millie was ill, Millie's constant insolence, and Anne's feeling that Millie was more of a friend than a servant. It all started to make sense as each piece of the puzzle fell into place.

"I told myself I'd never end up like my mother," Millie said, and again Anne marveled at how steely Millie's voice could be. "I didn't mind working for a living if it meant I could live a quiet and comfortable life."

Anne laughed. "I always felt the same way," she said, crossing her arms. "But life has had other plans for me."

"Miss," Millie said. "If you don't mind me saying . . ."

Anne laughed out loud at that. "Since when has that ever stopped you?"

Millie raised her eyebrows as if to say, *fair enough,* and continued, "Marrying a duke isn't exactly a sinful or shameful way to live out your life. It isn't like being his mistress. I know he's asked you—"

"Yes," Anne said, her voice clipped with anger, "Everyone knows."

"I know you care for him."

Anne narrowed her eyes. "Do you now?"

"Of course," Millie said. "And it's obvious he's in love with you."

Anne frowned. "Not to me."

Millie rolled her eyes and stood up. "I thought we were being honest."

"I am," Anne said as she stood and began pacing the room. "He's taken with me, sure. I'll grant it. He appears to respect me in some ways. I agree. But love?" Anne stopped and turned back to Millie. "I'm not sure it even exists."

"I wasn't sure either," Millie said. "But did you see Tobin today? Did you see those mothers and their children? Think back to your own dear mum. Of course, love exists."

"I'm not talking about that kind of love," Anne said, sighing. "You know what I mean."

"I do," Millie said, "But really, I'm starting to wonder: what's the difference?"

Anne sighed because while what Millie said made a lot of sense, Millie hadn't experienced what she'd just experienced out in the gazebo, or behind the curtain at the opera, or in that dark room at Chelsea. It was easy for her to say that love was love, but what Anne had felt seemed so much stronger and so much more dangerous than any love she'd ever known. Did Tobin and his wife feel that? Her mother and father had felt *that,* of course, it's how she came about. But was that *love?* To her, it seemed too dangerous, too fraught. She lost control of herself too easily. That didn't seem like it would be love at all. Love was supposed to be patient, and kind, and respectful. Love was supposed to be cradling a child when it was ill or teaching him or her to sing. It wasn't supposed to be feeling like your heart might explode, or like you'd never be whole again. Was it?

Millie brought Anne back to the wardrobe. "We won't figure this out right now," she said, "but we can get you ready for dinner."

Anne looked down at Millie, exasperated. "I told you I didn't want to go."

"You might not know how you feel," said Millie, "You might be scared, you might be unsure." She pulled a yellow gown from the wardrobe and held it up to Anne before frowning and shaking her head. "But you do know who you are. And you, Miss," she said, taking a green gown and nodding with approval, "are Miss Anne Heatherington—never one to back down from a challenge."

Anne laughed and snatched the gown away. "All right, I'll go to dinner, but stop fussing. This one will do just fine."

"I know, that's why I chose it," Millie said, turning to prepare the wash basin so Anne could freshen up.

"I'll tell you something else I know," said Anne, "I know I'm glad you're here."

Chapter Sixteen

"So glad you're here," Margaret said as Jonathan walked into the parlor before dinner. She patted the settee next to her, and Jonathan sat. "I heard you caused quite a row with the vicar."

Jonathan leaned back and looked up at the ceiling, pinching the bridge of his nose with his thumb and forefinger. "Can I not have just one pleasant, easy conversation today?" he asked.

"If you'd let me *finish*," Margaret said, "I was about to say how proud I am of you."

Jonathan sat up and looked into his aunt's wizened face. There was no furrowed brow this time. Only a small, proud smile. He nodded.

"Sounds like a row was just what was needed."

"I believe it was," Jonathan agreed. "He seemed quick to acquiesce to my demands."

"He saw the duke in you."

Jonathan frowned. "Perhaps. Or maybe he just saw it *on* me," he said, gesturing to his expensive breeches and jacket.

Margaret sighed. "Boy, when are you going to see yourself how I see you? You're so much like him."

"Like who?"

"Your uncle." Jonathan paused at that. Margaret so rarely spoke of her late husband, and Jonathan's parents had never mentioned him except to say that he'd died young of a sudden illness.

"He was stubborn. He lacked confidence. He never could see what I saw—a lovely, caring, and worthy man."

"He sounds wonderful," Jonathan agreed. "I'm sorry you lost him."

"So am I, my boy, so am I." She leaned forward and covered his hand with her own for a moment, then leaned back again and sighed before changing the subject back to the weather. "At least the sun finally came out today."

"How are the patients dealing with the heat?" he asked, imagining having a fever in this thick, heavy weather.

"We've kept most of the east wing quite cool, and the ice water is helping immeasurably. I believe most of them are as comfortable as they can be under the circumstances."

"That's good to hear." Jonathan looked out the window where the sun was finally beginning to set behind the trees on the estate. "It looks cooler already now," he said.

"Yes, my maid says she thinks a storm may be coming. Says her knee always hurts when the weather is changing."

Jonathan winced. He knew with this heat and humidity another storm front was probably inevitable, but he had hoped against hope it would miss them. It still could, he told himself. He just needed to remember to breathe and to try to be alone when it happened.

He realized he had been lost in thought and he looked up to see his Aunt Margaret's shrewd eyes watching him. "What?" he asked, trying to sound nonchalant, "Do I have a bug on my face?"

Margaret smiled that smile where just the corners of her

eyes crinkled, but it was enough. The moment passed, though not without the strange feeling that his aunt was reading his thoughts. She reached over and took his hand her own, and he once again marveled at the firm grip beneath the soft wrinkled skin of her palms. When she was young, those hands must have been the envy of the *ton,* he thought. They'd never had to work at anything a day in their lives. He narrowed his eyes a bit as he looked at his old aunt's face. There were many different kinds of work in the world. Perhaps she had done her share.

"What was uncle like?" he asked. He'd never thought to ask before. She'd always just been his old dragon aunt. He'd always loved her dearly, of course, but it had never occurred to him that she'd ever been anything but Aunt Margaret, living with his family and helping to raise him and his siblings after their parents had died. In fact, he'd never really thought about his parents as full people, either. He'd been young enough when they'd died, and distant enough, what with the governesses and Eton, so they were just figures to him. He wondered if David and Sarah felt the same way.

He had plenty of time for all of these thoughts because his aunt did not answer right away. She kept her hand over his but looked out the window as if lost in thought. "He was so kind," she began. "So gentle and loving."

Jonathan shifted a bit in his seat but did not speak. Margaret looked over at him. "He was the love of my life," she said with a frown. "You can't expect me not to mention it."

Jonathan colored in embarrassment and nodded. She was exactly right, of course. "I'm sorry, please continue," he said, turning his hand over under her palm to squeeze it.

"He was too gentle, one might have said," she continued. "And many people did say it. Especially when the orders came for the war."

"The war?"

"Yes," she said, "Charles was sent to the American colonies of course."

Jonathan wasn't sure why he had never realized that. He had known his Uncle Charles was in the Army, it was a long family tradition, but as far as he knew he had been the usual aristocratic military man—content to carry the title and help with the patronage, but not much more. He was surprised to hear that his uncle had gone overseas.

"He wasn't gone long," she continued, though her voice became quieter as she spoke. "He fought in one of the earliest battles, near Boston."

"Breeds Hill," Jonathan said.

"Yes, I think that was it," Margaret said, starting to remember. "At any rate, he was injured, not severely, a broken arm, but enough to be sent home, and when he got here, he was different somehow. All his gentleness was still there, but the kindness and sweetness I remembered had disappeared."

Jonathan nodded. He had heard this over and over again from his friends and colleagues who'd seen battle. There wasn't always a dramatic change, but there was a change. He wondered what he would be like if he had his memory—if that intervening year of recovery hadn't happened—and he'd gotten back and had to pretend like everything was normal. He'd come back from the war before, the first time, and that had been hard enough, but what he'd seen hadn't been nearly as horrific as Waterloo. It was a disconcerting thought.

"It must have been very difficult," Jonathan said.

"It was," Margaret paused, wincing. Even though it was forty years ago, the memories were still hard on her. He squeezed her hand again She continued, "I wanted a family, and we had dreamed of it before he'd left. But when he returned . . ." Margaret trailed off, then paused to wipe a tear that had fallen to her wrinkled cheek. She smiled at Jonathan and took both his hands in her own. "Luckily, I got you, your sister, and brother."

"Lucky for *us,* I know that," Jonathan agreed.

Margaret's characteristic toughness began to return. "That's why I'm so keen on seeing you settled and happy."

Jonathan rolled his eyes and leaned his head back. "Yes, so you've said." He sat up, laughed, and slapped his thighs with his palms before standing. "Shall we go in to dinner?"

He held his hand out to help her up, then tucked her hand into the crook of his arm as he led her to the dining room. They took their customary places at the table, and he sipped from the claret before clearing his throat. "I'm not sure Miss Batten will be joining us," he said.

Margaret's head swiveled toward him, and the look she shot him threatened to cut him to pieces. "Why ever not?"

"My valet told me that Millie told him she wasn't feeling well."

"Millie's not feeling well?" Margaret asked. "I do hope she's not having a reaction to the inoculation after all."

"No," Jonathan said, and he felt the color rising to his cheeks. "I mean An—Miss Batten was not feeling well."

"Well, after the day she's had, she deserves a good long rest," Margaret said, taking a sip of her own wine. "I did think she'd send word down if she wasn't . . ." At that moment Margaret's focus diverted to something over his shoulder and she stopped talking. Jonathan turned to see what his aunt was looking at, and he had to catch his own breath. Anne was standing in the doorway, and he wondered how it was that every time he saw her, she only became more beautiful. He stood and gave a silent bow before going to pull out the chair at Anne's place.

"Miss Batten," he said, nodding.

"Your Grace," she replied, her voice little more than a whisper.

"I, ah," he cleared his throat, "I was just telling Aunt Margaret that I feared you weren't well and might not be joining us."

"I'm very well, thank you," she paused, and the rest of her sentence was an interrogative, "For asking?"

Jonathan glanced over at his aunt, who was glaring at him. He cleared his throat again. "Yes," he said, "let me try that again." He dipped his head in a small bow, then continued,

"How are you feeling? Well, I hope?"

Anne smiled, and Jonathan's whole body felt like it was melting and hardening at the same time. "Thank you, I'm very well," she said, nodding at Margaret. "So nice to see you well, my lady," she said.

Margaret smiled widely, and Jonathan couldn't help but notice the difference between the disapproving glowers she'd been bestowing on him and the sunny disposition with which she was meeting Anne. He almost laughed out loud. He knew it was going to be a difficult dinner, and part of him wished Anne had taken her meal in her room. Now that she was here, he couldn't take his eyes off her, and he couldn't stop thinking about what had happened in the gazebo. His heart was breaking at the way they'd left off, but his body was suffused with warmth at the memory of what had come before. And now here she was, so beautiful in this simple green gown with the ruby she always wore hanging down in the cradle of her bosom. He would have to either make her his bride or never see her again. There was simply no other choice. He moved to change the subject as the servants brought the soup course.

"How's Millie?" he asked, trying to keep his voice level.

"She's very well," Anne said, taking a sip from her soup spoon and then blotting the corner of her mouth with her napkin. Jonathan thought of what it would be like to run his tongue along the edge of her lips right where the napkin followed.

"She's tired but seems to be recovering already. No sign of even a low fever. The pustule has formed and seems to be itchy, but hopefully, that's the extent of it."

"I'm so glad to hear it," Margaret said. "That little maid of yours could teach us all a lesson about forthrightness and strength of mind." At that, the old dragon glared at Jonathan, and he frowned at her before returning his attention to Anne.

"And Tobin, how is he holding up?"

"I haven't seen him since lunch, but he was well when I left him," Anne said, before adding, "I have to say, that man is an absolute treasure."

"I agree."

"He might make a good steward."

Jonathan agreed with this assessment and had even considered it before Anne mentioned it, but it somehow irritated him for her to be making suggestions about how he ran his estate. It galled him especially given that she had made clear on two separate occasions that she wanted no part of his life. He held his emotions in check and simply nodded.

But Margaret had no such compunctions. "What a splendid idea," she said, slapping the table to emphasize her point. "A capable man," she said, "But more than that, a caring and honorable one. Take it under advisement, Jonathan."

He forced a smile, then turned back to his soup. "Thank you, I will," he said.

The rest of the meal passed with pleasantries and some political banter, discussions of the gardens, and plans for the fall, and Jonathan did his level best to avoid staring at Anne or thinking lascivious thoughts about her, but truth be told it was probably the most difficult battle he had ever faced.

Finally, Margaret patted her stomach after the dessert course, and declared, "I couldn't eat another morsel." Dinner was over.

Jonathan rose. "Ladies," he said with a small bow to each of them, "Thank you for a very pleasant evening. I believe now I'll retire to my study to read a while."

Anne smiled, but it did not reach her eyes. "Thank you, Your Grace, rest well."

Margaret was watching the two of them between narrowed eyes, but Jonathan could not stay in the room one minute longer. He placed a quick kiss on his old aunt's head, left the room, entered his study, closed the door behind him, and slid to the floor, hiding his face in his hands.

When Jonathan left the room, Anne sighed and closed her eyes, leaning back against the chair. She must have been much more obvious than she'd intended, and her eyes flew open when she heard Margaret's soft cackling. Anne frowned at her, then stood.

"Lovely seeing you again, my lady," she said, giving a polite nod. "Have a pleasant evening."

She turned to leave the room but was stopped short by Margaret's insistent knocking of her cane on the floor as the old lady struggled to her feet.

"Would you care to join me in the parlor, Miss Batten?" she said, and her voice was much kinder than her cackle had been. "It's been an age since I've heard any good piano playing."

"Well, even if I play tonight, I'm afraid it still wouldn't be very good," Anne said, shaking her head. "I've got a passable ability, but not much talent."

Margaret smiled and beckoned Anne to follow her. "I'm sure that'll do just fine," she said, taking Anne's arm and leading her to the door.

As they entered the parlor, Anne realized it had grown quite dark even though it was not yet very late. She was just about to remark upon it when they both heard a distant peal of thunder.

"I was afraid we'd get a storm tonight," Margaret said. The old lady cocked her head, listening, but she sat down on the settee and motioned to the piano. "Would you?"

"Of course," Anne said. She smoothed her skirt beneath her and took her place on the bench. She ran a few scales and a couple of small melodies to warm up a bit, then asked Margaret what she'd like to hear. They heard the soft distant thunder sound again, and it was almost pleasant, thinking of being here in this candlelit room, playing the piano, while a storm approached. Just as she finished a light Scottish folk song she knew by heart, she heard a banging in the next room and stood up in shock, closing the piano and rushing to Margaret, who was staring at the wall.

"Could it be one of the patients from the east wing?" Anne

asked, worried. If the fever had taken any of them, they could hallucinate or wander and hurt themselves.

Margaret's face was pale, and Anne sat down next to her. "What is it, my lady?" she asked

"That's Jonathan's study," Margaret said in a whisper. She looked up at Anne, and her eyes were full of tears. "Go in to him, will you dear?"

Anne balked and tried to reassure the old woman. "I can escort you to check on him. Come, let's go."

"I can't go in there," Margaret said. "It's the storm. He's—I was afraid of this when I saw his face earlier today. Please, dear, please go take care of him."

Anne was confused, but she understood the urgency and sincerity of Margaret's plea, and as she rose, they heard the knocking again, so Anne picked up her skirts and ran to the hall, swinging open the door of the study without knocking. What she saw there struck her in the heart. Jonathan was lying on the floor, right next to the door, curled in a fetal position and rocking. It was his boots hitting the wall they had heard in the parlor. Anne knelt beside him and began to rub his back in slow, rhythmic circles. When the thunder pealed again, this time much louder and closer than before, Jonathan's whole body tensed, and the rocking became more pronounced. He seemed to be muttering, but she couldn't make out what he was saying.

"Hush," she said, continuing the slow circles on his back. "I'm here. It's all right. You're safe."

Jonathan's body relaxed a little at this, but he was still in a ball, and she could not see his face. When the thunder rumbled once more, he tensed again, and she knew it was up to her to help him through this. She had seen this kind of thing before in Chelsea, and she knew it would pass. The key was trying to keep him as calm as possible. She spoke in soft, soothing tones, almost sing-song, trying to match the rhythm of her hand on his broad back. She couldn't see his face, but his hair was slick with sweat. She sat down on the floor next to him and used her other hand to move the hair from his face.

When she lay her cool fingertips on his forehead, he lowered his arm and looked at her with unseeing eyes. She knew he wasn't present with her right at that moment, but she continued to act as if he were, talking and rubbing his back as if he were a child being put to bed. She breathed very slowly and very loudly, hoping he would match her. She whispered, "That's it, now, just breathe. Very deep. In, then out." Even though another roll of thunder rumbled by outside, she was relieved to hear the rain had begun. The water was very loud as it smashed against the windowpanes, and she hoped it would help drown out the sound of the thunder. It did seem to have that effect, and she could hear Jonathan's breathing start to slow and become more even.

She sighed and closed her eyes. She focused on her breathing, continuing to run her hand over his back until she felt his hand close over her arm and pull it away. She opened her eyes and was so happy to see him sitting up and looking at her like his old self that she flung herself around his neck, but he reached up and pulled her hands away. She backed away and was startled to see his eyes narrowed.

"What are you doing here?" he asked in a hoarse whisper.

"Margaret and I were in the parlor when we heard you fall," she said. "I ran to see if you were all right. How long have you been having these attacks?"

"None of your business," he said, standing and striding to the liquor cabinet. He kept his back turned to her, poured himself two fingers' worth of brandy, then downed it in one quick motion before filling the snifter again.

"I've seen it before," she said, trying to ignore the sting of his words. "I might be able to help."

"I don't need *help*," he bit off. "I just need to be locked away during thunderstorms."

"Have you had the attacks all this time? Since you returned from Waterloo?"

"No."

"There are triggers."

"Yes. We've established that mine appear to be thunderstorms."

"But not every thunderstorm," she said, and it wasn't a question.

"No, not every thunderstorm," he agreed. He turned from the liquor cabinet and sank into a deep leather chair nearby. He rubbed his forehead, sipped from the snifter, and motioned to the other chair, waving his hand like it was against his better judgment, which she supposed it was.

She sat, perched on the edge of the chair and staring at him. He leaned forward a bit and held the brandy glass with both hands in front of him, and she was again startled by how the darkness in the room made his gray eyes look almost black.

"Please don't be embarrassed," she said. "It's just me."

He uttered a soft bark of laughter. "You, Tobin, and about twenty people who saw me fling myself to the ground in Hyde Park."

"I'm sorry," she said, "but it's still nothing to be ashamed of."

He looked at her, the light from the candle reflecting in his dark eyes. "I'm not ashamed," he said, then looked away. "I just don't know how I'm supposed to run a household or care for my family when obviously I can barely care for myself."

"You know that's not true," Anne said. Her heart was aching for him. "Look at what you've accomplished here in just a few days. You're saving lives."

Jonathan laughed, but the sound was so completely devoid of any humor that it sent a chill up her spine. "No, *you're* saving lives."

"And you're the one who brought me here because you knew I could help," she said. She stood and walked over to where he sat. She knelt on the floor beside him and took his hands in her own. The silk of her gown felt strange against the scratchy surface of the wool rug that covered the floor, and his hands in hers had a similar contrast. She squeezed them and placed a kiss on Jonathan's cheek. "I know things between us are . . . complicated." At that Jonathan gave her a flat smile that did not reach his eyes. "But I need you to know how much I respect and admire you. There's nothing you could do that would change that." She stood up and then continued, trying to make her voice much lighter, "Except maybe refusing to get help."

He laughed and shook his head before finishing the brandy that was left in the snifter in his hands. He leaned his head back on the chair and covered his face with his hands, almost as if trying to wipe the humor off. When he looked back up at her, though, his smile was still there. "Very well," he said, "You win. What kind of help do I need?"

"I don't know that much, but I can write to some of the doctors I worked with in Chelsea," Anne said. "You're not alone, no matter what our relationship is. You know that." She made a move to leave, but his voice stopped her just as she pulled the door open.

"I think I'm starting to understand," Jonathan said. There was so much raw emotion between them that she felt her whole body tingle in response. "Thank you," He said. She just smiled and closed the door behind her. As she turned around in the hall to make her way back upstairs, she was surprised to see Margaret standing there in the shadows, leaning on her cane.

"Can't you bring yourself to love him, my dear?" Margaret said, with no trace of malice, anger, or manipulation.

Anne looked into the old woman's eyes, feeling tears in the corners of her own, and said, "My lady, that is not the problem, believe me. Now, if you'll excuse me." She barely got out the last words before they caught in a sob, and she ran upstairs.

When Anne arrived at the breakfast room, she was relieved to see no one there. She sat and ate a simple meal of toast and coffee before heading to the east wing to check on the patients.

When she knocked on the door to the East parlor, it was Margaret's face she saw first as she opened the door a crack. The old woman's face turned from annoyance to warmth when she realized it was Anne, and Anne was gratified. Margaret pulled the door open and put a finger to her lips. It was still early, and all the shades were drawn, keeping the room dark and cool so the patients could sleep as long as possible. Anne crept in behind her and shut the door.

"How is everything here?" she whispered.

"Well in hand," Margaret said, though the lines on her forehead deepened when she added, "Though there are some who may not make it."

"Yes, I'd feared as much," Anne said, shaking her head in sorrow. "It's a horrible disease."

"There are so many who are recovering, though," Margaret said, taking Anne's hand in her own and squeezing it. "Many whose fevers turned in the night. You've saved lives."

Anne smiled her gratitude at the old woman and squeezed back. "So have you."

"How's our Millie?" Margaret asked with concern.

"She's quite well," Anne said. "She's having coffee in my room now and coming down to head to the village in a few moments."

"Wonderful," Margaret said, then gestured to the sleeping patients who were just beginning to stir on the cots around the room. "Now, if you'll excuse me."

"Of course," Anne said, and on impulse, she pulled the old woman in for a quick hug. "Thank you."

When she left the east wing, she decided to take a stroll around the garden while she waited for Millie. She wandered a bit through the boxwood maze near the drive, admiring the absolutely breathtaking morning. The grass was still wet from the storm, but the sky was a clear, fresh, crisp blue. A soft breeze made its way through the trees and out to the open garden where she walked, and she took deep breaths as if to cleanse herself of everything that had happened the day before. She turned when she heard the front door open and walked to meet Millie as she emerged from the manor. Millie's eyes squinted and she blinked a few times before saying, "Rather bright, eh?"

Anne laughed. "Shall we?"

She and Millie began walking toward the village but had barely gone twenty steps before they saw a figure emerging from the bend in the drive ahead of them. Anne wasn't surprised when she realized it was Tobin. She smiled. "That man just won't let us walk alone," she said.

"A little domineering if you ask me," Millie frowned.

"A little kind and solicitous," Anne corrected, pursing her lips at her insolent friend before calling out a morning greeting to Tobin.

His gait quickened as he approached them, and he was almost out of breath by the time they met and he turned to walk with him. His words came so fast they had trouble hearing him at first. "My lady, you will not believe the church."

Anne's heart seized with fear. What if it hadn't worked? What if people who'd received the inoculation had fallen more ill than expected and scared off the townspeople?

"It's packed. I let them all in, but there's still a line out the door."

Anne almost giggled in her relief. "Thank God," she said, taking the man's hand. "Thank *you*, actually."

Tobin just bowed. "I'm so relieved, my lady."

Anne was thrilled, of course, but a new fear came to her. How could she inoculate so many in one day? It would be a long, tiring task, but she felt up to it. It would be good to be busy all day and keep her mind off everything else.

And that's exactly what she did. With Tobin and Millie assisting, they worked their way through every villager who came to them. Soon they realized they were inoculating people from nearby villages, people who had previously fallen victim to the vicar's lies. With just a short break for a quick lunch of bread and meat, they worked from just after seven in the morning until almost eight at night. As the sun was beginning to set, the last straggling patients were inoculated, and Anne began to pack up her things. Tobin took the cow back to pasture and returned to escort them back to the manor.

"My lady, I just don't know what we would have done if you hadn't come."

"You're quite capable," Anne assured him. "You would have figured something out."

"Well, at any rate, I'm so grateful you came," Tobin said.

Anne turned to Tobin with a serious face. "It's time for me to ask you for something," she said.

Tobin looked at her, brow furrowed. "I'm not sure what I can offer you, my lady," he said, "but I'm willing to try. What is it?"

"I need your help with the duke," she said, trying to ignore Millie's stare coming from her other side as they walked. "He had an episode last night."

Tobin nodded. "Yes, I was worried about that when I heard the thunder."

"He says you helped him last time."

"As much as I could. I just helped him with his breathing. A friend of mine taught me that trick when we got back from the war."

"Do you have other friends who've had episodes?"

"Too many to count," Tobin said. "Some just never could come back. They ran off, or worse."

"I've written to a doctor I worked with in Chelsea, but while I wait for him to respond I was wondering if you could talk to Jon—His Grace," Anne asked.

"I'll do what I can to help, but I don't know as he'll listen to me," Tobin said.

"I think he will," Anne said, then took the man's calloused hand in her own. "Thank you."

When Anne finally sank down in the softness of the big bed

that night, her body was exhausted but her mind was racing. She was starting to realize how deeply she cared for Jonathan, still reeling from discovering the truth about Millie, full of pride and accomplishment for the inoculations, and she couldn't stop seeing Margaret's tearful eyes when they'd realized Jonathan was having an episode. She tossed and turned most of the night, and when the first light of dawn started to come through the open window, she was relieved to have a reason to rise and start a new day.

She got up and threw on her dressing gown before sitting down to blot her face with fresh water. Something on her escritoire caught her eye as she began to pull a brush through her hair. Not just one thing, but two—a crisp white envelope with her name on it and the bundle of correspondence between her father and mother, which she was absolutely certain she'd left at Norwich House. She frowned and walked to the little desk, brushing her hair as she went. She stared down at both bundles. The envelope was addressed to her in Jonathan's strong, unmistakable hand. The bundle of letters was still tied with a brown string, their envelopes and stationery all different colors with varying degrees of fading and age. She didn't want to open either one.

She started when she heard the door open behind her. She turned on her heel and was relieved to see Millie's curls poking through. When Millie saw that she was awake, she came in and shut the door behind her.

"Sorry if I woke you, Miss," she said.

"No, I was up," Anne replied, then looked down at the table where the two items sat, both white in contrast to the dark wood of the desk, like the focal points in a painting.

"He brought it last night," Millie said. "I thought you would have read it by now."

Anne kept her eyes on that envelope, on the way her name was written in such bold lettering like it had made some kind of decision on its own.

"I was so tired last night I just went straight to sleep," she said. "What about my mother's letters? Did Jonathan bring those, too?"

"No, Miss," Millie said. "I brought them from Norwich when I came. I only put them out last night because I felt the timing might be right."

"How do you know?" Anne asked.

Millie sighed before she answered. "Just a hunch, I suppose." She went to the wardrobe and began looking through the day dresses.

"Just the yellow," Anne said. "And we should start to pack my trunk for the return to Norwich House."

Millie looked up, startled. "You aren't going to leave without reading it are you?"

"I don't know," Anne said. "I do know that first I need to face breakfast."

Once she was dressed in her simple yellow day dress, with her hair tucked back into a businesslike bun at the nape of her neck, she made her way to the breakfast room, steeling herself the whole way for the inevitable meeting with Jonathan. She patted the letter in her pocket both intrigued by and frightened of what might be written there. She wished he would just understand, that he would stop trying to convince her, but she knew very well that she hadn't done a good job of explaining herself.

When she entered the breakfast room, she was surprised to find Margaret at the head of the table in Jonathan's usual seat. She nodded a good morning to the old woman and took her seat at the left. She wanted desperately to ask about Jonathan, but she didn't trust herself to keep her voice steady. But Margaret, no trace of the dragon in her voice now, beat her to it.

"He's not here, my dear."

"Where is he?"

"He said he left you a note."

Anne cursed under her breath. "Yes," she said. "I didn't read it yet."

Margaret smiled.

"I take it you'll be going back to Norwich soon?"

"Yes," Anne answered. "I figured I would stay today to help with the invalids in the east wing and be sure everyone who wanted an inoculation has one."

"Yes, a day to tie up loose ends."

"Indeed."

"All the loose ends save one," Margaret said and lightened the mood by winking.

Anne had to laugh a little at that. "Yes, all but one. But it's not likely to be tied up any time soon, you know."

"Yes, some tangles take time to work themselves out," Margaret said, but those were her last words on the topic, and Anne was grateful to have the rest of the meal in comfortable silence, with some talk of the weather and of the Little Season coming in the fall. David and Sarah would of course be returning to London. Sarah had not yet fully experienced a season, Anne supposed Jonathan would be expected in Parliament, and they all had social obligations to attend to. But Anne was again surprised when Margaret said she was thinking of staying behind in the country.

"Whyever would you?" Anne asked, curious.

"I'm getting old," Margaret said, "I've been old for years, in fact. And the truth is, I'm tired. I like the country, especially in the fall."

"But won't you be lonely here?"

"I'll have Jonathan," she said. Then she closed her eyes as if remembering something. "That's right. You haven't read the note."

Anne's cheeks burned, but she said nothing.

They both finished their coffee in silence, and as soon as Anne was done, she stood, bid a good day to Margaret, and hurried to the hall to meet Millie and go down to the village.

Just as she had hoped, there were several people at the church who had come in from outlying farms to be inoculated. Just as she had also hoped, she was busy most of the day, again with the help of Millie and Tobin. They worked quickly and quietly, and by mid-afternoon, it was clear that their job was done. They had inoculated everyone remaining in the village. Only a few people had refused, and they had not remained, choosing instead to visit family elsewhere. When Anne and Millie had cleaned up and eaten a quick meal, Tobin came to accompany them back to the manor house. The pair was unusually silent. Anne had the feeling that they both knew what was in the note, but neither felt it was their place to talk about it, and she appreciated that. Tobin stopped and turned to her as they approached the drive up to Sutcliffe where he customarily took his leave.

"Miss, thank you for helping His Grace."

Anne was taken aback. She hadn't done anything, really, except show that she understood and cared. "Of course, Tobin. You know I'd do the same for you."

"I know you would, Miss. My own wife did."

Anne colored at the implication that Anne was to Jonathan was Tobin's wife was to him, but she said nothing. She understood Tobin's meaning. "Did he come to see you?" she asked, trying to keep her voice casual.

"He did. I told him where to go."

Anne's eyes narrowed. "Go where?"

"You didn't—"

"—read the note?" she cut him off. "No, I haven't. I guess I'm the only one who doesn't know what's in it."

Millie made a loud and obnoxious snort.

Anne took a deep breath and tried to keep her emotions even, or at least not let them show in her voice. "Well, whatever help you gave him, Tobin, I know he appreciates it, and so do I. We've done more than save a village from smallpox here. I feel I've made a friend for life."

Tobin smiled and took Anne's hands. "I hope I'm not being too forward, Miss, but I feel I've made four."

Anne laughed at that. "Margaret's more a dragon than a friend," she said, squeezing his hands right back. "But I will miss you when I go."

Millie chimed in, "As will I. And that ice cream . . . I'll miss that, too."

Tobin dropped Anne's hands to pull Millie into a big bear hug. They looked for all the world like father and daughter at that moment. Millie's smile disappeared for a moment as she embraced the older man.

Tobin took his leave of them and started to walk down the side road to his house. Just before he disappeared from her sight, Anne couldn't help shouting, "Please take care of him."

Tobin didn't look back, but his voice rang clear through the pine woods, "You know I will."

A short time and one carriage ride later, and Anne was back at Norwich House, settled in the parlor settee, *Love's Labor's Lost* sprawled on her lap, her hair loosened and a full pot of tea on the table in front of her. Her father and Harriet were nowhere to be found after the bustle of welcoming her back and eating lunch, and Millie had gone to take a nap. She realized it was really the first moment she'd had to herself since she'd gone to Sutcliffe. She sighed and just enjoyed the quiet of the empty room. She poured herself a steaming cup of the tea, dropped two lumps of sugar in, squeezed the small lemon wedge, and stirred the hot liquid. Pursing her lips, she blew on the amber brew, then brought it to her mouth.

"There you are," Aunt Harriet exclaimed, and Anne juggled the hot cup of tea to avoid spilling it everywhere.

"Yes, here I am, Aunt," Anne said, putting the cup back on its saucer and looking up at the old lady, frowning. She had missed Harriet and her father, of course, but she'd had her fill of meddling old people.

"I was hoping you'd tell me again about this inoculation method. I'm afraid your father cut you off too soon at lunch. He has a queasy stomach, but I don't." Harriet's eyes twinkled.

Anne laughed. "It really is fascinating. It was one thing to read about Dr. Jenner's work, but to put it into practice was quite another." She regaled her aunt with all the details of the inoculation, trying to make it extra interesting and gory, much to the old lady's delight.

She poured Harriet a cup of tea, and they continued talking, Anne telling Harriet about Millie and Tobin's singing until her aunt stopped her mid-sentence. "And the duke?"

Anne took a deep breath and a sip of her tea, looking away from her aunt to avoid showing her irritation quite so much. She tried to master herself, but she barely bit out a response between clenched teeth. "He's well."

"I heard he'd gone to—"

"Yes, he had already gone by the time Millie and I took our leave this morning." Anne cut her aunt off, partially to indicate that she'd rather not talk about the duke as if it could not be more obvious. But it was also because she still had not read the letter. She hated herself for it. It was like a lead weight in the pocket of her wide skirts. She had carried it with her the whole day, and every so often she reached her fingers in to brush it softly and make sure it was still there. But she hadn't read it. She didn't know where Jonathan had gone. She didn't know what was in the note. She still wasn't sure she ever wanted to read it. Almost against her will, she reached into her pocket once more and patted it.

"It sounds like you all did an admirable job at Sutcliffe, Anne," Harriet said. Finally, she was taking the hint.

"Thank you, Aunt Harriet. It was rewarding work. I haven't felt this capable since . . ." she trailed off, not wanting to hurt the old lady's feelings.

"Since we dragged you into the world of high society?"

"I would say 'gently led,'" Anne said, smiling.

"You want to go back to Bloomsbury?" Harriet asked, and Anne could sense the worry in her voice.

"No," she said, and it wasn't until that very moment that

she realized she truly meant it. It wasn't Bloomsbury she missed or her house. She missed her mother, of course. But what she desired most was feeling needed, feeling cared for. She had that here with her father and Harriet. She could see that in the old woman's eyes as she contemplated the idea of losing Anne back to Bloomsbury. She did miss the work, though, and while she'd been busy with the *ton,* she hadn't had any time to volunteer. She wasn't sure anyone would take her now that the rush of war-wounded had subsided. But she knew she couldn't live her life as a single ward of the Earl of Norwich forever, nor did she wish to live as the wife of some lesser nobleman or other. It was truly in taking care of others that she felt most alive, and so much so that it was more than a hobby or even a career—she thought of it as a calling. She knew that even better now that she had returned from her success in Sutcliffe.

"No," she said again, "I don't want to go back." She looked at Aunt Harriet and met the woman's worried gaze with what she hoped was a reassuring one of her own. "I'm happy with you and father. I truly am."

"But?" Harriet said.

"But," Anne replied, "I do think I need to do more than just lie about reading Shakespeare and taking occasional rides."

"Well, we'll go back to London for the little season, dear," Harriet began.

"Yes, more than balls and musicales, too," Anne said, smiling. "I want to be a doctor."

"A woman doctor?" Harriet said, and Anne braced for the worst, but the older woman did not laugh.

"I know it's not possible," Anne began.

"It hasn't been done," Harriet corrected her. "That doesn't mean it's not possible."

"Well, then," Anne said, correcting herself, "not *probable.* Certainly, no one will admit me into any school of medicine."

"What about the nursing?" Harriet asked.

"Yes, I thought of that, but I'm not sure they'd take me

anywhere now that the need is not so great."

"One never knows unless one asks."

"Yes, I suppose that's true." Anne smiled.

"Of course, one never knows what a husband might think of such a thing."

"One might not care," Anne said, and almost regretted it until she saw the crinkles at the corners of the old lady's eyes.

"No, I suppose one might not." Harriet stood. "Well, my dear, I just wanted to check on you. I'll leave you to your bard, then." She nodded at the book, still lying open where Anne had laid it down to pour her tea. "Until dinner?"

"Until dinner."

Anne watched the old lady leave, then poured herself a fresh, steaming cup and pulled the book back on her lap. She had left it to cool and just started Act II when she lifted the tea to her lips again. She took a deep breath of the hint of lemon, then tilted the cup to take a sip. Just as she did so, something on the desk in the corner of the parlor caught her eye. She brought the tea back down to the saucer and stared at the bundle of letters her father had given her. She uttered a curse out loud, directed at Millie even in her absence, and went swiftly to the little desk, lifted the lid, and threw the letters in.

Chapter Seventeen

Jonathan woke up when one single stream of light coming through the threadbare curtain fell across his face. He stretched and winced at the crick in his neck from the cramped cot on which he'd spent the night. He realized, though, that even with the pain and the aches in his various joints, and the piercing sun in his eyes, he had slept very well. Better than he had in over a week. He must have been making too much noise trying to unfold himself from the small space because it wasn't long before one of the dairymaids rushed in to make sure he was all right.

"Your Grace," the fresh-faced young girl said, curtsying low and making herself look as subservient as possible.

"No, no, that's not necessary . . . Lydia, is it?"

The girl nodded, blushing.

"Well, Lydia, I'm a guest here, but just like any other guest. Please treat me like one."

"Yes, Your Gr—"

"Jonathan," he said, "or Mr. Marksbury if you prefer."

"Yes, Mr. Marksbury," she nodded. "Do you need anything?"

"I'll come out and have some coffee in a moment. Is your father awake?"

"Yes, Your—Mr. Marksbury. He gets up at dawn to lead the milking."

"Wonderful." He nodded to Lydia to indicate that she could leave. He leaned back on the straw-stuffed pillow he'd slept on, and for all the world he felt like he was back in the army. It was bracing and comfortable. He liked the idea of not being a duke for a while. He opened the shutters of the window behind the curtain and breathed the freshness of the morning air. The farmers had begun haying yesterday, and the air was redolent with the sweet smell of the cut grass baking in the sun. He got up, performed some field ablutions, pulled his jacket on, and headed out to the kitchen where Lydia's mother, Mrs. Hyde, was cooking a simple, yet hearty breakfast for them all.

"Good morning, Your Grace," she said in a bright voice, but without any of the obsequiousness Lydia had shown.

"Good morning, Mrs. Hyde. Coffee?" She motioned toward a pot on the stove, and Jonathan poured himself a large mug. "Where's Mr. Hyde? Lydia said something about overseeing the milking?"

"Yes, he's out in the barn puttering around. The girls do all the milking, but he can't sit still, so he 'oversees,'" she chuckled, wiping her wet hands on her wide cotton skirts.

Jonathan smiled. "Thank you. When is breakfast?"

"You'll hear the bell," she said.

His aunt had balked when he said he was going to stay at the dairy farm for a few days, and her first reaction was to decry "that smell," but Jonathan realized he loved the smell of a dairy barn. It was earthy and real and solid. He breathed it in as he walked through the large double-hung doors, his eyes adjusting to the dimness. He squinted and looked around for Robert Hyde.

"Aye, there, Your Grace." The older man waved from a

milking stall where a hired maid, not one of Robert's girls, was milking a cow.

"Jonathan, Robert, please."

"Of course, force of habit. How did you sleep?"

"Believe it or not, very well," he said, clapping Robert on the shoulder. "I cannot thank you enough for your hospitality."

"There are not many dukes who'd sleep well on a cot off the kitchen," Robert said, laughing.

"Not many who cower like babes during a thunderstorm, either," Jonathan responded.

"More than you know of, I'm sure," Robert said. "Quite a few dairy farmers, too."

Jonathan and Robert shared a look. Jonathan wasn't sure how could ever thank Robert and Tobin for helping him. He opened his mouth to speak, then shut it again, unsure of his words, but when Robert looked back at him, his tawny disheveled hair falling in front of his kind blue eyes, Jonathan had an idea that Robert understood. It had only been two days since he'd jotted that letter off to Anne, dropped a kiss on his aunt's head, and fled on Percy out to the countryside, but it felt in many ways like a month. Just the knowledge that there were others who dealt with the same thing, and that there were people who cared enough to help him, gave him more hope and confidence than he'd had the whole past year.

He looked around and breathed the smell of the barn again. He stood to watch the milkmaid rhythmically squeezing the udder and listened to the steady sound of the milk streaming into the metal pail. He touched Robert's shoulder. "Could I try?" he asked.

"Well, of course, Your Grace." Robert pulled a three-legged milking stool into the next stall where a docile, big-eyed brown cow stood, swishing her tail. He motioned for Jonathan to sit and taught him how to milk a cow. It was not as easy as it looked, but with practice, he was soon settling into the rhythm of it. It was one of the most soothing and satisfying things he'd ever done. Maybe one day he could be whole again, he thought, maybe he could be *normal*.

When Anne retired to her room after dinner, she realized she was exhausted. It was the first day she *hadn't* been busy but having to pretend to be happy and normal with her father and aunt had been a constant battle and had taken all the emotional energy she had. She came into the room, shut the door behind her, walked to the bed, and turned so her back was to the mattress, then flung herself backward into the soft folds of the blankets. She spread her arms out to her sides and sighed—a long, ragged, exasperated sound.

"A little dramatic, isn't it?" Millie said, rising from the chaise in the corner. Anne took one of the little fringed pillows from her bed and threw it at the maid.

"What are you doing in here?"

"Here to help you change for bed," Millie said, batting her eyelashes.

Anne frowned and sat up on her elbows. "Well, I don't need help, so you can leave," she said, nodding toward the doorway.

"Of course, Miss, let me help you with your necklace."

Anne leaned her head back and groaned with annoyance before sitting back up and turning so Millie could undo the clasp of the ruby necklace.

"Is it still in your pocket?"

"Yes," Anne answered as she reached down to brush the envelope with her fingertips before realizing what she'd said, then quickly added, "Not that it's any of your business."

"No, of course not," Millie said as she tugged on Anne's elbow for her to get up so she could start undoing the laces in the back of the dress.

Anne stepped into her billowy white nightgown and pulled the little bun at her neck free of its pins before sitting down at the dressing table and dragging a brush through her hair. In the mirror she watched Millie behind her hang the silk dress in the wardrobe, arranging the chemise so it would air out overnight, laying the stays on the dressing stand so they wouldn't bend, stowing the little silk slippers back in the trunk with the other shoes. As Millie finished these tasks, she came back toward Anne and laid her hands on Anne's shoulders. Anne brought one hand up to cover Millie's and give it a quick squeeze before she scooted over on the bench and patted the empty spot. Millie sat and they looked at their reflection in the mirror together for a moment. Anne was taller and her skin paler. Millie was small, with those beautiful dark tight curls and that pixie-like nose and chin. They both smiled at themselves, and at each other. "We're quite a pair, aren't we?" Anne said, nudging Millie on the shoulder.

"Indeed, we are," Millie agreed, nudging right back.

"Millie, I need to talk to you about something."

"And I need to talk to you, too," Millie said, sounding relieved. They both spoke at once.

"I want you to go back to Bloomsbury."

"I want to go back to Bloomsbury."

They both laughed. Anne turned on the bench to face Millie and grabbed the young maid's hands. "I want you to have the Bloomsbury house. I want you to live there and make whatever kind of life you want. You're no one's servant, and you never should have been. You can sing or read or do whatever you like. My mother would love that."

Millie's eyes glistened. "Miss, I never would have dreamed to ask—"

"Of course not, that's why you deserve it," Anne said, with feeling. "As for me, I don't want to sell it, but I don't want to go back and live there, either. As much as I miss my mother, I have found a family here, and I can't leave them."

"I'm glad to hear that, Miss," Millie said.

Anne laughed. "But I don't want my mother's house to be cold and empty. I want it full of life, and who better than you to do that?"

"I happily accept the offer," Millie said. There was a pause as Millie looked down at her hands resting in Anne's between them. "I just need you to do one thing for me."

"What?" Anne said, taking Millie's shoulders, "Anything."

Millie reached out next to her and pulled the top drawer of the dressing table open. She never broke eye contact with Anne, but as the drawer slid wide, Anne glanced over and saw the bundle of letters, still tied with that rough brown string. She closed her eyes and sighed.

Millie squeezed Anne's thigh. "It's time."

Anne stood and grabbed the bundle. She walked over to the bed and sat down, pulling the string on the neat little bow so that the letters fell open and spread like a fan before her. Millie took a few steps toward the door, then said, "You know I'll come right away if you need anything."

Anne looked up at her, desperately afraid to be alone. "No, stay. I want you to stay. If you don't mind."

Millie smiled. "Of course, I don't mind. It's been everything I could do not to tear these open and read them myself," she exclaimed, hopping onto the bed and picking up the top letter. It was dated July 1791, six months before Anne was born. She pulled the brittle paper from the envelope and unfolded it with gentle fingers. There was her mother's own sprawling script, and it almost took Anne's breath to think of her mother holding this paper in her hands a quarter-century earlier. She took the letter from Millie, brought it to her nose, breathed it in, then laid it on the blanket in front of her and began to read out loud.

"My dearest Simon,"

"Simon is the earl?" Millie asked. Anne nodded and continued reading.

"The weather here in Naples is divine. I've just finished Magic Flute, and the house was packed for the whole run. Now I'm recuperating on the coast, taking the air, as they say, but every moment I think of you."

Millie whistled low and raised her eyebrows. Anne went on.

"I'm afraid this will be my last performance until the baby comes. I just know it will be a girl, and all I can think of is how she will look like you. Every day I will look at her and think of my beautiful Simon."

Anne started to feel like an intruder reading these intimate lines. She folded the letter carefully and placed it back in the envelope. "Just more of the same," she said, blushing.

"She really loved him," Millie said.

Anne took a deep breath and picked up another letter, this one from December, just one month before Anne was born.

"I know you want what you think is best, but I assure you no daughter of mine will be raised like a prize cattle and sold at auction."

Anne laughed. "So stubborn and so sure I was a girl. How could she have known?"

"A mother knows, I've heard."

"You must know how ardently I love you and how deeply I respect you, but your world is not my world." Anne flinched. She had said almost those exact words to Jonathan. She continued.

"Our daughter will be raised with the freedom your women are not allowed to have. She will be able to choose for herself. If I come to live with you, she and I will be prisoners in a gilded and cushioned castle."

So, the earl had asked Annelise to come to him. As his mistress? Anne could see why her mother would have been offended by such an idea. She took up the next letter. Marked March, from when she was two months old.

"She's so beautiful, Simon, and I was right. She looks exactly like you." Anne felt tears pricking the corners of her eyes, imagining her mother in that Bloomsbury house alone with an infant. The strength it must have taken.

"I must admit that your proposals have been wearing on me. That's why it's taken me so long to return your letters. I have teetered on the brink of acceptance these long months as

I gazed into our daughter's beautiful eyes, as I nursed her with my own body and rocked her to sleep at night. I have thought of the family we could make and I have been tempted. Oh, Simon, so tempted." Anne felt a single tear fall to her cheek, and she reached up quickly to dash it away.

"But—"

"Of course, there's a 'but,'" Millie interrupted, rolling her eyes, which Anne was surprised to find were also glistening with unshed tears. Anne chuckled, shook her head, and kept reading.

"But would I still be able to sing? Would Anne be able to choose the life she wants to live? I know in your world it would not be possible. Simon, I never expected to fall in love with you. You know you're not the first man I've ever known. But you're the only one I've ever loved. It was the first transgression I've made against my own better judgment. And I'll never love anyone like you again, I can see that now. You have given me the two greatest gifts of my life: your love and our daughter, and I will never forget those gifts or stop feeling gratitude for both. But I beg of you, please do not try to know our daughter. Please do not trap her in that cage of nobility. I will write you often and tell you of her. You deserve that much. But I beg of you please do not speak to me of love or marriage again. Please do not try to take my daughter from me."

Millie jumped from the bed to grab two handkerchiefs from the bureau, then came back to where Anne sat and handed her one. They both wiped their eyes and laughed. They rummaged through the rest of the letters, which were all updates on Anne's growth and life. They were endearing to read but held no more clues into Annelise and Simon's relationship. Apparently, it had ended just as she had asked for it to.

"That stubborn, prideful woman," Millie said.

"Look at what she did for me, Millie," Anne whispered. "She gave up her only love so that I could have a choice."

"Yes," Millie said, her eyes narrowing. "And have you made it?"

Anne reached into the pocket of her nightgown, where she'd almost mechanically transferred the letter from Jonathan from her dress when she'd changed. Her fingertips brushed it, and she lifted her head to meet Millie's eyes. Millie nodded. Anne nodded back. She pulled the letter out and almost ripped it with impatience. These long days she'd carried it like a weight, but now that she knew it was time to read it, she felt like she couldn't get to it quickly enough.

The thick ivory paper opened in her lap and it was just one sheet, written in Jonathan's bold, strong hand.

Anne,

You know I love you. I never thought love was actually real. No one I know has been in love, as far as I know. Not my parents surely, and not any of my friends. In the ton, we make advantageous matches and leave the love to our novels and songs. But the moment I first saw you that day in Chelsea, even though I did not know myself, I knew you. It was the sweetest transgression I've ever committed. And every day since then I've thought of you, somewhat scandalously if I am being honest.

But speaking of honesty, I have learned something from you. There are many forms of love. The love you have shown me as a friend has perhaps changed the course of my life. When I met you, I was quite literally broken. I've put myself together slowly, but it wasn't until you held me that night on the floor of my study that I realized I needed more help, and that I owed it to you to accept your refusal.

You are the most capable, admirable woman I have ever known. You would make a wonderful duchess, but you would also make a wonderful doctor. You should be free to choose. Though I cannot imagine a life without you, I also cannot imagine a life in which I've forced you to stay. Tonight, I'm going away to try and get

*myself righted. I want you to know that, even though
I will not intrude upon you anymore, it's important for
me to tell you how deeply and sincerely I love you.*

Jonathan

Anne just sat there, watching her tears fall and blur the words on the page. She took deep ragged breaths and did not notice at first that Millie was bustling around the room.

"What are you doing?" she asked.

"Packing."

"Packing for what?"

"Stop being daft," Millie said, rolling her eyes, and pulling the steamer trunk from the corner. "I've had just about enough of it."

"Millie, I don't even know where he is."

"A minor hitch in the plan that can be remedied with ease," Millie said, with complete confidence.

"It's the middle of the night."

"Well, of course, we'll wait till first light," Millie said, exasperated. Anne jumped up, hugged Millie, and began throwing petticoats into the trunk.

Margaret Marksbury was enjoying her customary early breakfast at Sutcliffe Manor when she heard a carriage on the drive. She smiled and stood, hoping against hope that David and Sarah had returned. When she got into the hall, though, she was surprised to see Anne Batten and the maid Millie standing there, Anne fingering a bonnet in her fidgety hands. The girl looked as lovely as ever but was clearly in a heightened state of agitation. Margaret narrowed her eyes, trying to parse out what was happening. She was shrewd, but she wasn't a mind reader. She walked forward with arms outstretched to them both. "What a wonderful surprise," she said.

Anne hugged Margaret then, she stepped back and cleared her throat.

Margaret rolled her eyes. "Spit it out, girl."

Millie stepped in front of Anne. "You'll not be speakin' to her like that, my lady."

Margaret felt duly chastened. She softened her voice. "I'm sorry, my dear, but you know you can just be frank with me. What are you doing here?"

Anne swallowed again but did not hesitate. She said, her voice even, "I need to speak to Jonathan."

Margaret felt her heart begin to beat so hard that she feared it would pound right out of her chest. She clutched it but tried to keep her face impassive. "Of course, my dear," she said, and she motioned them both into the parlor. "I hope everything is all right."

Anne's cheeks turned a bright rosy red, but she said, her voice faltering a bit now, "It's more than all right."

Margaret smiled but managed to keep her composure. She had longed for Jonathan and this girl to see the truth about how they felt for so long now. "I'll send a note right away."

Anne stood. "Actually, if you know where he is, I can just go to him now."

Margaret laughed out loud. "Of course, I know where he is." She motioned to a footman. "Have a horse brought round immediately for Miss Batten," she said, and the man went running off to the stable. "You're not in riding clothes, dear."

Millie rolled her eyes. "She can barely do more than trot," she said. "I'm sure if she gets some boots, she'll be quite fine."

Margaret called another footman and sent him up for some boots. While they waited, Margaret eyed Anne. She was wearing a worn yellow day dress. Though it was far from *au courant,* it brought out the girl's dark hair and eyes, and her beautiful complexion. "That's a lovely color on you," Margaret said.

"Thank you," Anne said, smoothing her skirt self-consciously. "It was always my mother's favorite."

Margaret smiled. "I think I would have liked to have known your mother."

"You would have been scandalized," Anne said, smiling. "She was an opera singer, you know."

"Is that so?" Margaret said. "No wonder you play the pianoforte so well."

Just then the footman arrived and bowed, indicating with an outstretched arm that the horse was ready. Anne slipped out of her traveling shoes and pulled on the riding boots. She hugged Millie, then pulled Margaret into a long embrace. "Thank you," she whispered into the old woman's ear, and Margaret smiled, rubbing the younger woman's back.

"Just be sure you don't break my boy's heart again," Margaret said.

Anne fought to keep the horse at a comfortable trot, knowing she was not a good enough horsewoman, and that the road was too winding, for anything faster. As she followed the directions the footman had given her to the Hydes' dairy farm in the country outside Sutcliffe, she heard the first rumblings of thunder. Another storm was coming. She felt as if she were racing against time. She had to get to Jonathan. She had to be there when the storm came. She urged the horse as fast as she dared and raced through the darkening forest toward her love.

When she saw the little farm cottage that must be the Hydes,' she forced the horse into a gallop for the rest of the short distance before pulling him to a halt in front of the house. She dismounted and tied the reins around a fence post, then ran inside, calling out, "Jonathan? Jonathan?"

She rounded a corner in a corridor only to run right into a matronly and kind-looking middle-aged woman. "Steady, my dear," she said, taking Anne's shoulders. "What's the rush?"

"I'm so sorry," Anne said, her face flushed with her urgency. "I'm Anne Batten. I'm looking for the Duke of Sutcliffe? Is he here?"

"Mrs. Hyde," the woman replied, breaking out into a smile from ear to ear. "Mr. Hyde told me he thought there was a woman in it somewhere. We just didn't know how lovely you'd end up being."

"Thank you," Anne said, trying hard not to sound impatient. "The duke? Do you know where he is?"

"I think he was up milking at the barn," Mrs. Hyde said, pointing to the large building across the way. "He really fancies the chore. Says it relaxes him. Though with a storm coming, I'm worried about him."

"Me, too," Anne called out behind her, already running to the barn.

When she burst through the doors, she was surprised at the pleasantness of the air in the large, open building. It was dim, but cozy somehow. The smell of cows, milk, and hay was reassuring, earthy. She saw some of the cows look up with startled eyes at her hurried entrance, and she closed the doors behind her. The barn seemed empty. She whispered, "Jonathan?"

She walked down the center aisle, peeking in stalls to either side. Apparently, milking was over for the morning. There wasn't a dairymaid in sight, and all the pails were neatly stacked awaiting the next milking. "Jonathan"? she whispered again, as loudly as she dared.

As she grew closer to the far end of the barn, she heard some movement and then deep breathing. In the last stall, which had been outfitted with a sort of cot, table, lamp, and single chair, clearly meant to be used as a makeshift office when necessary, she found Jonathan, sitting on the floor, his knees pulled to his chest and his chin resting on his arms crossed in front of him. He had his eyes closed and had not heard her. He was breathing deeply, rhythmically, tensing his shoulders, then releasing them. A flash of lightning lit the darkened sky outside, then a few moments later a distant peal of thunder sounded. She watched as Jonathan continued breathing, tensing, releasing, breathing, tensing, releasing. When the sound from the thunderclap had died down, she rushed to him.

"Jonathan," she whispered, touching his elbow. She knelt to look him in the eye. As his head raised and her eyes met his, she felt as if she were drowning in their gray depths. She put her hands on the sides of his face and just smiled, staring into those eyes, *her* Jonathan's eyes.

"Anne?" his voice was husky. Though he was not having an episode, it was obvious he was trying to stave one off. He took her hands from his face and brought them down in front of him. "Is it really you? How did you find me?"

"I read the letter," she said, and she laughed at the confusion on his face. "I finally read it. You gave me my freedom. You gave me a choice. Now I've made it."

She leaned in and kissed him then, kissed him like he was the last man on earth which, to her, he was. He seemed so startled that, at first, he did nothing. She darted her tongue in his mouth, unsure of his response, and, at that, he pulled her in and hugged her. He buried his face in her neck, and she felt him laying tiny kisses on the side of her face, her ear, in her hair. The whole time he was just whispering, "Anne, Anne, Anne."

She clung to him and sighed. "I know, I know."

They found each other's lips once more just as another roll of thunder echoed through the valley around them. Jonathan trembled in Anne's arms, and she pulled back. "Should we stop?"

"Please, no," he said, pulling her to straddle him where he sat on the floor. He ran his hands up and down her back, cupping her buttocks in his strong palms, and she moaned softly as she felt him harden against her thighs. She grabbed his face again and just drank him in, kissing his nose, his eyelids, that strong jaw that had been set so obstinately in so many of their conversations. His chin was rough with stubble from staying at the farm for a few days. She ran her fingers over it, then dropped more kisses where her fingers had led.

She grabbed the front of his shirt and began unbuttoning it, with each button going free, she kissed the skin that lay bare. Trailing kisses down his chest, she felt his body tense and shift in his passion. He reached up and yanked the neckline of her modest day dress down, freeing her nipples in one swift tug. Her back arched as he took one into his mouth, teasing it with his tongue as he suckled. She looked down and saw the other one, hard and tight as a little spring bud. Just as she was about to ask, he slid his other hand up over it and took it between his finger and thumb, toying with it just as he had the other with his mouth. She felt like she would lose control at any moment.

But it was her choice.

She gave it up.

Sitting up, she unlaced the back of her dress and pulled her arms free of the sleeves, then hitched the wide skirts up around her waist. She reached between them and tugged on his breeches. He scooted back against the wall to untie them, then she lifted up so he could stand and remove them. When his cock was free, she walked on her knees to him and took it in her mouth. He moaned but pushed her away a bit so he could come face to face with her. He kissed her there, on their knees, again and then drew her down to the floor. A shiver ran through her as her bare shoulders touched the cold wood, but soon Jonathan's tongue was running down the length of her neck, and she couldn't focus on anything else. His knee was wedged between her legs, and she bucked herself against it as he took her nipple into his mouth once more. She reached up and grabbed a handful of his hair at the nape of his neck, desperate to cling to anything at all. He came up to kiss her again, taking his time. Anne wanted him to continue, but she also wanted this moment to last forever.

"I don't want this to end," he said, his voice a hoarse whisper as he entwined his fingers in her hair. Another flash of lightning lit the dim space, but his eyes were on her.

"We can do it again later," she said, and when he smiled at that her whole body caught fire. She reached down and wrapped her hand around his hardness, rubbing the tip up and down her folds. She was slick with need, and she couldn't wait any longer. She wanted him to know that she claimed him forever. She pulled her arms around his shoulders and lifted her hips to invite him. He understood her need and thrust himself into her, deep.

There was a quick sharp pain as he took her maidenhead, but she barely felt it in the intensity of the moment, their two bodies having become one. She felt as if he were filling her whole body with his presence. He'd completed her in places she hadn't known were empty.

Jonathan stopped and did not move as he came up to elbows to look her in the face. She looked up at him, those gray eyes dark in a new way now, an expression she could read as plain as day. Just then another peal of thunder rumbled, much louder and closer this time, and instead of shuddering, Jonathan just held her and continued staring into her eyes. They lay there like that for a moment, and she took his face between her hands again, rubbing her thumbs on the stubble of his cheeks, then tracing his lips. She smiled and could feel tears in the corners of her eyes.

"I love you," she said. "You know I have since that day in Chelsea."

Jonathan turned his face to kiss her palm, then turned back to look at her as he rubbed his cheek against her hand.

"I know," he said, then his eyes narrowed in the intensity of his emotion. "But is it enough?"

"No," Anne whispered back. "It's not. I know that now. What matters is the choosing."

Jonathan smiled. "I choose you," he said. "Anne Batten, I want to do this every day for the rest of your life."

"I choose you, Your Grace, my Jonathan," she said. She pulled his face to hers for another kiss, and their tongues found each other as she thrust her hips up and took him even deeper. He groaned and moved against her, running his hand up and down the side of her body, cupping her breasts in his palms, kissing her everywhere he could reach. They were both so hungry in their need for each other, in the long wait, in the exhaustion of how they felt, that she exploded in her passion quickly, and he followed soon after. They lay there, spent, his head resting on her chest, and her stroking his hair, kissing his forehead, for long minutes before he had the energy to take himself from her and lie down next to her. He propped himself on one elbow and teased her by tickling her ribcage, tracing whorls on her skin. She had never felt so safe, so right. The thunder rumbled again; this time more distant. It appeared the storm was passing.

"We're going to have to explain ourselves to the Hydes," Jonathan said.

"I know Mrs. Hyde was worried for you when she saw the storm coming," Anne said, "But I also know she's a woman. A woman knows. There'll be no explanation necessary."

Jonathan laughed. "Robert kept asking me if there 'was a woman in it,'" he said, "But I didn't have the words to tell him about you yet."

"Well, there's definitely a woman in it," Anne teased, tracing his lips with her fingers again. "And she's not going anywhere."

Chapter Eighteen

When Jonathan and Anne rode together back to Sutcliffe, he had trouble keeping his hands off her. Their horses would come near, and he would reach out his hand to brush her fingertips or her shoulder. Halfway back to the manor they pulled the horses over near a stream to water and took their fill of one another on the mossy bank of the little creek. He felt he was making up for lost time with her, and he wasn't sure he'd ever be able to fill the deficit they'd created in their year of confusion. But he was determined to try.

She was an unskilled rider, but even her awkwardness was endearing to him. He watched her, talking to her horse, urging him around large boulders or gingerly picking their way through a meadow between the creek and the road. Even though she was obviously a novice at riding, she was not the kind of woman to balk at a new experience. As he watched her, tucking a stray hair behind her ear or leaning forward to rub the horse's neck, he realized he'd had it all wrong all this time. She wasn't his to claim or possess. What had happened between them was no transgression. Instead of breaking any rules, they had followed their hearts and come together to make something new. They had relied on each other's strengths and helped with each other's weaknesses. That was what love was, and it wasn't in the falling. It was in the choosing.

When they rode up the curve in the drive to the main grand entrance of the manor, Jonathan felt like he was seeing it for the first time. For the first time in his life, he knew he belonged here. He understood what his aunt had been going on about all these years. It wasn't just his duty to care for his brother and sister, or to fulfill some idea of what a duke should be; it was his duty to make a life he felt proud of. And he could do it right here, with Anne by his side.

The door opened just as they were dismounting, and Margaret and Millie ran out together. Millie was no longer dressed in her humble gray servant's dress. She was wearing a simple, slightly out-of-date, but perfectly fitting, green day dress. She and Margaret linked arms as they watched him and Anne mount the stairs. They looked for all the world like a couple of conspiring old bridge partners having just completed a suit. They even leaned their heads toward each other and tittered.

Jonathan couldn't help but roll his eyes, but a wide smile spread across his face regardless. He'd never been so full of love.

Anne ran to them both, and instead of taking their outstretched hands, she flung her arms around the ladies, and they all embraced, tears and smiles mingling in the morning sunlight.

Jonathan hung back a bit, giving them their space, but Anne and Margaret drew apart and Anne reached out her free hand to pull him in. He was so much taller and larger than all three of them, but he spanned his arms wide and pulled the women in close, resting his cheek on the top of Anne's warm brown hair.

When they pulled apart, everyone was full of questions and answers, interrupting each other and bustling with coats and bonnets as they made their way into the breakfast room. Once they were all seated and the coffee had been poured, Margaret stood and rapped her cane on the floor three times.

"If you don't mind, I have an announcement," she said.

They all looked up at her, curious. "I'd like to introduce Miss Mildred DiRossi, of Bloomsbury." She looked over at Millie, beaming.

Jonathan smiled wide. "So wonderful to meet you, Miss DiRossi." He bowed his head to her in deference.

The corners of Millie's eyes crinkled with delight as she bowed her head back. "Likewise, Your Grace."

They were just breaking into their coddled eggs when the door flew open. "Well, you have given us quite the chase," Sarah said as she burst in, tearing her bonnet off as she did and flinging it behind her. She stopped dead in the doorway, looking from one to the other of them around the breakfast table, then starting again, this time counterclockwise. David fairly skidded to a stop behind her.

Jonathan bit his lip to avoid laughing out loud and looked over at Anne's face. They both began to giggle. Margaret began to giggle. Millie began to giggle. The whole table erupted in uproarious laughter, and it was the release on a pressure valve that had been pent up since they'd arrived.

David and Sarah just stood, their mouths open, staring. This made Jonathan laugh even harder. He laughed until his sides hurt, then he stood and went to them.

"What am I thinking," he said, pulling them both into a hug. "Welcome home."

Sarah hugged him back, and David pulled back to pat him on the shoulder. "You're here a week early."

"We heard that Anne had left Norwich again with Millie."

"Miss DiRossi," Margaret corrected, clearing her throat and nodding pointedly toward Millie.

"Um, yes," Sarah continued, "And we were concerned the pox had returned. We knew if it had, you'd need our help."

Margaret smiled. "Good, good," she said, rapping her cane

on the floor to accent her words. "But I assure you we've got it well in hand."

"Then?"

Jonathan rose. He tapped his knife on the crystal water glass and cleared his throat. "I have an announcement."

They all stared at him in expectation, all of them except Anne, who looked up at him from her seat with a charming little wink. He rose his glass as if to toast.

"I'd like to announce that, with the earl's blessing, of course, Miss Batten and I are to be married."

"The earl's blessing?" Margaret grunted. "What about mine?"

Anne stood and went to the older woman. "My lady," she said, bowing a little, "It would mean so much to me if you would grant our marriage your blessing."

Margaret tapped the cane again and said, "It's about damned time." Anne bent down and kissed the old lady's head, and Margaret beamed from ear to ear.

David and Sarah still stood by the doorway in amazement. Sarah just blinked. David looked suspicious; one eye narrowed at his brother. Jonathan shrugged almost imperceptibly and raised his eyebrows as if to say, "How could you not have expected this?" In response, David laughed.

Finally, Sarah shook her head as if to shake her thoughts clear, then rushed toward Anne. "Anne," she said, taking his fiancée's hand and pulling her up from her seat. "We've got a wedding to plan." The two of them rushed off, Millie close behind them. As they left the room, Jonathan followed David's gaze to the former maid's swishing skirts as she hurried up the stairs. He smiled.

Margaret cleared her throat, and both men came to the table and sat. The servants cleared the ladies' plates and laid a fresh setting for David, and the family got around to the business of finally finishing their breakfast. David filled them in on all the latest goings-on in the country, the baron's continued pursuit of

Sarah, and the havoc the weather had been wreaking upon the roads. Margaret shared a look with Jonathan at the mention of the recent storms but said nothing.

They were finished with breakfast and sipping their coffee when a footman appeared in the doorway. "Your Grace," he said. "A Mr. Tobin here to see you."

Jonathan stood to go meet Tobin in the hall, but Margaret stopped him. "Bring him in, please, and pour a fresh cup of coffee."

Jonathan and David exchanged a look. Their old aunt, always a dragon and stickler for propriety, was surprising the hell out of them both this morning. Jonathan made his way back to his seat as Tobin came in, carrying his hat in front of him. "Lady Margaret," he said, bowing low.

"Mr. Smith," Margaret said, nodding her head. "What brings you here so unexpectedly?"

"Well, I wish I could say it was a social call, my lady," he started, "but I'm here because they've got the pox in Ripton."

"Bloody hell," Jonathan cursed right in front of his aunt.

"Yes, that's what I said, Your Grace. Surely some of them who refused to get inoculated and ran off were carrying the illness."

"Yes, we can be sure of that."

Tobin paused, looking at Jonathan. "You know of a doctor who can help?"

Margaret's eyes narrowed, and Jonathan could feel her glare without even looking.

"Yes, I think I do," Jonathan said, not fearing the wrath of his old aunt.

"Good, my boy," Margaret said, rapping the floor with her cane.

Jonathan stood. "David, will you run to the stable and have them saddle my horse?"

David jumped up. "Of course," he said. "But only if I can come too."

Jonathan laughed. "Better saddle several."

Jonathan leaped up the stairs to Anne's room two at a time. Sarah and Millie were scandalized when he burst in without knocking as they were standing over the bed filled with underthings and silk gowns. Sarah came in front of the bed, noting how improper it was for Jonathan to see all these items, but Anne, on the other side of the bed, lifted a pair of pink pantaloons and raised her eyebrows in question. He wrinkled his nose and shook his head, so she picked up a chemise with an extremely low neckline and held it against her. He smiled broadly, then remembered what he was there for.

"They've got the pox in Ripton," he said. "They need the doctor."

Sarah balked. "Who will you ask? Sutcliffe hasn't had a real doctor since the vicar drove Dr. Huxley away."

"It does now," Jonathan said, looking right at Anne. She smiled. He continued, "Can you be ready in half an hour?"

"Do I have a choice?" Anne asked.

Jonathan walked to where she stood and bent down to whisper in her ear, brushing her cheek with his lips, "Always."

Epilogue

David Marksbury, second in line to the Dukedom of Sutcliffe, looked at his brother Jonathan and Jonathan's bride, Anne, in the grand space of St. George's Mayfair. It was an ungodly hour in the morning, but the church was full to bursting with all of the *ton*'s most fashionable members, bowing their heads in prayer, but peeking up to look at everyone else and see what the new gossip might be.

David, as best man, stood a few steps down from the altar and was supposed to be facing the pews, but he could not stop looking back up at Jonathan and Anne and smiling. If he knew anything about affairs of the heart, and he did, or at least those of the bedroom, he wouldn't be second in line for the dukedom for long. David would bet a week's worth of faro winnings that Anne was already growing a little duke as the vicar spoke.

He looked out across the rows of gathered guests and caught the eye of Miss Jessica Weatherby, who waved her fan coquettishly at him, batting her eyelashes. David smiled, but then looked away. No, he thought, he wasn't the marrying type.

He caught a snippet of the vicar's speech.

"It was ordained for the mutual society, help, and comfort that the one ought to have of the other, both in prosperity and adversity."

David sighed. That did sound good, but, he thought, he already had the mutual society of his sister, brother, aunt, and new sister-in-law. The vicar droned on and on, and David looked over at Millie, Miss DiRossi, who was standing on Anne's side with her Aunt Harriet. Those devilish curls were popping right out of the little fashionable cap she wore, and her eyes were merry when she looked back at David. He raised his eyebrows at her, and the little minx had the audacity to wink back at him.

This day might be the one that bound Jonathan and Anne together, but now Sutcliffe would be taken care of, therefore this was the first day of freedom for David Marksbury.

About the Author

Renee Wilde is a writer, teacher, mom, runner, quilter, and Girl Scout leader living in the suburban wilds of Western Connecticut with her family. As a lifelong lover of language, teaching high school English was always her calling, but as a lifelong lover of historical romance, writing was always her dream. She grew up in rural Missouri and has a BA in English from Yale University and an MS in English with teacher certification from Southern CT State. She considers Henry Thoreau her spiritual guide, Julia Quinn her writer hero, and her cat Ewok her comic foil.

CPSIA information can be obtained
at www.ICGtesting.com
Printed in the USA
LVHW010120030122
707646LV00001B/14